Our Someday Family

1. ALABAMA
Late Bloomer—Peg Sutherland
2. ALASKA
Casey's Flyboy—Vivian Leiber
3. ARIZONA
Second Wife—Stephanie James
4. ARKANSAS
Bittersweet Sacrifice—Bay Matthews
5. CALIFORNIA
Hunter's Way—Justine Davis
6. COLORADO
Rafferty's Choice—Dallas Schulze
7. CONNECTICUT
Special Delivery—Judith Arnold
8. DELAWARE
Taking Love in Stride—Donna Clayton
9. FLORIDA
Marriage by the Book—Joan Johnston
10. GEORGIA
Baby, It's You—Celeste Hamilton
11. HAWAII
Daddy's Girl—Barbara Bretton
12. IDAHO
One of the Family—Kristine Rolofson
13. ILLINOIS
Above Suspicion—Andrea Edwards
14. INDIANA
Intrusive Man—Lass Small
15. IOWA
Count Your Blessings—Kathy Clark
16. KANSAS
Patchwork Family—Carla Cassidy
17. KENTUCKY
Heart's Journey—Cathy Gillen Thacker
18. LOUISIANA
Crazy Like a Fox—Anne Stuart
19. MAINE
Fantasies and Memories—Muriel Jensen
20. MARYLAND
Minor Miracles—Rebecca Flanders
21. MASSACHUSETTS
Only the Nanny Knows for Sure—Phyllis Halldorson
22. MICHIGAN
The Proper Miss Porter—Ruth Langan
23. MINNESOTA
Emily's House—Nikki Benjamin
24. MISSISSIPPI
Beloved Stranger—Peggy Webb
25. MISSOURI
Head Over Heels—Leigh Roberts

26. MONTANA
Renegade Son—Lisa Jackson
27. NEBRASKA
Abracadabra—Peg Sutherland
28. NEVADA
Chances—Janice Kaiser
29. NEW HAMPSHIRE
Racing with the Moon—Muriel Jensen
30. NEW JERSEY
Romeo in the Rain—Kasey Michaels
31. NEW MEXICO
Desperate Measures—Paula Detmer Riggs
32. NEW YORK
Honorable Intentions—Judith McWilliams
33. NORTH CAROLINA
Twice in a Lifetime—BJ James
34. NORTH DAKOTA
Letters of Love—Judy Kaye
35. OHIO
One to One—Marisa Carroll
36. OKLAHOMA
Last Chance Cafe—Curtiss Ann Matlock
37. OREGON
Home Fires—Candace Schuler
38. PENNSYLVANIA
Thorne's Wife—Joan Hohl
39. RHODE ISLAND
Somebody's Hero—Kristine Rolofson
40. SOUTH CAROLINA
The Sea at Dawn—Laurie Paige
41. SOUTH DAKOTA
Night Light—Jennifer Greene
42. TENNESSEE
Somebody's Baby—Marilyn Pappano
43. TEXAS
The Heart's Yearning—Ginna Gray
44. UTAH
Wild Streak—Pat Tracy
45. VERMONT
MacKenzie's Baby—Anne McAllister
46. VIRGINIA
First Things Last—Dixie Browning
47. WASHINGTON
Belonging—Sandra James
48. WEST VIRGINIA
The Baby Track—Barbara Boswell
49. WISCONSIN
Fly Away—Pamela Browning
50. WYOMING
The Last Good Man Alive—Myrna Temte

Please address questions and book requests to: Silhouette Reader Service
U.S.: 3010 Walden Ave., P.O. Box 1325, Buffalo, NY 14269
Canadian: P.O. Box 609, Fort Erie, Ont. L2A 5X3

Born in the USA

ILLINOIS

ANDREA EDWARDS

Above Suspicion

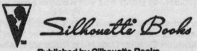

Published by Silhouette Books
America's Publisher of Contemporary Romance

SILHOUETTE BOOKS
300 East 42nd St.,
New York, N.Y. 10017

ISBN 0-373-47163-7

ABOVE SUSPICION

This edition published by arrangement with Harlequin Books S.A.

® and TM are trademarks of Harlequin Books S.A., used under license.
Trademarks indicated with ® are registered in the United States Patent and
Trademark Office, the Canadian Trade Marks Office and in other countries.

Printed in U.S.A.

Dear Reader,

We've traveled all over the United States and Canada, but as true blue midwesterners, born and raised here, we couldn't think of any other place in the world we'd want to set our stories.

What we like most about the Midwest is its variety, and Illinois is a perfect example of it. It has Chicago, one of the largest cities in the world, and towns so small they can't even afford a zip code. It has wide expanses of cornfields so flat you can play pool on them, and lush rolling river valleys. And it has wonderful little surprises tucked away in unexpected places.

Hinsdale, Illinois, is one of those. It's the perfect little town that you thought existed only in the movies—a small town with a distinct personality and flavor in the middle of suburban sprawl. Though just a half-hour drive from Chicago, it's an old town with an identity of its own.

Hinsdale is self-contained, with a vibrant downtown filled with restaurants, drug stores, boutiques and ice cream parlors. Small parks—the type where Dad takes the kids to play after dinner—dot the town. Modern new houses sit side by side with rambling old Queen Anne structures. Huge trees line the sidewalks, and everyone has a big backyard.

It's a quiet, peaceful town without a hint of danger and excitement. The type of place where everyone feels safe, where doors can be left unlocked at night and your kids can walk to school by themselves. Nothing scary ever happens in Hinsdale, which made it the perfect place to send a young, desperate mother.

Andrea Edwards

P.S. Thank you, Amy Evans, for the picture!

Prologue

The office was cold and intimidating. The air had been processed until it was as sterile as the music that was being piped in from unseen speakers. The glass doors leading to the reception area weren't marred by a single fingerprint, and even the magazines in the waiting area were perfect: recent issues with crisp, unbent covers. Claire Haywood clutched her purse and stepped up to the reception desk, feeling as out of place as the movie magazine the receptionist was reading. But Claire had no chance to speak.

"Ah, Ms. Haywood. You're here."

Claire turned at the sound of the man's voice. The door behind her had swung open. The balding man facing her smiled.

"I'm sorry I'm late," he said. He tossed some papers on the receptionist's desk and ushered Claire through the far door.

"I just got here myself," Claire admitted, though she wasn't certain the man was listening. She followed him into his office, another sterile cubicle with about as much personality as an ice cube. "Mr. Daniels—"

"Hey, the hair looks great." He perched on the corner of

his desk, his eyes suddenly probing, and he inspected every detail of her appearance. "I guess this means you've decided to take the job."

Claire touched her newly lightened curls, not yet used to the bounce her normally straight hair now had. "If it's still open."

"Oh, it is." He got up and went around the desk to sit in his chair. "I told you we want to get proof of whether or not Jonathon Tyler's been taking bribes, and you're the only one that can help us do that."

She sat down in the chair in front of his desk. The leather surface was slick. Its disapproving chill shot through her thin summer dress. "I guess I can't believe that this is real," she said. "I know I'm going to wake up and find it's all a dream."

"I hope not," Daniels said with a chuckle. "I've looked for months for Sarah Tyler's double. With your hair curled and dyed, the resemblance is uncanny."

Claire fingered the short curls again, trying to convince herself that she'd made the right decision. But what choice did she have? Brad was being hounded by loan sharks, and he was hounding her in turn because of threats they had made against their little girls. Since his creditors didn't seem to care about divorce decrees, she needed the money to buy his freedom— and theirs—and then help her and the girls start a normal life far away from him. Molly seemed happy enough now, but the doctors all said Katie wasn't likely to start speaking, as long as she was always being left with baby-sitters. Quitting college to marry Brad had been Claire's biggest mistake, but divorcing him had shown that she had some sense after all. Taking this job was further proof.

"So what now?" Claire said, a little more loudly than necessary. She cleared her throat, hoping to clear away her fears. Some Muzak version of a Broadway show tune played faintly in the distance. "So when do the girls and I move?"

Daniels pulled an envelope from the top drawer. Ripping off one end, he poured the contents on the table: two sets of keys, some papers, a bankbook and a few pictures. He pushed one set of keys and a paper toward Claire.

"Here's the lease on your apartment and the keys. You've got it for two months. That should be more than enough time." He dropped the other set of keys on the pile. "These are for the red Ford Escort that's down in the parking lot behind the building, space 11."

She nodded and picked up the keys and stuffed them in her purse.

"We've put money in your account at the First National Bank," Daniels said, pushing the bankbook across the desk toward her. It was open. "Half the money has already been deposited. You'll get the rest when that notebook is found and Tyler is either cleared or brought to trial."

The numbers on the page seemed to jump out at her: $10,000. This was a dream, something her feverish nerves had conjured up to tease her.

"There's got to be a catch," she said quietly. "That's all I've been thinking since you approached me last week. Why are you willing to pay me all this money for doing practically nothing? What is it you aren't telling me?"

"Ms. Haywood." Daniels's words slid off his tongue, pushed by a gentle, mocking laugh. "Twenty grand isn't that big a deal, given the department's total budget. You're a temporary agent going undercover. Obviously it would have been more sensible to use one of our own people, but as I've said, none of them bear the strong resemblance to Sarah Tyler that you do."

She'd heard all that last week. "Yes, but—" She swallowed her own doubts. This job was the answer to her prayers. It offered a real chance to earn the money to finance a move to a place where Brad and his gambling cohorts would never find them. If Daniels was crazy enough to give her twenty thousand dollars for doing virtually nothing, why should she complain? She took a deep breath, running the strap of her purse through her hands. "I won't be breaking any laws, will I?"

Daniels sighed. "Ms. Haywood, we want to find that missing evidence, but we also need to find out how it got lost in the first place. If Tyler just misplaced the notebook after his wife's death, all we want to do is to get it back. But if he's deliberately hiding it to scuttle an investigation, we want him to pay. Since we don't know what happened, we can't afford the slightest hint of impropriety in what you're doing. All we ask is that you get close to Tyler and keep an eye open for that notebook. If you see it, let us know, and we'll subpoena him for it."

"What if I can't get close to him?"

"He was devoted to his wife and son, and he isn't over their deaths. Once he sees you, you'll have no trouble."

Maybe, but she was no femme fatale, skilled at attracting men. She pushed the thought aside. She'd just have to learn.

"You're sure the girls won't be in any danger?" she asked.

"We're afraid Tyler might be a crooked lawyer, not a loan shark," Daniels pointed out, smiling slightly when she started. "Yes, we know about your husband's gambling problems. We knew about them before we ever approached you."

"My ex-husband," she said stiffly. "We were divorced eight months ago."

He shrugged and leaned back in his chair, putting his feet up on the desk. "Whatever. We found him to be of little importance regarding this case."

His disinterest in Brad's compulsion, a compulsion that had torn her life apart and caused her endless days and nights of torment, made her push all the harder. "But how do you know you can trust me? Maybe I'll run off with the money and give you nothing in return."

Daniel's eyebrows rose. "You? Your checking account has been overdrawn fives times in the last six months, and you've worked hard to cover each bounced check. If you've got a larcenous streak in you, it's buried deep—real deep."

Claire flushed and stared at the framed black-and-white geometric print on the wall behind him. "It's been a tough eight months. Brad had nothing to give us." Except trouble, she thought, clutching the bankbook even tighter and swallowing hard. "Do you have anything else for me?"

He unfolded a piece of paper and laid it on the desk. "Tyler's normal routine. He's been at a law enforcement seminar in Washington for the last two weeks, but he's normally a creature of habit. You won't find it hard to meet him.''

She folded the schedule up again. The show tune had ended, and something new was playing over the loudspeakers. It was an ancient Elvis Presley song, but without the words, and changed from a plaintive wail to an upbeat tempo. Nothing was sacred.

"And here's some pictures of Tyler," Daniels went on. "Study them so you'll recognize him."

She looked down at the photos. One was a newspaper clipping with the caption U.S. Attorney Jonathon Tyler to Conduct Racketeering Hearings. Dressed in a three-piece suit, his face somber, he was hurrying up some courthouse steps. The next photo showed him in jeans and a plaid shirt. His hair was dark, with slight streaks of gray at the temples, and his brown eyes were laughing as he and the little boy in his arms smiled at someone unseen. The last photo was of him with a blond woman who had to be Sarah. He was looking at her with such love and tenderness that it made Claire's heart ache with loneliness. He looked like such a gentle man, a loving husband and father with an honest, open face. How could Daniels suspect him of any wrongdoing? Intruding on his grief by playing this absurd game seemed a crime in itself.

Her face must have shown her thoughts quite clearly, because Daniels slipped the pictures back into the envelope. "You know, by watching him and being on the lookout for that notebook you may very well be helping Tyler. You could be clearing his name and removing the cloud of suspicion that's been hanging over his head for the last few months. He'll very likely have reason to thank you when all this is over."

Claire nodded slowly and watched as Daniels slipped the pictures back into the desk. Maybe Tyler did need her help. The possibility might make sleep come easier at night. "The little boy," she said suddenly. "Was that his son?"

Daniels nodded and went on. "Tyler's coming back tonight, so you should move in by tomorrow morning. I trust that's enough time?"

To do what? All she had to do was settle the last overdraft and pack up their belongings, which would barely fill two suitcases. They could leave today right after lunch. "Yes, it'll be fine." She gathered her things together, thinking of what this job would mean to the girls, of the smiles she'd be able to bring to their faces. "I want to thank you—"

He cut her off, apparently embarrassed by her gratitude. He thrust a card into her hand. "Here's a number where you can reach me. If I'm not there, leave a message on the machine. Don't *ever* call the agency. You don't have the proper clearance, so they won't put you through."

She nodded. So much to remember.

"I'll be in touch once you've settled into the apartment."

She felt like one of those dogs she sometimes saw in the back windows of cars, their heads bobbing on springs, nodding automatically. She got to her feet, her throat dry and her stomach twisted with tension now that the job was actually beginning.

"I'll do my best," she said.

"We know you will." His smile said he had more faith in her than she had in herself.

Daniels sat there smiling until she closed the door. Then he got to his feet and walked over to the window in the corner. In a little while she appeared down below. His eyes followed her until she got into the red Escort and disappeared down the street. Then he went to the phone on the desk. He dialed a number and waited for it to be answered.

"It's on," he said quietly. He hung up without waiting for a response. Elvis's mournful lament played cheerfully on.

Chapter 1

The cab pulled to a stop in front of the familiar white colonial-style clapboard house, and Jonathon Tyler got out. He stood there for a moment, taking in the neatly trimmed lawn and the perfectly shaped mounds of yellow marigolds surrounding the bases of the trees in the yard. America's dream home in a dream suburb. Maybe he should hire someone to smuggle in some dandelions.

The cab driver had finished unloading the suitcases from the trunk, and Jonathon reached into his wallet and pulled out several bills.

"Thanks," he said, handing the man the fare, plus another five.

The cabdriver grunted and pocketed the money, then got back into the cab and drove away. It only took a minute for the sound of the car's engine to fade, and even less for the vehicle to disappear around the corner.

Jonathon stared after it, slowly allowing the normal mid-June sounds of the Hinsdale, Illinois, neighborhood to penetrate his consciousness. A gentle breeze rustled the leaves. Birds chattered. The distant sounds of traffic drifted over from the Illinois Tollway, located a half mile to the east. Snatches of music came faintly from a house down the street. The peace of the country, close to the convenience of Chicago. Wasn't that the argument Sarah had used to persuade him to move out here? But lately its perfection had made Jonathon want to scream.

Taking a deep breath, he turned back toward his house, shaking off his strange moodiness. The flight from Washington had seemed unbearably long, and the *New York Times* crossword puzzle even more incomprehensible than usual. He was plain tired. His suitcases had somehow tripled in weight, the walk to the front door suddenly seemed a mile long.

Why hadn't he taken that earlier flight? It would have been much more convenient. He could have unpacked quickly and gone to the office for a few hours. He'd been away for two weeks. There had to be a mountain of things that needed his attention.

Jonathon put his cases down on the step and fumbled in his pocket for his key. He had trouble sliding it into the lock. It was almost as if he were waiting for someone to open it for him. Open it and throw her arms around him, laughing about how long he had been away and how much she had missed him. But those days were gone forever.

The key finally turned in the lock, and the door opened onto the dark, deserted foyer. Suddenly he dreaded stepping inside. He wished again that he had taken that earlier flight and had this moment behind him—or that he'd caught a later flight, so that the moment hadn't arrived yet. This was the hardest part of losing Sarah, the time he felt her death the most, when he came home to the dark and silent house. The waiting emptiness mocked all his brave claims that he was fine.

He picked up his bags and carried them into the foyer, leaving them at the foot of the stairs to the second floor. The house smelled of new paint and wallpaper paste, not the welcoming fragrance of a roast in the oven or freshly made peanut-butter cookies. He pushed his thoughts aside and flicked a switch. The living room lit up. Another few flicks and the dining room and the kitchen were bright. He frowned at the new red checked curtains over the sink, then went back to his suitcase.

"Jonathon? Is that you?"

He was halfway up the stairs, and he stopped at the sound of his sister's voice. "Yes, Marilyn," he called down. "Be there in a minute."

Without bothering to turn on the lights in the bedroom, he left the suitcases at the foot of the bed and went back downstairs. Marilyn stood in the kitchen, unloading a bag of groceries.

"Hi," she said with a smile, pausing a moment in her unpacking. "Have you seen the house? What do you think?"

It seemed as lonely as ever, but he didn't say that. It wasn't part of the role he was trying to play. "It seems great. I just got in, and I haven't had time to look around. The yard's in good shape."

Marilyn grimaced. "It ought to be. You're paying your nephew a fortune to take care of it."

"I'm going to be his summer job, eh? Good thing I didn't sell this place after all."

A touch of the bleakness in his heart must have flashed across his face, because Marilyn laid a gentle hand on his arm. "Why don't you come over to our place tonight? You can eat with us and sleep in the guest room."

He shook his head. "Stop fussing. I'm fine…just tired, that's all. Why don't you show me what you did with the house?"

Marilyn put a few things in the refrigerator, then glanced around the kitchen. "There's just new wallpaper and curtains in here. I decided against plants, even though that windowsill is begging for them. With your schedule, they wouldn't last a week."

"Good idea. I'm not a plant person." A vision of that same windowsill covered with ivy and ferns came into his mind. Lord, how ridiculously guilty he'd felt when they'd died—as if he'd somehow failed Sarah's memory.

Marilyn led him back through the dining room. "I couldn't see getting rid of the dining set. It's in gorgeous condition, so

I only had the seats reupholstered." She waved her hand toward the wide window. "More new drapes and wallpaper."

"You left the china," he noted quietly.

"You have to eat off something."

"I could afford a new set."

Marilyn sighed. "Look, Jonathon, when you asked me to redo the house while you were gone I told you I thought you should do it yourself. My taste isn't the same as yours—or Sarah's."

"That's why I asked you to do it. I wanted the place to look different." He felt impatient. He'd thought they'd covered all this before. "I wanted all this stuff gone so I could start feeling alive again. I want to be free of the constant reminders."

Marilyn shook her head. "Give yourself time, Jonathon. The memories will fade."

"They *are* fading—but then I come back here and her china pattern sets them off again." He ran his finger through his dark hair. "How much longer do you expect me to live with the ghosts?"

"The ghosts aren't in the china cabinet. They're inside you." Marilyn went back into the kitchen. When she spoke again, the impatience was gone from her voice. "Look, if you don't like the place, make whatever changes you want. Throw out all the furniture. I won't be offended."

She unpacked the rest of the groceries and folded up the bag, smoothing out the brown paper just the way Sarah always had. Only when it was perfectly flat did Marilyn look up at him. "Just remember that it's hard to undo things once they're done. If you get rid of everything Sarah ever touched, what happens if you change your mind and want it back?"

"What for? To hand down to her child?" The sudden bitterness in his voice reflected his pain.

"Jonathon, I loved them, too. You aren't the only one who's suffering."

He closed his eyes and sighed. Some of the tension and anger left his body. "I know, Marilyn. It's just that I need to start living again and I don't really know how." He opened his eyes and looked at her. "I really do appreciate what you've done with the house. Why don't you go back home to your family? I'll be fine."

"Are you sure?"

Jonathon nodded silently, and Marilyn picked up her purse from the kitchen table. "Come on over if you want," she told him. After giving him a quick kiss on the cheek, she left.

Jonathon sighed as the door closed behind her. He walked quickly across the kitchen to the freezer. Luckily, Marilyn's changes had only gone so far. He took out the pint of Häagen-Dazs that would be his dinner, grabbed a spoon and went upstairs.

During the weeks he'd been away he'd prepared himself for this. He'd been ready to find the reminders of Sarah gone. The china she had loved would be gracing someone else's dining room. Her favorite chair would no longer be positioned in front of the television. The pictures she had painted would be replaced by mass-produced prints with aluminum frames.

He'd been ready to get on with his life. He hadn't wanted to live with the memories any longer, yet still they'd haunted and tormented him. Longer and longer hours at the office hadn't seemed to help. Whenever he'd stepped into the house, all the pain had returned.

Suddenly, last month, he'd decided that he couldn't go on living in a shrine dedicated to Sarah. His first instinct had been to sell the place, but he couldn't quite do that. Despite his recent feelings, he actually liked both the neighborhood and the house itself. No, he had to take the memories away. And he'd thought Marilyn could do that for him.

Jonathon frowned as he glanced around the bedroom. The walls were papered in the same soft peach tones as before, and the dark brown rug had been shampooed, not replaced. Damn that Marilyn. She always was too careful with the pennies.

He took another spoonful of the ice cream. He couldn't seem to taste it anymore. The room across the hall beckoned, but his eyes avoided it. Did he dare see what changes she had made there?

By the time he'd put the carton of ice cream in the bathroom sink he knew he had to take those few steps. He couldn't keep acting as if the room weren't there. He went across the hall. Fumbling only slightly, he found the switch and bathed the room in light.

Marilyn had done her job well here. The nursery was a guest room now, with pale blue walls and bright floral-print drapes. Two twin beds were covered with dark blue spreads, and a deep-piled white rug covered the floor.

Jonathon walked slowly across the room, dropping into an armless chair that was the same color as the bedspreads. It was as if Timmy had never existed. Where had the tiny white crib gone? And the huge stuffed panda that had sat in the corner?

Jonathon closed his eyes to force his sudden tears away. This was what he'd wanted, he told himself. The reminders were supposed to be gone. He'd asked Marilyn to destroy the ghosts so that he could find peace. He jumped to his feet, unable to stay in Timmy's old room any longer. Was there no escape, no way to avoid the nightmares? Somehow, somewhere, he had to find a way to live again.

The sound of a lawn mower woke Jonathon. It was Saturday, and someone was getting an early start. He frowned in confusion as he reached for the clock on the nightstand. Eight-thirty wasn't really all that early, he supposed.

He went to the window and pulled aside the curtain, surprised to see his nephew Paul cutting the grass. Frowning, he watched as the boy moved carefully past the bushes and then along the white picket fence that separated Jonathon's yard from his neighbors'. He stopped suddenly, his head turning. Then he left the mower to lean on the fence. The neighbors' teenage daughter was washing her car, a Chevette whose color matched that of the string bikini she was wearing. Some things never changed.

Jonathon let the curtain fall back into place, a smile touching not just his lips but the frozen edges of his heart. When had he ever been as carefree as Paul? Not lately, that was certain. For the past year his thoughts had been consumed entirely by his work. Once he'd gotten over the initial numbness after the accident he'd thrown himself into investigation after investigation. His office had made a record number of indictments and convictions. They'd broken a major drug ring, uncovered an international smuggling scheme out of O'Hare and closed down a slew of illegal gambling operations. He had a lot to be proud of, yet his emptiness hadn't diminished.

At first he'd thought it was because he wasn't busy enough. Now he wondered if he'd been wrong to try to bury his grief in work. Maybe it was time he faced it, worked at easing its hold.

He dressed for his usual Saturday-morning jog, then hurried downstairs to find that Paul had moved into the kitchen to fry some bacon. The boy looked up as Jonathon entered. "The front lawn's done," he said.

"And it's time for breakfast?"

Paul shrugged. "Want some?"

Jonathon shook his head and got his running shoes from the top of the basement steps. "Not now. I wouldn't mind if you left me something, though."

Paul laughed as he broke two eggs into the frying pan. "Mom wants you to call her today."

Jonathon concentrated on putting on his shoes. He was certain Marilyn was dying to fix him up with some friend or other of hers. She meant well, he knew, but he just didn't want to be "fixed up." When he started dating again, he wanted a private affair brought about by a woman's teasing laughter or the warmth of her smile, not a therapeutic evening out prescribed by Marilyn.

"I'm going into the office today. Tell her I'll call when I get back."

Paul grinned. "Hiding from her?"

"Of course not. I'm too old to hide from people."

Paul clearly wasn't fooled. He grinned again and plunked a couple of slices of bread in the toaster, then rummaged through the refrigerator.

"Where's the jelly?"

"In the jelly section of the grocery store. I used the last up weeks ago," Jonathon said with a laugh as he went out the screen door. "Lock up if you're done before I get back." Paul waved and closed the refrigerator sadly.

Jonathon took the driveway slowly, then turned onto the sidewalk. Maybe Paul was right, Jonathon thought. Maybe he was hiding—but from life, not Marilyn. Maybe he ought to sell the house and be done with it. In spite of Marilyn's re-decorating, it was still Sarah's house, and it always would be. Could an attraction to another woman ever grow strong if his memories of Sarah always blocked the sunlight?

He ran a few blocks. Right foot, left foot. Keep the stride even. Then he turned into the park. The heat seemed to press down on him even in the shade of the oak trees, but he pushed himself all the harder, jogging the length of the baseball field, around the play area and then past the picnic benches. He needed the exercise to clear his mind. They were close to bringing in indictments involving a major construction kick-back scheme, and there were some fish on the line that he was determined not to lose.

He circled back around the baseball field for his second circuit, glad the park was empty, as it usually was at this time of the morning. There was nothing worse than dodging bike riders or pop flies to the outfield. As it was, there were only a few other runners in the park—and a woman playing with two little girls on the swings. They'd arrived while Jonathon had been by the picnic tables.

He wasn't certain why he watched the woman as he ran. Maybe it was because it was easier than keeping track of his breathing, or maybe it was because she kept hesitantly glanc-ing his way. It was almost as if she were watching him. He rounded the corner of the baseball field and came up past the play area. She glanced up then, her eyes nervously meeting his. He stopped dead in his tracks.

"Sarah?"

The word was out before he could stop it, and his feet were taking him closer to the woman even as his mind shouted that he was mistaken. The woman stared back at him. She had

Sarah's blue eyes, Sarah's short, mussed blond curls and Sarah's gold hoops in her ears.

"Excuse me?" the woman said. She wasn't Sarah. He could see that now.

"I'm sorry," he said lamely, embarrassment mingling with disappointment in his voice. The woman's eyes were a blue-green, like the sea, not a clear blue like the sky. The hair was more a reddish blond, and the earrings were just earrings, not souvenirs of their honeymoon in Mexico. "I thought you were someone I knew."

She looked at him with the same nervous hesitancy that he'd noticed before. Then she smiled. It was a garden celebrating after a summer rain. "I'm sorry I'm not," she said.

And somehow he knew it was true. He smiled back. Now that he was closer he could see that she was shorter than Sarah, with more determination in her jawline. The resemblance was only superficial and only from a distance. And yet, even though the traces of Sarah had disappeared, he had no desire to leave. This woman's smile held peace, protection from baying memories, even if just for a few moments.

"You live near here?" he asked. "I don't remember seeing you in the park before."

"No," she said, then stopped. "Yes, we do. We just moved in yesterday. The girls were anxious to try out the park."

They both turned to watch the girls playing on the slide. They were about three and five years old, Jonathon thought, blondes, with braided hair and bright ruffled sunsuits. Their canvas shoes were too white to be anything but brand-new. He smiled at them, but they just stared back, silent and suspicious, so he turned back to their mother.

"Where'd you move from?"

"From the city, the northwest side."

Jonathon nodded. "You and your husband buy a home here?"

She shook her head and looked away, watching the girls—not, Jonathon thought, from an interest in their play, but to avoid his eyes. "I'm divorced," she said awkwardly after a moment. "I thought we needed a change." She paused. "We're just renting an apartment."

The pain of separation. He certainly understood that. "Well, you're going to find it a lot different out here. I'm sure your kids will love it," he said lightly. He really should go. He had work waiting for him but when her eyes came fleetingly back to his, something there made him want to stay. A tiny flicker of warmth came to life in his soul and promised that something better would soon follow.

A child's voice broke into his thoughts. "Mommy! Mommy! Katie fell and cut herself!"

The older girl was leading the tearful younger one over to them, and when the woman stooped down the little girl silently ran into her arms. "Oh, little Katie girl," the woman said. "Did you hurt yourself? Let Mommy see."

It was just a skinned knee, a tragedy for a little person, but not enough to throw a parent into panic. Timmy used to— He stopped the thought, but not before the pain came.

"It'll be okay, you'll see," the woman crooned, and for a blinding moment, Jonathon thought she was talking to him. He had a second's fleeting certainty that she could make everything all right, but he cut off that thought, too, as the woman struggled to her feet, still holding Katie.

"Do you live close by?" he asked. He saw no car. She must have walked to the park.

"In that apartment building down by the railroad station," she said. Then she turned to the older girl. "Molly, could you get my purse for me? It's over on the bench there."

"But those apartments are at least six blocks from here," he protested, though he didn't know why. "You'll never be able to carry her that far. Why don't you let me?"

Katie had buried her face in her mother's neck, and her little hands were clutching her mother's blouse. At Jonathon's words, her hands clenched even tighter. "No, thank you anyway," the woman said. "It's kind of you to offer, but I'll manage."

It was obvious to Jonathon that she couldn't. He followed as she started toward the edge of the park. "At least come to my house, then," he said. "It's only two blocks away. We can clean up Katie's knee, and then I'll drive you home."

The woman said nothing for a long moment, so long that he wondered if she'd heard him. She stopped and turned to face him. Her jaw was clenched, and her eyes were clouded. "Thank you. That would certainly be a big help."

Then why did it seem the opposite? "Here, it's just down this street," he said. Then he realized they hadn't introduced themselves. "I'm Jonathon Tyler."

"Claire Haywood," she said, shifting Katie and sticking a hand out.

He took it, surprised by the electricity of her touch. Her eyes were troubled as they gazed into his, but there was also a depth and a quiet determination that intrigued him. He shook the daze from his mind and patted the sniffling Katie on the back.

"Hang in there, Katie. My house is just down the street here." For the first time in a year he didn't dread going home.

Chapter 2

"There. Does that feel better now?" Claire asked.

Katie nodded, and Claire lifted the silent girl off the kitchen table, where she'd been sitting while her knee was bandaged. Then Claire picked up the wrapper and the paper towel she'd used on Katie's knee and threw them away, careful to avoid Jonathon's eyes. He was so nice, so kind. She hated the game she was playing.

"That's an awfully nice bandage," Molly said wistfully, looking at the strip on her sister's knee, which had a teddy bear printed on it.

Jonathon offered her one, still in its wrapper. "Want to take one home with you in case you ever fall down?"

Molly's eyes grew wide, but she turned to Claire. "Mommy?" Claire nodded reluctantly and the little girl took the bandage from Jonathon. "Are you sure you won't need it? Our daddy used to cut his finger sometimes, and then he needed a bandage."

Jonathon stooped down so that he was eye-to-eye with Molly. "Daddies don't get to use teddy-bear bandages," he said. "They only work on little girls and boys."

"Really?" Molly looked down at the bandage in awe. Claire turned away and stared out the kitchen window at a teenage boy working in the yard. She washed her hands in the sink, wishing she could wash away her guilt as easily.

The job had seemed so straightforward when she'd agreed to it: meet the man and watch him. She hadn't meant for the girls to be part of the bait. If only she could take them and run away from this house, from this town. If only she could give the money back to Daniels and tell him to forget the whole thing. If only there were a way to take care of her children and still be able to face herself in the mirror in the morning.

Her children. She stopped her silent rantings with a sigh. Her needs might be negotiable. Theirs weren't. She turned from the sink with a bright smile on her face.

"We certainly appreciate your help," she told Jonathon as she dried her hands. "But if you don't mind driving us home, we'd better get going. We haven't had breakfast yet, and we've got lots to do today."

"You haven't had breakfast yet?" he repeated, letting a grin creep across his mouth. "Then you can't leave. I haven't had any, either, and I hate to eat alone."

A little voice inside her ordered her to refuse, to get out while she still had her self-respect, but her daughters' giggling over the teddy-bear bandages drowned it out. "Well, if you're sure it's no trouble..." she said slowly.

"None at all," he said. Then he looked down at the girls. "Now what do you normally have for breakfast? Chocolate cake? Ice cream?" Molly giggled, and Katie looked uncertain.

"Eggs," Claire said.

"Aw, Mommy," Molly said. "How about French toast?"

"Molly! This isn't a restaurant."

"French toast sounds great," Jonathon said. "Tell me how to make it and it's yours."

The eagerness in his eyes and voice tore at Claire's heart. "No," she said firmly, "tell me where you keep your eggs and bread and I'll make it."

A few minutes later she was alone in the kitchen while

Jonathon turned on the Saturday-morning cartoons for the girls in the living room. Claire broke the eggs into a bowl with far more force than was necessary, hating herself for having finagled the invitation. The man was so obviously lonely that it was a crime to take advantage of him.

But then she thought of Molly's happiness that the parade of baby-sitters was over and of Katie's appointment with a speech therapist. She thought of Brad's whining admission that if he didn't get the money he needed the girls would be in danger, and of Daniels saying that she could clear Jonathon of suspicion. That was what she would do, she vowed, beating the eggs as if they were Brad or Daniels or herself. She'd clear Jonathon's name. She'd help him, not hurt him.

"That's a great set of kids you've got there," Jonathon said from behind her.

She started, then looked over her shoulder at him, not daring more than a brief glance for fear that her will would collapse. "Thank you." She concentrated on stirring the milk into the eggs.

"Katie doesn't talk much, does she? She this shy with everyone?"

Claire fiddled with the slices of bread. "She doesn't talk," she said curtly, and was immediately sorry for her terseness. She turned and gave him a quick, apologetic smile. "The doctors all say there's nothing physically wrong. It was just the trauma of the divorce and all the changes in her life. She'll talk once she feels secure again."

"And in the meantime you're carrying a load of guilt."

She stared at him.

"Over the divorce, I mean," he explained. "Wondering whether or not you did the right thing."

She plugged in his electric frying pan and stared at the square of margarine sliding over its surface as it melted. "No, that's one guilt I was spared. I never doubted the divorce was right. I was only sorry I married him in the first place."

"The marriage gave you two beautiful daughters." His voice was gently reproving.

"Yes. Maybe having them was worth all the pain that came later."

"Maybe?" he asked teasingly.

She laughed. It was her first real laugh in weeks. "You're right. No maybes. They're worth everything. Life wouldn't be the same without them."

Her happiness faltered when she saw the look that crossed his face. She wanted to say something to comfort him. She wanted to hold him, to have him lay his head against her chest and let her ease just a little the painful memories that smiling children must bring. But that she wasn't supposed to know about his wife and son.

"Who's Sarah? You called me that at the park, and I just wondered…" He looked stunned, and she hurried on, cursing herself and Daniels. "It doesn't matter. Forget I asked, and tell me where the plates are."

"She was my wife," he said simply. The words were edged in pain, and she could hear the lonely nights and the empty, wakeful hours just before dawn in his voice. "She and my son were killed in an automobile accident last year."

"I'm sorry." The words seemed so inadequate, so meaningless. She dipped the bread into the batter she'd made. "Do I look like her?"

He started setting the table. Bright plastic dishes in crayon colors that made the room smile despite everything. "Yes and no. From a distance you do," he said. "But there are a lot of little differences when you're up close. Your eyes and hair are slightly different colors. Your voice is nothing like hers."

She forced herself to ask the question that was eating away at her. "Does it bother you to see me here?" She turned the French toast, careful to keep from looking into his eyes.

"No. Shall I pour some milk for the girls?"

Wait, her heart cried out. There was more she wanted to know. Was it because of her likeness to Sarah that he didn't mind her presence? Or did the differences between them keep him from seeing Sarah in her face? But she couldn't ask.

"Yes, milk would be fine." She piled French toast on a platter as Jonathon called the girls into the kitchen. Sarah no longer mattered, she told herself. She had to keep her own heart strong. "Girls, how about if you sit over here?"

She got everyone seated, then served. She helped Katie pour syrup on her French toast and gave Molly sugar to sprinkle on hers. By the time she began eating her own breakfast her good feelings were almost genuine, but the silence got to her. She could almost feel Sarah's presence in the bright, cheery kitchen.

Claire sipped at her coffee, then put the cup down. "So tell me something about Hinsdale," she said to Jonathon. "We actually ended up here by accident."

Jonathon's smile was apologetic. "About all I can tell you is that it's been home for the last three years."

"You've lived here for three years and can't tell me a thing about the place?" She shook her head in mock disapproval. "I've only been here for two days and I can tell you there are more big trees on your block than on all of Devon Avenue. Why, I used to go for days without seeing a tree."

"But, Mommy, we had a tree in our backyard," Molly told her with a frown and a mouthful of French toast. "Remember, you used to give it a drink every day."

"That was before, honey," Claire said. "There weren't many trees around our last apartment," she explained.

She could feel Jonathon's gaze on her face, and she looked up to meet it. His eyes were warm with understanding. "If it's trees you like, you can have all of mine," he said. "Especially come October."

"Can we really?" Molly was in awe.

Claire shook her head gently. "Mr. Tyler's joking," she told her daughter. "He meant we could come and rake up all the leaves in the fall." Long after their two months here were over.

"It wasn't totally a joke," Jonathon said. "You're welcome to come use the trees anytime you like. I think they're a bit high for climbing, but you can have all the shade you want."

"Do you have a swing?" Molly asked. "Angie O'Neal had a swing from her tree."

"Molly!" Claire protested. "We have that lovely park we were just at."

But Jonathon ignored her and focused his attention on the little girl. "I don't have a swing up now, but I do have a helper who might be able to put one back up." The back door opened. "Ah, speak of the devil…"

Molly's eyes widened at Jonathon's words, and she leaned over toward Claire. "Mommy?"

"No, he isn't, really," Claire whispered as the teenage grass cutter came in. The boy was tall and tanned, with an easy smile that froze when he saw Claire sitting at the table.

"Yes, it throws you at first, doesn't it?" He put his hand on the boy's shoulder and drew him forward. "Claire, this is my nephew Paul. Paul, this is Mrs. Haywood, Katie and Molly. We met in the park."

Paul mumbled a "How do you do?" and shook Claire's hand as briefly as possible. Claire knew he wasn't so much impolite as shocked. Why hadn't she thought through all the implications of her little job?

Jonathon punctured the awkward silence. "Molly here's interested in your swing-hanging abilities."

Paul seemed relieved to be able to focus on the little girl. "My swing-hanging abilities? Do I have any swing-hanging abilities?"

"You'd better," Jonathon told him. "If Angie O'Neal has a swing in her tree, we need one, too."

"Can't let old Angie beat us," Paul allowed.

"I think there's an old swing in the garage," Jonathon said, glancing at the girls' empty plates. "Maybe you two would like to go out and help him."

Claire nodded her permission, so Molly took Katie by the hand and led her out after Paul. "What kind of swing is it?" she asked the teenager. "Angie's swing was red." The door closed on Paul's answer, and Claire took a deep breath.

"I feel we're imposing on you terribly," she said, forcing herself to meet his eyes. "You've given us first aid and breakfast. Shade trees and a swing really are above and beyond the call of duty."

Jonathon shook his head, bleakness warring with sadness in his eyes and losing. "You've given me company at the breakfast table and a reason to smile. I think that leaves me owing you a bundle."

Unable to bear his gratitude, she got to her feet and hastily stacked the dirty dishes. "Good thing you're not an accountant, if that's the way you think. You'd be in the red all the time."

"How do you know I'm not an accountant?" He took the dirty dishes from her and carried them over to the dishwasher. "Maybe I just know the real value of things."

The teasing laughter was gone from his voice now, and her mouth suddenly went dry. But it was from the anguish in his voice, not her slip. She turned to the sink to wash out the frying pan. "You can't be an accountant," she said quickly. "You haven't once said the words debit or credit."

"You're too clever for me," Jonathon said. "If you have lunch with me, I'll tell you what I really do."

"Lunch?" She spun around to face him. "But you've already given us breakfast."

"Dinner, then."

Her heart wanted her to say yes. He was a handsome man, and the spark she felt every time they accidentally touched warmed her all the way to the far corners of her soul. Even his voice set her heart to pounding. Her mind wanted her to say yes. It was her job to get close to him. Their fresh start, the new life for her and the girls, depended on her doing just that. But her conscience said no. It wouldn't let her take advantage of the loneliness in his eyes.

"Jonathon, we've only just met." She put her hand on his arm and was stunned by the needs that stirred within her. She didn't want to feel that way again. It could only lead to heartbreak. She turned back to the table, grabbed the syrup bottle and put it away. "We certainly appreciate your kindness to us, but you must have other things to do than feed us."

He picked up the frying pan. "In other words, you have other things to do."

"Well, we did only arrive yesterday," she pointed out gently.

"How about tomorrow?"

"Let me see how the girls are settling in. Can I call you?"

"Sure. Let me write down my number for you."

He went off down a hallway, and she turned to the window over the sink. No swing was in sight, but Paul was cutting lilacs, and each girl was holding a bouquet. Katie was trailing along behind Paul and Molly, stopping every few feet to bury her face in the flowers. Claire could feel the child's delight all the way inside the house. Damn that Daniels. Damn her own inconvenient conscience. If she did her job well, she could buy Katie ten lilac bushes.

"Here you go."

Jonathon was back with a piece of paper for her. It had his name and address and his home and office phone numbers.

"Want my birthday or my social security number, too?" he asked.

Embarrassed by his intent stare, she laughed and slipped the paper into her pocket. "I think this'll do for now."

He smiled and took her hand. "I can't tell you how nice it's been to hear laughter in this place again. Don't wait too long to call. Patience isn't one of my strong points."

"No, I won't." She forced a smile onto her face. "Could you drive us home now?"

Claire had never known that silence could be so accusing. If it wasn't Katie's silence, reminding her of the security that money would bring, it was the silence of the phone, reminding her that she could call Jonathon anytime.

She did the grocery shopping and carefully arranged all her things in the cabinet. Then she made the girls lunch. She promised herself she would clean the rest of the apartment in the afternoon. Since she'd cleaned half of it yesterday, it was barely two o'clock when she finished. She sat down at the kitchen table, staring at the worn Formica surface. Now what?

The phone rang, as if in reply, and she nearly jumped out

of her skin. The sound was so loud, so insistent. She grabbed the receiver.

"Claire Haywood. May I help you?" The silence that followed sent prickles down her spine, but she didn't hang up.

"Neatly done," a voice rippling with laughter said. "You work fast."

Her hand tightened on the phone. "Hello, Mr. Daniels." Despite the man's friendly manner, the room suddenly seemed to take on a chill. The sun-warmed summer air blowing through the screened windows seemed unable to reach her. "What can I do for you?"

"I thought you might have something to report," the man said, his tone comfortable and smooth, as if they were discussing a normal business transaction or the health of her aunt Millie. There was no reason for the chill to stay in the air, yet it did.

"Not yet."

"You were in his house for over an hour."

"How—" She bit off the words. They were watching her. Embarrassed by her naiveté, she spoke quickly. "How about if you give me a clue as to where this notebook might be?"

Katie came into the kitchen, still carrying her lilacs, and climbed into Claire's arms to give her a silent hug and then a wet kiss. It was enough to put the most stubborn conscience to sleep.

"I briefed you," the man said.

"All too briefly." She smiled at her own bravado, then let Katie slip to the floor and reached over to hand her a cookie. Katie grinned and scampered into the other room with it.

"You said I was supposed to get close to Tyler and look for a notebook," Claire went on. "What does it look like? Everybody has notebooks in their house. How will I know which is the one you want?"

Daniels just laughed. "Don't bring me every notebook you find in the man's house, please. The one we want is small—about five by seven inches—and red, a half-inch thick and filled with columns of numbers. You'll know it when you find it. When are you seeing him again?"

"Soon. Maybe this afternoon," she said. "If not, then this evening."

"You're as good as a pro. I'll be in touch." Then there was silence as he hung up.

Claire slowly followed suit, letting out her breath in a long and ragged sigh. She'd taken the job. It was time to start working. She pulled the paper from under the magnet on the refrigerator door and dialed Jonathon's number with shaking fingers. This was right, she tried telling herself. For the kids' sake, she had to do it. He answered before she had time to change her mind.

"Jonathon? It's Claire. I'm afraid I'm going to ask a huge favor of you."

"Good," he said. "I'm at my best with big challenges."

She laughed, but it didn't touch her heart. "Better wait until you hear it. The washer's broken in the laundry room here, and the kids have nothing but dirty clothes that I hadn't had a chance to get to because of the move."

"So bring it all over here."

"Are you sure you don't mind?" She felt she had to offer a token protest. "I know I've got real nerve, barging in and demanding your washing machine like this."

"I'll mind only if you refuse to stay for dinner."

"And I'll accept only if I can bring some dessert."

"If it's chocolate, I'll let you use my clothes dryer, too."

She laughed then, a real laugh that brought the sunshine back into her kitchen. "It's a deal, then. We'll be over about four o'clock, all right?"

"Fine by me."

She hung up, grabbing for her cookbook at the same time. What was she so worried about? She and the girls needed the security that that twenty thousand dollars would bring. Jonathon needed to learn to smile again. And Daniels needed to be shown that Jonathon was innocent of the wrongdoing he suspected him of. No one could possibly get hurt.

Jonathon looked perfect standing in his open kitchen door, worn and faded jeans defining his muscular legs, a simple sport shirt hinting at the broad power of his shoulders. Unfortunately, the ache of loneliness in her soul had grown stronger. But she closed her heart to its persuasive murmurings and listened only to the strict scoldings of her mind. Her reasons for being here had nothing to do with the inviting strength of his arms or the melting warmth of his voice.

Love had scorched her in the past, and she wasn't going to let that happen again. She was here to do a job, to earn money for her and the girls' new life. In doing so, she'd befriend a lonely man, but that was as far as she'd let it go.

"I really owe you one for this," she said, carrying her laundry basket past him into the kitchen. Her arms brushed his stomach, causing a tightening in hers. She forced lightness into her voice when she spoke again. "This is really an imposition."

"True," Jonathon replied. "But I'll forgive you if that's a chocolate pie Molly's carrying."

"Katie has the whipped cream," Molly told him. "It's in a can that squirts all funny."

"Sounds like we're having a party," he said.

Or was it a hanging? Trying not to let her dour thoughts show on her face, Claire put the laundry basket on the kitchen table so that she could take the pie from Molly.

"This needs to be in the refrigerator," she said. "And so does the whipped cream."

Jonathon opened the refrigerator door for her. "Anything else you need?"

How about his arms around her, reassuring her that everything was all right? Claire shook the thoughts away and slid the pie onto a shelf, putting the can of whipped cream next to it. "No, this should do it," Claire said, straightening and closing the refrigerator door. "All set for a scrumptious dessert after my laundry is done."

Jonathon nodded toward a hallway as he picked up the laundry basket. "The washing machine is this way."

"I can carry that," she protested.

He shook his head, his dark eyes gentle. "And then what would you need me for?"

For strength to lean on and a hand to hold when the shadows of darkness got too close. But those were the ramblings of her unstable heart, ramblings that have to be ignored. Her mind knew better than to trust in emotions or to try to reach for impossible dreams.

"I need you to show me how to work the washer," she pointed out. Before she followed him to the laundry room, she turned to the girls. "You two want to try out that swing Paul put up for you this morning? I'll come out when I've got the wash started."

"Okay, Mom." Molly took Katie's hand and led her out the door to the backyard.

"How did your husband ever agree to part with them?"

Claire spun around, startled to hear Jonathon's voice so near her. She'd thought he'd be halfway down the basement stairs by now, but instead he was right behind her, the laundry basket in his arms. He slowly looked away from the girls to look into her eyes. There was a knowledge in those dark depths that made her uneasy.

"I'm not sure," she admitted hesitantly.

His gaze flickered, and the piercing quality faded. "Forget I asked," he said quickly. "It's none of my business. Not every man wants to share the wonder of his kids."

He turned, and she hurried after him, needing to talk, needing to tell him that Brad had never found the joy in the girls that she did.

"I didn't run off with them, if that's what you're thinking," she told Jonathon.

He laughed and looked back over his shoulder at her. "Believe me, the thought never crossed my mind. You're not devious enough for that."

His words stung her already-burdened conscience. "How would you know?" she asked. "You only met me this morning."

The stairs led into a family room paneled in knotty pine, complete with a long-unused fireplace and a Ping-Pong table. He went past them as if they didn't exist and into an unfinished part of the basement that held the washing machine and the dryer.

"I'm an excellent judge of character." He put the laundry basket on top of the dryer. "I could tell in those first few minutes that you were incapable of lying or taking advantage of anyone."

"And how could you tell that? Everyone's capable of lying."

He shook his head, folding his arms across his chest and leaning back against the laundry tub. "Not you. You didn't even want to let me help you when Katie fell."

"Maybe I'm just not as fast a judge of character as you are," she said. "How was I supposed to know if I could trust you or not?"

"By my honest face?" He grinned. "What made you decide I was safe?"

The assignment Daniels had given her. She looked away, sorting through the girls' clothes—shorts and shirts and the new pajamas she'd splurged on after she'd left Daniels's office.

"I'm not sure," she said. "You seemed nice, and so honestly concerned. I really couldn't have carried Katie all the way back to the apartment."

"Ah," he said with a laugh. "My honest eyes, and necessity."

She couldn't help but laugh with him. She looked up, her eyes dancing. "Surely your excellent immediate assessment of people told you that though."

"Of course." A spark flickered in his dark eyes, and she turned back to the laundry.

"Do you have anything that needs washing?" she asked after filling the washer about halfway with their white things.

"Only about two weeks' worth of dirty clothes," he said. "I just got back from a business convention and haven't quite gotten caught up yet."

"I'm impressed," she told him, stepping aside as he went over to an enclosed bin that had to be beneath a laundry chute.

"I never met anybody who had enough underwear to go two weeks without washing clothes."

He carried over an armload of clothes. "Actually, I only have enough to last a week. I sent my clothes out halfway through the conference."

"What a shame." She pulled some shirts off the top of the pile and tossed them in the washer. "Now you've lost that aura of mystery."

She reached for another shirt, but he caught her hand. His touch was electric. The current raced through her blood and set her heart on fire.

"Is mystery important in a man?" he asked. "I can easily put some back."

She pulled her hand away in an attempt to casually measure the laundry detergent. "Don't be silly," she said.

"I wasn't." He paused, and his sudden silence began to eat away at her composure.

She looked up at him and saw him leaning against the dryer. Even in repose he seemed to dominate the space, to fill the low-ceilinged basement with a sense of sleeping power and danger.

"How long ago was the divorce?" he asked quietly.

The question surprised her, and she frowned at him as he straightened up to start the washer. "About eight months," she said. "Why?"

He shrugged. "Just curious."

"It was a congenial parting," she told him. "Brad was very cooperative."

"Was he that cooperative when married to you?"

She shook her head and wiped away a bit of soap she'd spilled on the top of the washer. "He was never *un*cooperative. Actually, he wasn't all that hard to live with most of the time. We were happy for a while, and I loved him. It was just that—" Somehow she couldn't tell him about Brad's gambling, about the way he'd repeatedly jeopardized their safety and their future, always refusing to admit that he had a problem.

"It was just what?" Jonathon asked gently.

She straightened up from the washing machine. "He had some interests outside the family that occupied him far more than we did. Hobbies," she added quickly when she saw Jonathon's eyes flash. "I never had reason to believe that Brad was unfaithful to me. Still, I was surprised when he gave me complete custody of the girls."

"Maybe he loved you too much to fight it," Jonathon suggested.

"I don't know. At one time I might have agreed, but I'm not sure I ever really knew him at all."

"Mommy." A little voice floated down the stairs to them. "Mommy, when are you coming out?"

"Right now, honey," Claire called back, smiling at Jonathon. "It's too nice a day to spend worrying about Brad's motives. I promise not to even think about them, if you promise to let me do the rest of your laundry."

"How can I refuse such an offer?" he said with a laugh.

Katie and Molly were waiting for them on the stairs, all eagerness and excitement. "We need good pushes," Molly told them. "We want to go all the way up so our feet touch the branches."

"That's pretty high," Jonathon pointed out.

"I can touch the branches when I swing on Angie O'Neal's swing."

"Then I guess you'll have to touch the branches here," Jonathon said as he followed the girls upstairs.

Claire relaxed in spite of her resolve not to as she climbed the stairs. Jonathon was so good with the girls, so gentle and patient. It was as if—

Claire stopped at the dining room door. Out the front window she could see a woman hurrying up the driveway, an intensely curious woman, if the speed at which she was moving was any indication. Fingers of panic clutched at Claire's stomach. It was time to play the part again.

Chapter 3

Jonathon followed Molly and Katie through the kitchen. He felt alive again, as if the sun had finally chosen to melt the ice in his soul, and it was all because of a certain lady. Even simple, everyday chores like laundry and eating had become special again. The house seemed to be happy again, too. It wasn't the echoes of the past that he heard in its corners, it was the promise of children's laughter.

They went out onto the porch, and as the screen door swung shut behind him he spotted his sister hurrying up the driveway. He stopped at the foot of the stairs. Was it only yesterday that he'd complained to Marilyn that the house still overwhelmed him with memories? It seemed a lifetime ago.

"Hey, Marilyn," he called out, the urge to tease and play raging strong in his heart. "Where's the fire?"

She slowed her pace slightly, tiny spots of embarrassment highlighting each cheek. "It's almost dinnertime and I'm missing some items."

"My kitchen is your kitchen," he said with a broad sweep of his left arm.

"Actually, I need a bundle of things, and came by to see if

you needed anything, too," she explained, her gaze slipping away from him to find Molly and Katie at the edge of the backyard. "You know, as long as I'm going to the store anyway."

"How kind of you," he said, keeping almost a straight face. He felt as he had years ago, when he'd been a little boy with a smug smile and an empty box and his big sister had been screaming at him to show her what was inside.

"I can't think of anything I need," he replied.

Marilyn's eyes flickered back to him for a moment, then returned to the girls. He could almost see the questions dancing in the air above her head.

"Are you sure you don't need anything?" she asked. "Milk? Bread? Ketchup?"

"Positive." Jonathon controlled his merriment and winked at the little girls. "I think I even have enough spinach." He heard Molly giggle as he turned back to his sister.

"Well." Marilyn's sigh burst upon the lazy June day like a cherry bomb on the Fourth of July. "I guess I'd better get going if I'm going to feed my family."

"I guess you'd better," Jonathon agreed.

"Did you want to borrow the washing machine, too?" a little voice asked suddenly. "Mommy didn't bring that many clothes."

Jonathon turned to find that Molly had come closer and glanced back at Marilyn in time to see a potpourri of emotions skim across her face. Curiosity finally won out over the rest, and she raised her eyebrows.

"Laundry?"

Jonathon nodded, fighting back the urge to laugh.

"I realize that a person doesn't get rich on a government salary," Marilyn said slowly, "but I thought a trained attorney might have other ways to supplement his income."

"Yeah," he agreed. "But they all violate the conflict-of-interest statutes."

The curiosity stayed on her face, growing even stronger. "So you're taking in laundry."

"I'm not actually taking in laundry," he said. "I'm just letting people use my facilities."

"You're running a Laundromat in your basement? I'm sure there have to be zoning laws that forbid that kind of thing in a residential neighborhood."

Unable to contain himself any longer, Jonathon threw his head back and laughed. In the time it took him to compose himself, irritation replaced curiosity in Marilyn's eyes.

"I'm sorry, Marilyn," he said.

The irritation melted away, and her face softened. "I don't appreciate being laughed at," she said, "but it is good to see you acting like your normal insane self again."

"Believe me," he said, giving his sister a quick hug," I would never laugh at you."

"Right. You're laughing with me."

"I just feel relaxed," he said.

"That's nice."

Jonathon waved toward the girls, who were staring at him, obviously as confused as Marilyn. "Molly is the older girl and Katie is the younger. Their mom is using the washing machine. Girls, this is my sister Marilyn. Paul's mother."

"Hi, girls," Marilyn said.

"Hello." Molly's greeting was quiet. Katie merely clutched Molly's hand.

Jonathon smiled reassuringly at them. He didn't want to see a shadow cross their faces, not while they were in his home. "I met these lovely ladies and their mom while I was running in the park this morning."

Marilyn looked at him pointedly.

"She's divorced," Jonathon said. "They just moved into that apartment house down by the train station."

"The one without a laundry room." Marilyn's voice was light and teasing, but Jonathon sensed a darker vein in it, a concern.

"The machines were broken," he explained.

"*All* of them?"

"I don't know." Jonathon paused a moment, then shrugged and grinned at the girls. "You two want to get that swing all ready for branch-touching rides? I'll be there in about two seconds."

"Okay." Molly gave Marilyn one last look, then took Katie into the backyard.

Jonathon turned to his sister again. Her mood had affected him, made him sharper, more protective. "They needed a bit of help, and I'm glad to be able to offer it."

The worry in Marilyn's eyes didn't totally disappear, but she forced a smile into them as she came over and placed a light kiss on his cheek. "I guess I was being a little overprotective."

"Hey," Jonathon said with a laugh. "I'm a little big to need protection."

"You're a heck of a nice guy, Jonathon Andrew Tyler," she replied. "And no one is ever too big for a little looking-after."

He put his arm around her shoulder and pulled her close. "Don't worry. There's nothing going on. Claire was divorced not too long ago, and I'm just helping her settle into the community."

Marilyn stepped back, pinning him with her gaze. "Paul says she looks just like Sarah."

"There's a resemblance, but it disappears after a minute or two, and you see only her. She's nothing like Sarah."

"She's a two-fisted drinker who swears like a trucker and chews tobacco?"

"Of course not." Had Marilyn come over here to protect him from some wild hussy he'd picked up? He took her hand and pulled her down on the steps next to him. "She's quiet and gentle, cares deeply about her kids and wants to make a good life for them."

Marilyn's face showed no humor now. "And how is that different from Sarah?"

The unexpectedness of her attack left him annoyed. "Come on, Marilyn," he snapped, getting to his feet. "You'd be happier if she was a floozy?"

"I'd be happier if she didn't look like Sarah." Marilyn grabbed his hand to keep him from stalking away. "Jonathon, don't try to bring Sarah back by clinging to someone who resembles her. Sarah's gone. No one else can take her place.''

Marilyn's worries were trying to block out the sun, trying to steal the warmth from the day, but he wouldn't let them. "For God's sake, let up," he cried, pulling his hand away. "I just let someone use my washing machine. It's not a betrothal rite, I'm just being neighborly. You don't have to rush me off to a therapist."

"I don't want to see you hurt."

"But do you want to see me happy?" Even as he said it he knew it was unfair. His anger quickly disappeared, and he sank down next to his sister on the step. He put his arm back around her shoulders. "Hey, I'm sorry. I know what you're worried about, but you can relax. I like Claire. I like her kids. They need someone to lean on a little, and it feels damn good to be leaned on again, even if it's only in terms of a washing machine."

"I know that," Marilyn said. "But if you could find—"

"No." He shook his head. "I don't need to find someone who's the exact opposite of Sarah, because I don't see Sarah when I look at Claire. I really don't."

Marilyn sighed. "I wish you didn't feel the sudden need to run a Welcome Wagon."

Jonathon hugged her again. "Hey, I'm only being a good neighbor and sharing my trees."

"Your trees?"

"I don't have anything else," he replied.

"Don't sell yourself short," she muttered, getting to her feet. "You have a lot to offer a woman."

Trees were all this woman seemed to need though. Trees, and a washing machine. But he grinned at Marilyn and said nothing.

Claire stood in the doorway between the kitchen and dining room. She should go outside, she knew, if for no other reason than that it was rude to eavesdrop. Not that she could really hear what Jonathon was saying. Only bits and pieces of the conversation were floating in on the soft, summer air.

Still, she shouldn't stay hidden like this. She should march out there and meet this woman whose walk reminded her of the cavalry coming to the rescue. Yet telling herself to get out there and actually doing it were two different things. It had been hard enough to steel herself to meet Jonathon in the first place, and with each passing minute the deception grew harder. She felt like the fraud she was.

She took a step toward the door. She'd taken the job, and she'd finish it, she told herself firmly.

"They need someone to lean on, and it feels damn good to be leaned on again," she heard Jonathon say.

Why had those words come into the room so clearly when everything else had been muffled? Because this whole thing was wrong, that was why.

She took another step forward and glanced out the window. Molly and Katie were taking turns pushing the swing. She sighed, feeling her heart arguing with her mind. She was in this, like it or not, and the only way out was to find the notebook. Then her job would be over. Jonathon would not be hurt, and neither would her kids. And what about her? Her soul had cried out with joy when she'd met Jonathon, but this wouldn't come to anything. She knew better than to let her heart do her thinking.

Her resolve strong, her heart's pleas safely silenced, she carefully retraced her steps, peering around corners and into doorways. To the right of the basement was a room that had to be Jonathon's home office. Papers littered the surface of a large rolltop desk. A briefcase stood open on the seat of an upholstered swivel chair, and leather-bound volumes—legal texts, no doubt—filled the shelves on the wall to overflowing.

She made her way to the end of the hallway. Looking through the kitchen, she could see outside. Jonathon was still talking to the woman on the porch. It looked as if they were laughing and sharing confidences. Was this a woman who had her cap set for Jonathon?

Clenching her jaw tightly, Claire eased herself back to the office. She wanted the best for Jonathon. She wanted him to be happy, and if that meant finding another woman, then—

She stopped herself short. Another woman? Other than herself? Her heart had been leading her mind astray, and she hadn't even been aware of it. Jonathon wasn't hers, except in her fantasies, and those were easily ignored.

She paused at the door of his office, taking deep breaths and trying to bring her heart rate down to somewhere near normal. The lump in her throat pained her, and she tried to swallow. Oh, God, she told herself, she'd never do this again. She wasn't cut out to hurt people she respected. She wasn't cut out to be a burglar.

That thought brought the heat of anger into her cheeks and enough strength into her legs to propel her into Jonathon's office. She wasn't a criminal. A burglar was a criminal. She was a citizen, doing her duty for justice and her government. And you're earning a few bucks on the side, a little voice whispered in her ear. But she marched resolutely toward the desk and its litter of official-looking papers.

Her hands were quivering slightly, so she clasped them in front of herself as she stared at the desktop. Legal-size documents—briefs, probably—letters with official government headings and notes marked From The Desk Of were scattered all over. The desk also seemed to have a zillion pigeonholes that contained more notes, folded letters and envelopes. Where was she to start?

She started with another deep breath. At this rate she would still be standing here arguing with herself when Jonathon sent in a search party for her. She tiptoed to the door and looked out. She could still see him standing on the driveway, laughing and chatting with his visitor. She hurried back to the desk.

The letters and the legal briefs were of no interest to her, but the notebook might be buried among them. Claire pushed down on them, trying to feel for a rectangular lump approximately four by seven inches. Nothing.

The notebook Daniels had described was fairly thin, and the pile of papers was so thick that she might not feel it, so she began lifting up individual groups of papers. She came up empty here, too, and berated herself for her stupidity. Would

Jonathon leave a valuable item like the notebook lying on top of his desk?

Maybe the pigeonholes held a clue. She began to poke through them, keeping an ear cocked toward the kitchen. The screen door had squeaked when she'd opened it, but did it do the same for Jonathon? It should, unless he had an owner's special touch. Her body shivered slightly as his strong hands came to mind. The way he'd lifted Katie onto the countertop for knee-mending. The way he'd carried her laundry with one arm, as if it weren't heavy at all. The way his hands promised security and safety in even her most worried moments. Oh, he did indeed have a special touch.

She forced herself to concentrate on the pigeonholes. No more daydreaming, or she'd never find that notebook. And if she didn't find it by the time her two months were up she wouldn't get the other half of her money and the pall of suspicion would still be hanging over Jonathon's head. And neither of them would be any better off than they were now.

The pigeonholes yielded nothing but checkbooks, bills arranged by date of payment and other such miscellaneous papers. Nothing resembling a notebook. She scanned the shelves around the room. If Jonathon were innocent, why would he have hidden the notebook? Claire closed her eyes for a long moment. Nothing made any sense at all.

When Claire opened her eyes she was looking straight at a shelf that was filled to overflowing with Jonathon's personal life. Pictures and trophies from his past. Group photographs of Little League teams and high school basketball teams, and trophies, mostly swimming awards from college. Again her heart cried out at this intrusion into his life, but that didn't stop her from going closer.

Along with the team photographs, there were many family pictures. An older couple who were probably Jonathon's mother and father. A family photo, with Jonathon as a boy and two other children, a boy and a girl. Probably brother and sister. It was obviously taken on a farm.

A picture of a woman and a little boy were also on the shelf. Sarah and Timmy. Sarah did resemble her, not like a mirror image, but there was a strong resemblance. Yet it was to Timmy that her eyes were more drawn. He had Jonathon's mischievous eyes and impish smile. Just seeing the boy's picture and knowing of his tragic death hurt her. How could Jonathon leave this picture where he'd see it every time he walked into the room? Wouldn't the pain be unbearable?

Claire closed her eyes, trying to imagine what it would be like if Katie or Molly was taken from her like that. Would she want their picture out in the open, or would she prefer to bury the photos in a family album? Actually, in a situation like that, it probably wouldn't matter what she did with the pictures. She'd see them no matter where she went: swinging in a park, riding in a grocery cart in the supermarket or standing in line in front of a school. She'd hear their voices floating on the lazy breezes of a summer's day or skipping across the sharpness of the winter cold. The photographs could be hidden, but the images would live in her heart forever.

Shaking her head violently, Claire focused her attention on the room around her again. This wasn't getting her anywhere. She wasn't being paid to stand around and daydream. She was supposed to find that notebook.

The rows and rows of books called for her attention. She remembered a detective show on television in which the villain had hidden a gun in a hole cut out of a book. Not that Jonathon was a villain, she thought. A person didn't have to be a villain to hide something in a book. But then, if one wasn't a villain, why would one want to hide something?

Claire took a book from the shelf. It was heavy. She flipped through the pages. All were full pages. No holes—not even a tear. Replacing the book, she took another. And then another. Nothing. Nothing but pages filled with words. This was ridiculous, she thought suddenly. Most of these books couldn't hide a notebook. Besides—

On a shelf up above her, just out of reach, was a small, thin red book. Could it be the one?

The creaking of the kitchen door echoed through the house.

Chapter 4

"Claire?" Jonathon called out.

Her heart hadn't really stopped, not for good, she told herself. She pulled her hands away from the thin red book. With a bright expression on her face that belied the quaking of her knees, she went out into the hallway. "The girls are certainly having a great time. I was just watching them out the window here, and you'd think they'd never seen a swing before."

"They're just what the swing's been waiting for, too," Jonathon said without a trace of suspicion shadowing his eyes.

His obvious trust hurt her, but she tried not to think about it. "You've been nicer than we could ever have hoped for."

"Then you've been hoping for too little." He put his arm around her shoulder and led her toward the door. "Come on outside. There's someone here who wants to meet you."

To meet her or to check her out? Claire said nothing to indicate that she was aware of the woman's presence and went out onto the porch. Jonathon's proffered arm offered her a safety she didn't deserve.

The woman was waiting in the driveway. Her smile was vague and aimed at some distant tree, and her stance indicated suspicion. The main emotion that flashed across her face as Claire came out the door was total astonishment. Claire swallowed hard, then forced a look of innocence into her eyes.

"Claire, this is my sister Marilyn. Marilyn, Claire Haywood," Jonathon said.

His sister? No wonder she was rushing to his rescue. Claire's heart grew heavier with guilt, but she forced her smile to grow warmer. "Hi," she said. "You certainly have a nice brother."

Marilyn's smile almost touched her eyes. "I know." Her voice held a strange mixture of defiance and sadness. "I met your girls. They're darling." Her voice was softer now, that of a mother speaking to a mother.

"Thanks. And, thanks to your brother, their newly cleaned clothes will help them stay that way." Claire glanced over her shoulder at Jonathon. The warmth she saw rocked her to her soul. Was he offering her much more than clean clothes, or was her delirious heart trying to read caring and comfort into his gaze?

Claire turned back to Marilyn. "Does your family all live in this area?"

"We grew up west of the city, outside Joliet. Our other brother lives in Wheaton."

"How lucky you are that you're all close. My parents are in North Dakota, and my sister's in Missouri." She felt a sudden sadness at the way they'd drifted so apart.

"Yes, we are lucky," Marilyn said, and her tone suggested that she intended to see that they stayed that way, relying on each other, not on strangers.

There was nothing Claire could say. Marilyn was right to want to protect Jonathon, she was right not to trust her.

"Well, I'd better be off," Marilyn said after a moment, "or else my family will starve to death. You sure you don't need anything from the store?"

"Positive," Jonathon replied. Even Claire was aware that he was telling her to go, to stop worrying about him.

"Okay," Marilyn said. With a shrug and a wave, she started back down the driveway. "So long."

Claire watched until Marilyn had disappeared behind the hedge, then turned to Jonathon, her heart heavy. "Your sister seems very nice."

"Yeah, but she's a worrier."

Maybe she had reason to worry. "Were she and Sarah good friends?"

"Reasonably." Jonathon fell silent for a moment, and a pensive expression settled over his face, clouding his eyes. "They both believed their families came first, so they became friendly, especially once we moved out here."

Claire understood. Her family came first with her, too. A sick feeling started in her stomach and worked its way up to sting her eyes. Her presence here might seem likely to hurt Jonathon, but she would make sure it didn't. She'd make certain that the cloud of suspicion hanging over him dissipated.

"Aren't you guys ever gonna push us?"

Claire woke from her thoughts with a smile ready for Molly, but Jonathon spoke first. "We were just coming," he said, putting his arm around Claire's shoulder and heading her toward the backyard.

"Great." The little girl turned and started to run ahead, then stopped. "I told Katie she gets to have the first turn."

"That's nice of you," Claire said. The feel of Jonathon's arm around her shoulders put her conscience on alert, as well as her mind. Her heart was fluttering too rapidly under his attention, and her cheeks were flushed with a pleasant warmth. Didn't she have any sense? Couldn't she remember all the hurt her love for Brad had brought her? Stay on target and clear Jonathon's name, her mind told her.

"Being older sometimes means you have to wait longer," Molly said with such mournful wisdom that Claire couldn't help but smile up at Jonathon.

It was an instinctive sharing of a moment, natural and sweet. His eyes met hers, and a moment of silent laughter passed between them. It shouldn't have been any more than that. But even more than his touch, his heated gaze ignited needs in her heart she had thought long dead. Longings, hopes and impossible dreams suddenly sizzled between them, charged with the belief that all things were possible.

His lips brushed hers. It was the merest touch, yet, like the kiss of rain on parched earth, it gave life to her soul. His closeness, his strength, brought her hope that emotions she had thought buried could be revived. The world seemed young, filled with the promise of springtime.

"Was that lady really Paul's Mommy?" Molly called over her shoulder.

Reality returned, and with it the knowledge of what she was doing. Claire gently pulled away from Jonathon's side and caught up with Molly. "Yes, she was, sugar. Why do you ask?" She mussed Molly's hair fondly.

"Paul said she'd come over. Come on, Katie. Don't you want to swing?"

Katie appeared from a flower bed, where it looked as if she'd been digging with a stick. "Oh, dear. Hope she didn't wreck anything you treasured," Claire said to Jonathon.

"The things I treasure don't usually frequent flower beds," he said, teasingly.

His voice was lighthearted, but his words touched something in Claire's heart—that vulnerable spot that only he seemed able to awaken. She looked away, busying herself getting Katie onto the swing. Stay strong, her mind ordered. Stay strong.

This job was her lifeline, her salvation. The only way to keep her kids safe from the consequences of Brad's gambling. She couldn't let herself be distracted from her target. And that might very well be on a high shelf in Jonathon's office.

"Need help with the pushing, or am I extraneous?"

Claire felt safe with the kids between her and Jonathon. She could focus once more on her priorities. The broadness of his shoulders had no effect on her, and neither did the promise of his smile. "Actually, you can do the pushing, if you'd like," she told him. "I need to run in and check on the laundry."

"Sure you trust me to push right?"

"'Course Mommy does," Molly said. "When's it my turn?"

"In just a minute," he said. "When Katie gets up to thirty swings back and forth."

Jonathon adapted to the pushing rhythm easily, and he assured Molly that he wasn't getting cheated out of a turn. Claire swallowed a sigh as she turned away. Everyone out here was happy. She was free to go inside and continue spying on Jonathon. A bitter taste came to her mouth, but she ignored it and marched resolutely across the lawn.

It wasn't fair that Jonathon was so wonderful and Brad was a first-class rat. It wasn't fair that she should meet a man who could bring her happiness only after she'd been so badly burned. But life had never been fair, and it wasn't likely to start being so soon.

The screen squeaked as she pulled it open. The laughter of the children echoed through the kitchen, mingling with Jonathon's deeper tones. Claire got her feet moving in the right direction. Across the tiled kitchen floor, through the carpeted hallway and into the office. The laughter was still in the air, but she could ignore it now. She slid a hassock across the floor and stood on it.

The volume almost jumped into her hands. But once she was holding it, she could see that it wasn't a notebook. It was an address book, labeled clearly on the front and filled with addresses and Christmas-card notations.

She was almost giddy with relief. He hadn't stolen the evidence and hidden it in his house. She was convinced that he was innocent, just as her heart had told her all along.

A little voice tried to point out that the notebook might still be hidden here somewhere, but she refused to listen. She put the address book back in its place and moved the hassock. She could enjoy the evening, and when Daniels called next she'd tell him Jonathon didn't have it. Her heart applauded her decision.

"I can help Katie with her pj's," Molly said, her bright face framed with tendrils of hair that were still damp from her bath. "I always used to do it when we had baby-sitters."

"Well, you don't have a baby-sitter tonight," Claire pointed out, "so you can just climb up into bed and relax."

Molly did as she was told, but not without an argument. "I thought you said you were tired," she told Claire. "I could do it, 'cause I'm not tired."

"You ought to be. You had a busy day with all that swinging." Claire pulled Katie's pajama top over her head and placed a kiss on her nose when it reappeared. Katie giggled.

"He's a real nice man, isn't he?" Molly said around a small yawn.

Claire didn't have to ask who Molly was talking about. There was only one man in their lives these days who fit that category, though "nice" somehow seemed to restrictive. How about "handsome"? "Bold"? "Strong"? If the truth were known, she couldn't think of a single word that described Jonathon. She'd need multiple words, multiple sentences, multiple paragraphs. A person could write a book about a man like Jonathon Tyler.

"Isn't he?"

Molly's plaintive wail brought Claire quickly back to the present reality—the two-bedroom apartment by the train station, her two little girls and that damn notebook. Would Daniels call tonight? How could she convince him that Jonathon didn't have it, that he never would have kept it? Her heart had known the truth long before her mind had admitted it. The trouble was, it was Daniels's mind she had to convince. How in the world would she get him to believe her?

"Yes, Mr. Tyler is very nice." Claire picked Katie up and carried her over to her bed. Daniels would believe her. He had to. "Anybody need a last drink of water before lights-out?"

"Don't we get a story?"

"Moll, it's late. Way past your bedtime. How about if you have two tomorrow night?"

"We won't be able to get to sleep without a story," Molly mumbled. "If you're too tired, we could call Mr. Tyler. He said to call him anytime we needed anything."

"I don't think he meant reading you girls a story."

But Claire could see herself calling him and asking him to

read the girls a story. She sighed as she realized how glad he
would be to come. Maybe she ought to ask him to bring his
favorite bedtime story for her and see if it would banish her
nightmares. There was no doubt that lying in the dark listening
to his deep voice would banish any and all bogeymen from
her nights. Her cheeks grew hot and her breath caught at the
thought of it. Only the sound of the phone ringing allowed her
to escape from the room and her vivid imagination.

"Whoops! There's the phone." She gave each girl a quick
kiss and a tuck-in, then darted out into the hallway.

"If that's Mr. Tyler," Molly called after her, "tell him we
need a story."

"It won't be," Claire said. "And get back in bed."

Little footsteps had been about to follow her. Instead, there
was a weary sigh and a slight creaking of bedsprings as Claire
hurried into the kitchen. It would be Daniels, not Jonathon.
She took a deep breath and told herself that she wasn't afraid.
She wanted to talk to him, she had to talk to him, had to tell
him about Jonathon's innocence. But it wasn't Daniels. It was
Brad.

"What do you want?" she asked.

"Is that any way to treat the father of your children?"

That remark had always brought guilt tumbling down
around her shoulders in the past, but all it did now was fan
the flames of her anger. "I'm sure they would enjoy seeing
their father once in a while," she pointed out.

"I've got things to do," he replied. "Besides, little girls
need mothers. They've got nothing in common with fathers."

Her lips came together in a straight line. She remembered
how both girls had opened up to Jonathon's gentleness and
how they had laughed at his antics. Little children, boys or
girls, needed a mother and a father. But Brad didn't understand
that. He never had.

"I'm sure you must want something," Claire said. "You
never call just to be sociable."

"Boy—" he snorted "—it appears that you don't hold me
in high esteem."

"I don't see how you could have any doubts about that. I don't, and I don't pretend to."

"Maybe things would have worked out for us if you'd pretended a little more," he growled.

Pretend what? That he cared about any of them? "Brad, I'm tired. Now tell me what you want or I'll hang up and go to bed."

"I'm being pressed," he said. "Hard."

Claire felt sick and tired. Brad's gambling debts weren't their fault, yet she and the girls had to suffer for them.

"They're going to start squeezing the kids if I don't pay soon."

"I know that," she said, weariness and anger merging into fear.

Tears rolled around the edges of her eyelids, ready to spill over. Her lower lip was quivering, and she took it firmly between her teeth. It wasn't fair. Fathers were supposed to protect their daughters, not bring them harm.

"I'm well aware of the danger the girls are in," Claire said after a moment, pleased that her voice was coming out calm and cold. "You've told me often enough."

"Would you rather not know?"

Ignoring the question, Claire went on. "I am working very hard to get you the money. You keep those goons away from the girls."

"I'm trying, kid. I'm really trying. You get the cash and we're all home free."

But would they be? A great weariness sat on her shoulders. Would she ever be able to stop living in fear? Would she ever stop seeing shadows lurking in every corner?

"You still there, kid?"

"Yes," she said wearily. "But not for long. I'll get you your money. Good night."

She put the phone down firmly, but that was as far as her blustering determination went. She stood in the lighted kitchen, suddenly feeling as if she were onstage. The curtains on the windows were open wide, exposing her to the watchful eyes of the night. She pulled them closed, but she still felt exposed. She flicked off the lights and walked into the darkened living room and over to the front window.

Was someone out there even now, watching and waiting for a chance to get at the girls? The night seemed so still, so peaceful. How could it hold danger? Yet it did, and the only way to stop it was to keep sneaking around a nice, gentle man, to keep living this lie and using his pain to her advantage. What choice did she have?

Claire sighed and walked into her bedroom. She was exhausted, but she knew that sleep wouldn't come tonight.

Chapter 5

Daniels didn't call all the next week, and he didn't return Claire's calls, either. She felt as if she were in limbo, suspended from unseen puppet strings and forced to dance to a tune she didn't like. Except she didn't completely dislike her situation. Spending time with Jonathon was not a hardship, as long as she concentrated on proving him innocent. She was almost able to put on Brad's call and its attendant worries out of her mind.

"So what flavor are you going to have?"

"Oh!"

Claire started, and her hand flew to her throat when she realized that they'd stopped in front of the ice-cream parlor. She swallowed, waiting for her heartbeat to slow, as Jonathon frowned in concern. It was Friday evening. It had been seven days since they'd met—seven days of dinners and walks and laughter that would break her heart with sweetness if she let it. But it had also been seven days of sneaking around Jonathon's house, looking for that notebook, every chance she got. Seven days of watching the girls like a hawk, jumping at every passing car and every innocently friendly stranger. Then, this evening, Jonathon had wanted to take Molly and Katie for ice-cream cones. Fear had warred with her desire for the girls to have a normal life. She'd given in, then spent the next fifteen minutes questioning her wisdom. What if the girls got too close to Jonathon?

"Sorry if I scared you," Jonathon said. "I didn't know ice-cream selection was so terrifying."

She found a smile to convince him that she was fine. "I was daydreaming, that's all," she said. "It just didn't register that we'd stopped walking."

He pushed open the door and let them all inside. The air smelled of air-conditioning and chocolate, reassuring scents that told her not to worry. They were with Jonathon, and they were safe.

"I see," he said slowly. "So answer my question, then. What flavor are you going to have? Terrifying tutti-fruit or daydreaming macadamia?"

"Very funny," she said, moving past him to take the girls' hands and lead them up to the counter. "Two chocolate single-scoop cones, please."

The teenage girl behind the counter moved off to fill the order, and Claire felt Jonathon come up behind her. Her senses tingled, and her body warmed to his nearness. She stiffened her spine and resisted the sensations.

"No, the real question is whether you are a chocolate person and a single-scoop person," he whispered, his breath tickling the back of her neck.

Her determination to resist him faltered.

"Don't tell me. You're chocolate, but never a single scoop. Double or triple, maybe, but never single."

The counter girl returned with Molly's and Katie's cones, and Jonathon handed them down to them. "There's nothing like chocolate, is there, girls? True food for the soul."

Molly frowned at him as she licked her cone. "I like mine in my stomach."

"And on your face," Claire said with a laugh, wiping a smear of chocolate from the girl's face with a napkin. It felt too right to be here with Jonathon like this, to be doing such family things. She needed to put some distance between them. Claire turned to the waiting teenager. "A single scoop of vanilla for me."

"Vanilla?" Jonathon repeated under his breath.

"That's right," Claire said briskly. "I don't like the richness of chocolate or all the calories in a double scoop." *See?* she was telling him—and her own heart. *We don't have that much in common.*

"Actually, I knew that was what you'd have," he told her as the girl brought over her cone. "You see, opposites attract and complement each other. Man and woman. Chocolate and vanilla."

That was a bit much even for her weary heart, and she laughed. "Single and double scoop."

"Right."

He grinned and ordered two scoops of chocolate, just as she'd known he would. Then, after paying for the cones, they wandered outside. The evening sun had long since disappeared from the streets, leaving only long shadows and faint heat shimmering up from the streets as a pleasant reminder of the day's warmth. Somewhere in the next block a lawn mower was running. A dog barked. Kids squealed delightedly in neighboring yards. This was exactly what a family neighborhood should be.

"So," Jonathon said after a long moment, "have you noticed what a great guy I am?"

She turned to stare at him. How could she not have noticed? "I beg your pardon?"

He shrugged. "Actually, I could be a Boy Scout. Loyal, honest, trustworthy and square. Isn't that their pledge?"

"I wouldn't know."

He grinned and ate some of his ice cream. "Never a Boy Scout? I wasn't, either, but I could be now. I'm good with knots, I can start a fire in the woods, and I help little old ladies across the street."

She let his silliness become contagious. "Just what is the point of all this?" she asked, biting into the teeth-tingling cold

of the ice cream. "Do you want my endorsement for Eagle
Scout of the Year?"

His teasing attitude fell away as he reached for her hand.
"I want you to tell me what's wrong."

His hand closed around hers tightly, a lifeline for her to
cling to, if only she dared. But she didn't. Instead, she stared
at her ice cream. "Wrong? Why do you think something's
wrong?"

"Because you're wound up tighter than a drum."

She shrugged. "I'm just a tense person. You don't know
me very well yet."

He shook his head, and his hold on her hand tightened. "I
know you better than you think. Is it money? I've got some
put away I can loan you."

The differences between him and Brad seemed to leap out
at her. She started, pulling her hand away from Jonathon's.
"For goodness' sake, don't go offering money to strangers.
For all you know, I might be some con artist." She caught up
with the girls and wiped some of the dripping chocolate from
their faces.

"If you were a con artist, you'd accept it." He joined her,
still eating his ice cream. "You aren't a con artist, and you
aren't a stranger. I just wish you'd let me help you."

A moment's contemplation of an approaching bed of marigolds helped Claire regain her control. "I don't know where
you've gotten the idea that I need help," she said lightly. "I
admit I've been rather distracted lately, what with the divorce
and settling into a new place. I'm not quite ready to relax."

"Then you need me to help you."

Oh, how she did. But instead of jumping at the offer the
way she wanted to, she jumped at the excuse it gave her.
"Actually, that might be the problem—or part of it." She
returned to her cone with vigor. "You've really been wonderful—too wonderful, almost—and I guess I'm just a bit gun-
shy at the moment."

A curtain seemed to come down over his eyes. He took a
deep bite of his ice cream. "I see."

She wasn't sure what he thought he saw, but she knew that

sudden chill in his voice had nothing to do with the ice cream. "No, I don't think you do. You're so nice, so easy to be with, that I could easily just start leaning on you all the time, and that wouldn't be fair to you."

"Do you hear me complaining?"

She shook her head. "It's just that the girls and I need to build a life for ourselves." She bit into her cone again. It was almost gone. What would she use for a distraction when it was?

"Girls, stay with us! Don't go running ahead!"

"Hey, don't worry," Jonathon said. His hand touched her arm, then caught at her hand, pulling her back from the edge of terror. "They're just going to see the Willoughby's cat, Rufus. He comes out to say hi to all the kids who go by."

Sure enough, a fat old tabby cat was sitting invitingly on the sidewalk of a house two doors ahead, but the girls had obediently slowed down to a walk. Claire sighed at the way their shoulders slumped.

"I guess I was too hard on them," she said, wishing desperately that she could tell him the truth.

She finished her cone and let her glance wander over Jonathon's face. Surely his broad shoulders could support a heavy load. Why not confide in him? Why not let him help her? Wasn't he offering to? Yet, as it was, she was using him. To lean on him, to ask him for help, would just be using him more. She had to be strong, to tie her heart up securely so that it wasn't in danger, and think only of what she needed to do for her kids.

"Isn't he cute, Mommy?" Molly was purring along with the cat. "I wonder what his name is."

"Rufus," Claire said.

Molly frowned at her. "How'd you know that?"

"Mommies know everything," Jonathon said.

The girls looked skeptical, and Claire joined in when Jonathon laughed. Her storm of worries was dissipating. Nothing would happen to the girls. She would get the job finished and buy their freedom. And then what? that nagging little voice asked her. What about Jonathon and the way he made her heart race with joy?

She bent down to pet the cat, firmly keeping her eyes away from the man who so occupied her thoughts. She didn't know what then. Mommies didn't quite know everything, but she wouldn't let that stop her.

"I'm thirsty, Mommy."

Claire dumped the grocery bag on the counter Monday afternoon and turned her attention to the demanding screams of the telephone.

"There's some lemonade in the refrigerator, Molly," she said as she picked up the receiver. "Pour a glass for Katie, too." Then she turned her attention to the mouthpiece. "Hello."

"You've been calling."

"Mr. Daniels," she said, relief flooding her heart. She sank into the nearest chair and kicked her shoes off. "I was beginning to think I'd dreamed you up."

"You found the notebook?" There was no mistaking the eagerness in his voice.

"No. He doesn't have it."

"He doesn't have it?" Daniels voice was tinged with sarcasm. "And how can you be so sure of that?"

"I've looked," Claire said quickly. Her certainty was based on the honesty in his eyes and on his gentle understanding and compassion, but she knew that none of those things would carry any weight with Daniels. "I've looked everywhere." Even to her, that argument sounded weak.

Daniels sighed impatiently. "We know he has the notebook, Ms. Haywood. He signed it out and never returned it. Your not finding it isn't a good sign. It may mean he destroyed it."

"No! He wouldn't have," she said. Her heart cried out, as well as her voice. "That would mean he was trying to hide it."

"That always was a possibility,' Mr. Daniels reminded her.

As far as she was concerned, it had *never* really been a possibility, not once she'd met him and felt the gentle strength in his eyes. She knew he wasn't hiding evidence. But those weren't things she could explain, or wanted to explain, to Daniels. She had to retain her objectivity if she was going to help Jonathon.

Taking a deep breath, she steadied her rocky heart and voice. "I know it was a possibility," she said quietly. "I just don't think it's likely since I've started searching. He seems so conscientious."

"Conscientious people are susceptible to bribes also, Ms. Haywood."

Unbidden, the thought of the money Jonathon had offered to lend her came to her mind. No! It couldn't have come from a bribe. It was savings, or insurance money. Jonathon was honest. Her heart couldn't tremble at the sight of someone she couldn't trust. She had never felt this overpowering wave of emotion about Brad.

"Shall we get a search warrant?" Daniels asked, his voice suddenly seeming to carry a threat.

"No," Claire said. "Not yet. I'll keep looking. I'll find it."

"Good."

The line went dead and the silent air was filled with the scents of threats. The girls and Jonathon—innocent targets, all of them—with only Claire to keep them safe. Was she strong enough?

She reached over and hung up the phone, but even as she took her hand away from it the room was filled with its ringing again. Was it Daniels again? Her hand trembled, echoing the fear in her heart. The phone rang again, and she just stared at it, wanting to run from the danger it suddenly seemed to hold.

"Mommy, the phone's ringing," Molly said from the doorway, her tiny face creased with confusion.

"Yes, honey." Claire swallowed, forcing her face into a smile. "I was just going to get it."

She reached out, trying not to show that her mouth had gone dry with fear. It was Jonathon. Relief, peace, safety washed over her, and she leaned against the wall for support.

"Hi," she breathed.

"What a greeting," he said. He had to have heard the need

in her voice and the gladness in her heart at finding out it was him. His voice was soft, not mocking. "I'm going to call more often."

Call as often as you like, she wanted to shout, but she said nothing of the sort. "You're lucky you caught us. We just got in after a busy day of park visiting, the speech therapist and then a little grocery shopping. We are certainly glad to be home, or at least I am. How was your day?"

"Duck soup," Jonathon said with a laugh. "Almost dull, compared to yours."

"Mondays aren't hectic days for you?" she asked. "I thought everyone waited for the weekend to get arrested."

"The police are busy over the weekend," he said. "But once things reach us lawyers the wheels of justice turn very slowly."

"You make it sound as if all you lawyers do is sit around all day."

"Shh," he whispered. "Don't say it that loud. If people know the truth, the whole lot of us will be selling pencils out on the street."

"I doubt that." As if by magic, her worries were fading away and a warm glow of contentment was taking their place. There was another feeling smoldering inside her, also, not a comfortable contentment, but a knot of delicious tension in the pit of her stomach. Her knees wanted to turn to jelly. She wanted to lean her head against his chest and draw on his strength. There was such a sense of power about him. Her fingers ached to explore it, and her heart longed to feel the wonder of him.

Claire sighed and opened her eyes. She couldn't remember closing them. Molly was staring at her.

"Can we watch television?" the girl asked.

Claire nodded her assent as Jonathon cleared his throat. "Actually, I have an ulterior motive in calling you," he said. "I'm in need of a little assistance."

"Certainly," she said. "Ask and you shall receive." Claire rubbed her bare feet against the cool vinyl floor.

He laughed. "Shouldn't you find out what it is first?"

"I trust you."

"I'd appreciate a ride from the train station this evening. My car's in the garage for the day."

"No problem." Would that all her problems could be solved so easily.

"I get in at 6:20," he said. "Why don't the three of you pick me up, and then we'll head on to the Cypress for a bit of dinner?"

"You don't have to take us out."

"I don't have to do anything," he replied. "I want to. Anyway, if I don't have food in my stomach by 6:45, I turn into a ravaging beast." His gentle baritone, rumbling deep within his chest, called forth images of laughing brown eyes, strong, tanned hands and arms that were just made for holding her.

"A raging beast? I—"

"*Ravaging*. I said *ravaging* beast. You're not paying attention."

Claire found it impossible to suppress her laughter.

"You're also not taking this seriously," he continued.

"I'm sorry."

"I was going to forgive you." Each word exited the speaker wrapped in sternness. "But it's no more Mr. Nice Guy. I want you and your troops at the station at 6:20 sharp, ready and willing to move on to dinner. That's an order."

"Yes, sir," she said. Chuckles flavored her words.

"See you in a little while." He'd switched back to wrapping his words in a gentle tone.

"Yes, sir," she repeated.

The dial tone signaled the end of the conversation, and Claire lazily laid the handset in its cradle. She leaned against the wall. In a little while. He'd said he'd see her in a little while.

In a little while! Her eyes opened wide, and she pushed herself away from the comfort of the wall. It was already past five o'clock. It really was just a little while. She ran into the living room.

"Girls, turn off the TV. We all have to shower and dress up, and we don't have much time."

Her heart pounded through showers and combing tangled hair while little girls squirmed impatiently, through her own shower and a frowning inspection of her hair, which was really Sarah's hair. Would Jonathon care about her with brown hair instead of blond? If it was longer and straight instead of short and curly? Now was not the time for introspection, she told herself, hurrying the girls into the car.

The station was crowded, but she found a place to park down the street and climbed out of the car. He hadn't told her where to wait, and the crowds seemed to be growing all the time. Would he find them?

Another train pulled into the station, and Claire smoothed down the front of her cotton dress for the umpteenth time. She'd never been to the Cypress, but she'd driven by it once and remembered that it had looked rather fancy. She hoped her cotton dress would be all right. It was the middle of June, and the weather was too warm to dress all that formally.

The train came to a stop and Claire glanced back at the two clean, shiny faces hanging out the car window. Both were anxiously searching the train for signs of Jonathon. She turned away as a sharp tightness rose in her stomach. The girls were becoming attached to Jonathon, but soon her summer dress would be out of place, and so would they. Her assignment would be over, and they'd be moving on.

"There he is," Molly shouted, and Katie began waving vigorously.

Jonathon's tie was loose, his briefcase was in his left hand, his coat over one shoulder. He looked tired, but he had a huge smile on his face. Claire's initial joy was quickly drowned by a bittersweet thought. Jonathon looked so happy. Just like any other commuting husband being greeted by his family after a hard day of work in the big city.

"Hi," he said, bending down to kiss her lightly on the lips.

She raised herself up slightly on tiptoe to receive his kiss, which was all too brief. "Hi," she said.

"Hello, ladies," he said to the girls.

They responded with huge face-covering grins.

"Can you put this in the trunk?" he asked, indicating his briefcase.

Claire stared at it for a moment. Was the notebook in it? She squashed the thought angrily and moved quickly to open the trunk. She didn't have to look for the stupid notebook twenty-four hours a day. She and the kids had a right to dinner and a little easy conversation.

"Do you know where the Cypress is, or would you like me to drive?" he asked.

"It's up on Route 34, isn't it?" Claire said. "Sit back and relax. I'll drive."

"Thanks." His tone was full of gratitude as he slumped in the front passenger seat.

"I thought you'd had an easy day," Claire said after she'd backed out of the parking space.

Jonathon shrugged. "I might have lied a little."

The rest of the short trip was made in silence. Once at the restaurant, they were seated quickly in a secluded booth near the back. With the restaurant's natural dim lighting and the location of their table it was as if they were alone in the world and safe. Claire felt herself relax as she stared at the long menu the waiter handed her. It seemed that everything was à la carte and expensive.

"Do they have a children's menu?" she asked.

"Not officially," Jonathon replied. "But they'll fix a hamburger or fried chicken for kids."

"Good," Claire said, nodding. "They both like chicken."

"Do they got French fries?" Molly asked.

"Hey, does the queen live in Buckingham Palace?"

Molly turned a puzzled glance on Claire, then looked back at Jonathon. "I don't know," she replied.

His eyes softened. "I'm sorry, honey," he said, taking Molly's hand. "I was trying to be funny, and I'm too tired to make it."

"That's okay," Molly assured him, her face solemn.

"Thank you," he said.

"Do they got French fries?" she asked again.

"The best."

Her little face still solemn, she thought a moment. Then she said, "Okay, I'll have some."

"You got it, kid."

"Katie likes French fries, too."

"Two orders of French fries," Jonathon said. Turning to Claire, he asked, "And how about a carafe of white wine?"

She nodded. As Jonathon turned to get the waiter's attention, she felt a sharpness behind her eyes. The girls were so happy, and everything was so nice. They were acting like a real family. She smiled, hoping it looked natural. She wasn't going to think about Daniels or the notebook or Brad or his shylocks. They were just going to have a nice dinner.

Dinner was over all too quickly, and their safe cocoon was given to another set of diners. Jonathon drove Claire and the girls back to the apartment, while Claire tried to hold on to the peace of the evening. There were only scraps of it left by the time he pulled into her parking lot, but a different sort of emotion was beginning to grow in its place. A hypnotic spell was weaving in and around her heart, telling her that the fire in his eyes was a reflection of the passion in his heart, that the longings in her soul could overcome the lies in her life, that dreams could come true if one wished hard enough. She had to keep remembering Brad and all the pain her love for him had brought her, but even that didn't work to keep her strong.

As the girls scrambled from the car and skipped across the lot, Jonathon reached for her hand. "It was a nice dinner," he said.

"It's been a nice week."

"Has it only been a week?" Jonathon asked with a quick laugh that echoed warmly in the gentle evening sun. "I guess in some ways it has been, but in others it's like you've given me a whole new life."

"No. That life was always there, waiting for you to want it."

"All right, so you made me want it." His hand reached out to touch her cheek gently, to stroke it tenderly. "But in both cases the common denominator is you."

His touch mesmerized her, made her powers of speech and thought desert her. His hands and his eyes captivated her; her heart called out to his.

"Is it?" she said vaguely as they pressed closer together to get between two parked cars.

He was close—oh, so close—and her soul hungered for him to come even closer. Longings her body had forgotten came alive under his gaze and the sweetness of his touch. For a marvelous, magical moment his lips came down on hers and all the shadows melted. Her life was sunshine and happiness, and birds sang of love and contentment and belonging. Then he pulled away, and the memory of distant storms prodded at her.

"The girls," she said slowly. "I have to find the girls."

"They're fine," Jonathon said. "What can happen to them at home?"

What indeed? Her heart knew the answer to that all too well. She hurried quickly across the parking lot. "Katie, Molly," she called out.

The girls had been at the door, squeezing their way into the vestibule of the apartment building, and now they came racing out.

"We have a letter, Mommy," Molly told her as Katie waved the white envelope over her head. "It wasn't in our mailbox. It was sort of stuck in the side."

Claire reached for the letter.

"I thought the mailman already came today," Molly said.

"It was probably put into someone else's box by mistake," Jonathon told them as Claire glanced idly at the envelope. Suddenly the air had turned cold. Her whole world had lost its sunshine. She felt the cold starkness of reality.

"Who's the letter from, Mommy?"

"Just an ad, honey. Nothing important," Claire said, stuffing the envelope into a pocket and hurrying them up the few steps toward the apartment building. Even out of her sight, though, Brad's handwriting still danced before her eyes. "Come on, girls. Let's get inside."

"Can't we play outside for a while?" Molly asked. "It's still early."

"No," Claire snapped. It didn't matter that the evening was warm or that the sounds of a Little League game were floating over from the park. Everything appeared comfortable and safe, and yet she couldn't help shivering. She felt chilly.

"No," she repeated, her voice gentle this time, but just as firm. Aware of Jonathon's puzzled glance, she smiled at the girls. "Tomorrow's your first swimming lesson, Molly, so I think you should get a lot of rest tonight. Don't you?"

Molly's face clearly showed that she wanted to argue, but her concerns about her first encounter with a real swimming pool apparently won. With a gigantic sigh, she took Katie's hand and led her toward the door. "Come on, Katie. Let's go in."

Jonathon stopped Claire with a hand on her arm. "Claire, what's wrong?"

"Nothing," she said brightly. "Nothing at all."

His eyes said that he didn't believe her, but he let her pass by him and sweep the girls into the apartment. But even as she opened the door, a wave of terror washed over her. Were they any safer up here? This apartment building was no fortress. Who was to say someone wasn't waiting inside right now? But the door opened onto silence, shadowed and still.

"Well, let's see if there's anything on television," Claire said.

Jonathon turned the set on, flicking the channels as the girls watched. The letter seemed to be burning a hole in Claire's pocket, but all she did was push it down deeper inside.

"Hey, wasn't there a cartoon on?" she said. "Try channel five."

"Oh, boy," Molly cried as Jonathon flipped back to the station that had previously had a cereal commercial on. An animated restaurant scene was now on.

"Can we watch, Mommy?" Molly pleaded. "Can we stay up and watch the whole thing?"

Jonathon joined in. "Can we, huh? Can we?"

Claire had to laugh in spite of her fears. "All right," she replied. "But it's bedtime right after the show is over."

Katie and Molly nodded. "Okay," Jonathon agreed. "I promise, too. When the show is over, it's straight to bed."

His eyes teased her. She half wanted to join in and half wished she could run and hide. She saw the desire in his face, along with concern and a pleading for her to confide in him. But once she started baring her soul she wouldn't be able to stop, and then the caring in his eyes would turn to anger and hatred.

"You guys excuse me?" she asked, and slipped down the hall to the bathroom. With shaking hands she closed the door behind her and opened the envelope. A letter came out, and a photograph fell to the floor.

The letter was short and to the point: "They want the money, now. These people don't play around."

Claire took a deep breath, then forced herself to pick up the photo. Her heart stopped. It was a picture of the girls playing on the swings in the park down the road. Their faces were smiling, and trust and happiness filled their whole beings. The message of the picture was as simple and clear as the letter. If someone could get close enough to take the photograph, he could get close enough to do anything else he wanted.

The fears that had been lurking in the corners of her soul broke free to consume her. She began to shake uncontrollably. She wrapped her arms around her body to try to contain herself, but the trembling was too strong. Afraid that Jonathon or the girls might hear her, she choked back her sobs.

What kind of animals were these people to be totally unaffected by the trust that shone forth from these children's faces. These people were beasts. Unfeeling, twisted beasts that had no place in God's plan for the universe. She would not let them get her girls. Shoving the letter and the picture back in her pocket, she splashed cold water on her face until the redness around her eyes faded. She would find a way to keep her family safe.

The cartoon was coming to an end as she eased herself onto the sofa. Both girls were crowded on Jonathon's lap and giv-

ing their attention to the fat orange cartoon cat on the screen.
Jonathon's eyes went to her immediately, and she knew that
he could see her distress.

"Is anything wrong?"

Claire forced a smile onto her face and grabbed at the first
lie she could think of. "I guess I had a little more wine than
I should have."

"I'm sorry." He reached over to take her hand. "You
shouldn't have had it if you didn't want it."

"It was good. I didn't think it would bother me."

Jonathon squeezed her hand and looked deep into her eyes.
She saw a bit of pain there, but mostly his expression indicated
questioning concern.

What picture were her eyes giving Jonathon? Could he see
her fears? Could he tell that all she longed to do was fall asleep
in his arms and wake up by his side, safe from all her worries?
Could he tell that underneath all the battles she was fighting
was a desire to bring sunshine into his life?

She blinked back sudden tears and turned away. What kind
of fairy tale was she feeding herself? She wanted love and
trust and safety, but was she offering him the same? How
could she spy on him and yet expect something wonderful to
develop between them? Only a fool would let herself think
this way, even for a moment.

"Come on, girls." She stood up abruptly. "Bedtime."

"Can't we wait to see what else is on?" Molly asked.

"Nope."

"Will you read us a story?"

"How about letting me read you one tonight?" Jonathon
said. "I'm a good bedtime-story reader."

"Are you really?" Molly asked.

"Scout's honor," he said, holding up two fingers.

"Oh, boy!" Molly whooped and ran for the bedroom, and
Katie, her face flushed with excitement, pattered rapidly behind.

"You don't mind, do you?" Jonathon asked Claire. "I
thought if you weren't feeling well..." His voice trailed off,
but his eyes finished his statement of concern for her.

Claire forced the now-familiar fake smile onto her lips. "I'm feeling much better, but no, I don't mind. The girls will consider it a wonderful treat and will probably con you into reading all their books."

His smile seemed to offer her the world. "Don't worry," he said. "I'll put up a strong fight. I won't read any more than six or seven."

She laughed in spite of the growing agony in her soul, then fled to the girls' bedroom. This was getting too complicated.

For once, the girls were amazingly cooperative about getting their pajamas on. Arms went in the right holes, and so did buttons.

"Maybe Mr. Tyler can tuck us in, too, Mommy."

Claire stopped unbraiding Katie's hair in surprise. "Don't you want me to tuck you in?"

Molly climbed up on the edge of her bed, swinging her feet. "You get to do it all the time," she said.

Claire went back to the unbraiding. "It's not really Mr. Tyler's job to read you stories and tuck you in."

"But he said he wanted to."

"I know." Claire finished Katie's hair and gave her a hug. "Mr. Tyler is a very nice man, but this is our family, and we have to take care of ourselves."

Molly solemnly pondered her words. "Mr. Tyler doesn't have any family, does he?"

"No, he doesn't."

"So, if he wants to read stories and stuff, why don't we just let him?"

Why don't we just let him? Oh, Molly, it would be so easy. There was so much that she would just like to let him do. But someday Jonathon's trial of pain would be over. And some-day—someday soon, she fervently hoped—she would find that damn notebook. Then Jonathon would know she was a spy, and everything would be over. Summer would be gone, and winter would come early. There wouldn't be any autumn.

A light rap on the door interrupted her thoughts.

"Are you girls ready?" Jonathon called, poking his head in.

"Yes," Molly shouted, and Katie vigorously nodded her head.

Forcing the worry lines from her face, Claire squared her shoulders and stepped aside to let him in. The girls quickly dragged him over to Molly's bed.

"We always sit here," she said, pointing to her bed, which was over by the wall. "We can lean back against the wall and you can let your feet hang down."

"That sounds fine."

"And be careful, because Mommy gets mad if you put your shoes on the bed," Molly warned.

He gave Claire a quick wink. "We certainly wouldn't want Mommy mad at us."

"No, you wouldn't," Molly agreed. Katie shook her head solemnly.

"What would she do if she got mad?" Jonathon asked.

"She'd make you stay in your room."

Jonathon shrugged. "So what? I could watch TV and read comic books."

"Uh-uh," Molly said. "She'd take them all away."

"I'd make paper airplanes and throw them out the window."

In spite of Claire's heavy heart, Molly's stern countenance was almost enough to make her burst out laughing. Jonathon was acting like an ornery little boy, and Molly was being firm, like the teacher she always said she wanted to be.

"She'd make you stay in bed all day," Molly said.

"Oh?"

Claire's senses woke with a start. It was amazing what meaning could be conveyed by a single word. The look in Jonathon's eyes increased her heart rate, brought a warmth to her cheeks and weakened her knees.

"She'd only let you out to go potty and eat."

"Hmm."

Claire concentrated on the clown sitting on the little chair by Katie's bed. She could feel Jonathon's eyes on her, hot eyes that were stripping away her facade. She knew she mustn't look up. If their eyes met, she was lost. He would read all the fears and desires in her soul, and there would be no hiding her heart again.

"And if you didn't do like you were told you'd get a big spanking," Molly finished.

"Sounds good to me."

Jonathon and the girls all laughed, breaking the tension and forcing Claire to chuckle along with them. How good he was with the girls, so free and easy and tender. Her eyes suddenly found his, and her breath caught in her throat. She was playing with fire, but somehow she was forgetting to be afraid of getting burned.

"Molly," she said, her voice sounding hoarse and strained, "better pick out your story."

"Let me," Jonathon said. Leaning over to the small bookshelf between the beds, he pulled a book out. "How about this one?"

"No," a little voice said firmly.

Claire's shoulder slumped with weariness. Things were really getting out of hand. She couldn't walk by Jonathon without her heart doing flips, and now her kids were treating him like a big brother. Things could not go on like this.

"Molly—" she started.

But Molly was staring, mouth hanging open, at her little sister. Then the voice slowly penetrated the fog that lately seemed to be Claire's mind. The word was simple and definitive, but it had its own unique timbre and tone—one she hadn't heard before. Her emotions were stretched so thin that Claire thought for a moment she was going to faint. It wasn't Molly who had spoken, it was Katie.

"This one." Katie pointed at the book she wanted. Molly closed her mouth, but her eyes remained as wide as two saucers. Claire thought her heart had surely stopped beating.

"Okay," Jonathon said, his voice easy and offhand, as he picked up the chosen book. But his eyes darted to Claire's and silently shared her joy.

Katie was speaking! Claire wanted to shout it from the rooftops, wanted to hug the girls, wanted to hug Jonathon, but her joy died quickly as a sense of agony overtook her. The doctors had all said that Katie would start speaking once she was comfortable with her environment and felt secure with the world around her. Jonathon had given her security. Jonathon, the man Claire was spying on, the man who trusted her, the man she was using. Claire felt sick to her stomach.

"This one all right with you?" Jonathon asked Molly, who nodded solemnly. He leaned back against the wall, and both girls snuggled up to him, one on either side. Molly smothered a little yawn.

Not trusting herself, Claire let herself out of the room. In the silent emptiness of the living room, she sank wearily into a chair and let her tears flow. Things just couldn't go on the way they were. Everyone would get hurt. It was time for the truth.

Chapter 6

"Well, the girls are on the sleepy-bye train and rolling into dreamland," Jonathon said, pausing in the living room doorway to stretch his shoulders and work his neck. He was out of shape. Two little girls hugging him for the length of three stories and he was all stiff. He'd have to get back in training. He took another step into the living room and smiled at Claire as she stared out the front window.

"Hey," he said. "Wasn't that the greatest thing? In another few weeks I'll bet Katie will be yakking a mile a minute. I think she's going to be—" He cut himself off.

Claire wasn't acknowledging his presence at all. She was still looking out the front window. Her back was to him, but Jonathon could sense her strain.

"Claire?"

As she slowly turned to face him, Jonathon could see that her eyes were rimmed with red and that her nose also sported a touch of red. Her face had a scrubbed-with-cold-water look, probably achieved over the kitchen sink with the piece of paper towel she was clutching in her hand.

"Claire." He moved toward her. "Baby, what's wrong?"

"Don't come near me, please."

"What did I do?" he asked. "Tell me so I won't do it again."

Her face was filled with such pain and weariness that it took all his will to keep from running up and crushing her in his arms. A feeling of anger rose up to join the tenderness he felt for her. He wanted to destroy whoever had hurt her this way.

"Just sit down," Claire said. "There are some things I have to tell you."

He walked slowly toward a chair and dropped into it. His feet seemed to have moved of their own accord. His mind was certainly in no shape to direct them. It was a jumble of anger, pain, longing and bewilderment. In the silence he heard nothing but the ticking of the kitchen clock.

Claire shook her head. "I don't know where to start."

Jonathon was unable to think of anything to say. Pain was seizing more territory, squeezing out anger and longing. This had all the makings of a confession.

"I'm not who you think I am," she said.

"You're not Claire Haywood?"

Bewilderment made her eyes widen, giving them a wild look. "Yes, I am Claire Haywood. I guess I mean that I'm not *what* you think I am."

"You're not a divorced mother of two."

She looked around like a trapped rabbit looking for a way to escape.

"Damn!" she exclaimed. "I don't even know how to tell the truth anymore."

The legal orderliness of Jonathon's mind was starting to sort things out and prioritize them. Emotions were relegated to the background, and calm was brought in to restore cool, analytical thought to his mind and soft gentleness to his voice.

"I want you to sit down, too," he told her. "Sit down and take a deep breath. Then start at the beginning so we can get everything out on the table."

She did as he ordered her. In fact, she did even more. She took several deep breaths before she began to speak in a low monotone, her voice totally lacking its usual sparkle.

"Things had not been going well for the girls and me the last few months."

She was close to tears. Jonathon considered taking her in his arms and fixing everything. He wasn't rich, but he certainly didn't have any money problems. But Claire regained control of herself before he could act on the impulse.

"Molly worries along with me instead of being a carefree little kid, and Katie's been so upset about things that she wouldn't speak," Claire went on. "All the doctors I saw said she needed a stable home life, but how could I be home with her and still earn a living? I don't have much more than a high school diploma. When my neighbor down the hall offered me a job at her restaurant, I took it. The pay wasn't great, but I was close to home and it had flexible hours. It was the best I could do."

One half of his brain wanted to reach out and ease the suffering of this struggling young mother and her family, but the other half—the cold, analytical half—involuntarily began reviewing the facts. She was a young mother of two. She said she was divorced, and though she might have had financial problems she didn't appear to be hurting now. She had a new car, a nice apartment—not luxurious, but very nice—and she was now taking Katie to a private specialist. What had happened?

"Only it wasn't good enough. My checking account was overdrawn several times," Claire continued. "I was in debt, overdue on my rent and about to be evicted."

Jonathon remained silent as she paused. To have come from the depths of near-poverty to a comfortable middle-class existence would have required quite a bit of money. Past bills would have had to be paid and deposits made on the new apartment, and even if her new car had been bought on credit, she would have had to make a down payment.

"Then, early last month, a man came to see me."

Claire paused again to fight the emotions raging within her. Jonathon took a deep breath himself and resigned himself to hearing her confession. She was doing something illegal. She was involved in a scam. That was why she was set up here.

"His name is Mr. Daniels, and he works for a government agency. I met with him in his office downtown."

Government agency? Jonathon had to close his eyes for a moment. Was Claire part of the scam, or was she a victim?

As his eyes opened, they focused on the misery that showed so clearly on Claire's face. She'd need a lawyer, a good defense lawyer. He'd call Swanson tonight. Jonathon didn't always agree with his methods, but the man was the best in the business. He'd make sure that Claire was given every advantage the law allowed her.

"Why don't you get some rest?" Jonathon suggested. "We can get together in the morning and start putting things in order."

Claire stared at the far wall and went on as if she hadn't heard him. "Daniels offered to pay all my debts, buy me a car, set me up here and pay me twenty thousand dollars, tax-free."

"Claire, we can talk about it in the—"

"All I had to do was get close enough to watch you."

"Claire—" He tried to speak, but no words came out. Total confusion took over his brain. What had she said? His lungs were screaming for air, and the scene before him had become a hazy blur.

"Watch me?" he repeated dumbly.

She nodded without looking at him.

"Get close enough to watch me?" He couldn't raise his voice above a whisper.

For the first time since she'd started her confession, Claire looked straight into his eyes. "This isn't my real hair color, and I've never worn it in this style."

All he could do was stare. She had confessed to spying on him, and now she was discussing hairstyles. Was he going insane?

Then it hit him like a bolt of lightning. *Sarah.* His chest hurt, as if it were being squeezed in a vise. "That whole thing in the park," he said. "It was a setup."

He hoped against hope that he was wrong, but Claire merely nodded her head.

"Why?"

"My hair was cut, styled and dyed to look like Sarah's." It was as if she hadn't heard the question. "They thought the resemblance would be close enough to get your attention."

"Damn it!" He sprang up and grabbed her by the shoulders. "I asked you why! Who wants to spy on me?"

"The government. They suspect you of corruption."

"Bull," he roared, and flung himself away from her. "What government agency is behind this? What kind of corruption?"

"I don't know." Her voice was almost a wail now. "It was some kind of federal agency."

"Are you stupid? Didn't you ask for any ID?"

"Yes, I did." He ignored what appeared to be a pleading light in her eyes. He knew he had to be strong now. "I saw an official ID with Daniels's picture on it. He had a regular office, with furniture and a receptionist, just like a social security or tax office."

He had to turn away from her before he softened, before he remembered how alive he'd felt these past few days. "What about the kids?" he asked through clenched teeth. "Did you rent them by the week or month?"

"They're my own children. I wouldn't lie like that."

Jonathon couldn't help laughing. A short, bitter snort spit out past his lips. "I'm sorry. For a moment there I forgot about your high moral standards."

Tears were pouring down her cheeks now, but they didn't move him. Her betrayal burned through him like a raging fire, destroying the tender feelings that had begun to grow. All that was left was gnawing pain. It had all been a lie.

"I only wanted to find out the truth," she said. "I was sure I could prove your innocence."

"How would you know what was the truth?" he asked. "All you've done since I met you was lie."

He couldn't stay any longer. The pain was too great. Everything he had thought was growing between them had been an act, a careful, calculated act on her part. There was no future to hope for, not here with her. He strode across the living room and slammed the door. His vision was blurred. It wasn't until he was standing outside in the parking lot that he remembered that his car was still in the garage. He decided the walk would do him good. It should help clear his mind.

Unfortunately, the walk did nothing to help. A reddish, pain-filled haze surrounded him all the way. He was sure that a few people spoke to him, and he had a faint recollection of having responded, but he didn't remember who they were or what was said.

All he knew was the pain. There had been pain when he'd lost Sarah and Timmy. This time was different, but it hurt almost as much. True, he'd had more time with his wife and son, but Claire and the girls had filled a void that had already been there. She'd bandaged and patched wounds that he'd thought would never close. Now he was without her, and added to his pain was the knowledge of her betrayal. It had all been a lie.

The house seemed even emptier than usual when he stepped into it, but he welcomed that emptiness, that silence. It was a known pain, a pain that he'd already learned to cope with. He'd always been a loner, anyway, so it was just as well that this little incident with Claire had ended the way it had. It would be easier to live with loneliness than with betrayal.

The slamming of the door echoed through the two-bedroom apartment. Claire stood up and walked numbly to the bathroom. She felt as if the slamming door echoed the sound of her crumbling life falling to pieces around her.

After washing her face, Claire stared in the mirror. A red-eyed stranger, her face drawn and haggard, stared back at her.

"I'm sorry, Sarah," she said aloud. Then, a sudden purposefulness filling her soul, she turned on the shower.

She had imposed on Sarah's eternal rest long enough. The very first thing she had to do was to let the woman rest in peace. Pulling Timmy and Sarah back into the real world was one of the things that had always bothered her about all this.

Claire couldn't do much about her hair color without alerting Daniels that things had changed, but she could try to rid herself of Sarah's curls. For once she was grateful that her hair was so hard to curl. She could wash the curls out now and never curl it again. That, at least, was simple.

As she washed her hair though, she kept remembering how Jonathon had looked when she'd told him the truth. He'd been so angry. Not that she could blame him. It was easy to understand that he would feel cheated and betrayed, but she wished with all her heart that he'd given her a chance to explain.

Some soap got into the corner of her eye, and she almost started crying again. She wasn't proud of having deceived Jonathon, but it wasn't as if she were a cheap tart ready and willing to sell anything—even her self-respect and honor—for a buck. It wasn't like that at all. She rinsed her hair with special vigor.

"It was for the girls," she said aloud, wrapping a towel around her hair. It was to give them some kind of a reasonable life, away from the danger Brad had brought to them.

She took off the towel and shook her hair, combing through it with her fingers. Good. That was a start. She was beginning to look more like Claire Haywood now. A grin twisted her face. How did this make her feel better? Did she feel more honest now?

Avoiding her own questions, she took a brush and comb and pulled her hair out into the straight, simple style she had always preferred. She had never wanted to be Sarah anyway. A person had to be herself.

Her eyes watered slightly. All right, so at times she had wanted to take Sarah's place at Jonathon's side. It hadn't been a real wish. She hadn't really expected it to happen. But she hadn't wanted it to end with such pain and anger. She dabbed at her eyes with the towel and fought to keep the tears from flowing again.

The telephone rang, diverting her attention. She eagerly hurried to answer it. At this point, a wrong number would have been welcome, but her heart was hoping against hope that the voice at the other end would turn out to be the rumbling baritone that had become so familiar.

"Hello," she said.

The laughing response had such a dirty feel to it that she knew immediately that it wasn't Jonathon. "Hello yourself."

"What do you want, Mr. Daniels?"

"Boy, you sound a tad touchy." He snickered. "What's the matter? You little lovebirds have a little argument?"

"I beg your pardon?"

"I saw the man leave a bit ago," Daniels said. "He walked home."

Claire had known all along that they were watching her—after all, the agency's investment was rather large—but she still didn't like it.

"I know the distance isn't that great," Daniels continued. "Especially for a big, strapping fitness freak like Tyler, but it sure doesn't look friendly."

She felt a dryness in her throat. Was there a suggestion of a threat in Daniels's voice, or was she just getting paranoid?

"No," she replied. She swallowed hard to disperse the squeak that always wanted to creep into her voice when she was nervous. "The girls are in bed and Jonathon thought he could use the exercise after a heavy dinner."

The silence that followed her statement was heavy. She didn't think Daniels believed her, but right now she was too tired to care. Not that she wanted to go to sleep. It was more of a tired-of-it-all type of tired. A tired that would only be cured by walking away from everything.

"So, how are things going?" he asked.

"The same as they were earlier today when we talked," Claire said. "I haven't found the notebook yet."

"Have you looked everywhere?"

"I've been thorough with his house," she answered. "I've even checked out his car somewhat. Maybe it's in his office, but I have no way of getting in there," she said. "You should be able to do that."

"Yeah," Daniels said. "I'll have to talk to my section chief about it."

"I really don't know where to go from here," Claire said. Yes, she did. Away. Far away from all this.

Daniels grunted.

"I mean I really need more direction. You'll have to tell me what to do. You know I've never done this kind of thing before."

"I'll check with headquarters," Daniels said.

"You'll call me, then?"

"Yeah."

Claire slowly hung up. She had a feeling she'd never see Jonathon again, and she didn't think much of her chances of getting the rest of the money she'd been promised.

She squared her shoulders and went into her bedroom. She had almost enough money left to buy them freedom from harm. Maybe the three of them could get in the car and find a place where no one knew them. A place where they'd be safe, even if she still couldn't quite face herself in her mirror.

The glow from the digital clock flickered with each new minute. Two-seventeen. Jonathon sighed and turned over. It wouldn't help, he knew, but he turned over anyway.

The darkness had always had such memories, swaying images of the past that had haunted him until he'd slept out of sheer exhaustion. Those memories had faded with time. He guessed that in three or four centuries, these new memories would also fade.

Why, Claire? he asked himself. Why did it all have to be a lie?

Some of his anger had fled. Raging anger always burned out eventually. But what was left was no picnic. He felt tired and very much alone. He'd been a fool to build such dreams in only a week's time. But time had become precious to him. When happiness could be snuffed out in the blink of an eye, it seemed a crime to waste a moment in indecision.

A crime.

He turned over again. What kind of crazy story had Claire related, that he was suspected of corruption? He'd hardly listened to her story once he'd realized the whole setup had been a lie, staged for some obscure reason and resulting in his pain. She wasn't what he'd thought, she hadn't really understood his every look and read his silent fears. No, she'd been acting a part, playing a role. But for what purpose?

Hands folded behind his head, he stared up at the ceiling. Weird, elongated shadows stretched from the windows like thick tentacles reaching for him. A breeze stirred the leaves of the trees, sending a gentle sigh through the air even as it turned the flickering shadows into nightmare material. Nightmares might be a relief after what he'd been through lately.

He frowned. He was a logical thinker, trained to get through masses of details to the truth, yet here he was, letting his thoughts get sidetracked. Think the thing through, man, he told himself. What was most important?

That Claire had lied.

But when? What had been the lie? She'd pretended to care about him, pretended to feel the same fire that flickered inside him. She hadn't said anything, but it had been there in her eyes promising a joy he had never known. But had that been a lie?

Was this a new thought that nagged at him, or was it just an old hope trying to spring to life again? Think, man, think. Don't blow everything because of stubborn pride.

All right, backtrack. Claire had been picked for some sort of scam because she resembled Sarah. It had worked. He'd fallen for the bait. No argument there. But then why had she revealed the setup? Was it part of the plan? He couldn't figure out what anyone stood to gain that way. Or had her conscience gotten the better of her?

He thought of Katie when she'd finally spoken tonight, thought of the real joy and triumph he'd felt at her victory. He'd thought Claire would want to celebrate, to break out some champagne, if only symbolically, and—

Maybe that was what she'd done. Maybe confessing had been her champagne. Did that mean she cared? Or did it only mean that she couldn't live with the lies?

He sat up in bed and threw aside the covers. Why had he gone off, refusing to listen to anything she'd said? Damn it, he hadn't learned anything in the thirty-eight years he'd been alive. He was still acting like some junior-high kid with hurt feelings. Why was he assuming all was lost when no one had said that?

He reached for the phone, only to stop when he saw the blinking red numbers of the clock. Two-forty-three. Claire would be asleep now, and so would the girls. He couldn't call and wake them all up. Besides, this wasn't something he should handle over the phone. He had an early-morning meeting tomorrow—no, today. Then, suddenly, he remembered the briefcase he'd left in Claire's car. Well, that made it simple. He'd postpone the meeting, go over to Claire's and take them all out to breakfast. They'd settle this whole issue of just what was a lie and what wasn't. They'd worry about the scam later.

Jonathon lay back, sighing as his head hit the pillow. Tomorrow, Claire, he promised. Tomorrow and tomorrow and tomorrow. The whole future lay ahead for them.

"Are we going to have dinner with Mr. Tyler tonight?" Molly asked early the next morning.

Claire put her knee up against the wall to provide support for the heavy bag of groceries while she searched her purse for her housekeys. She had to get these groceries put away before picking up Katie at the speech therapist's. Her early appointment was a blessing this morning; it meant that much less time for Claire to lie in bed and think.

"I really don't think so," Claire said. "He has a lot of work to catch up on."

"But he promised."

Damn, where were those keys? She really should clean out this purse. "Promised what, honey?" she asked as she finally found the keys.

"He promised to buy me an ice-cream cone when I learned to count to a hundred, and I can now. I've been practicing."

Claire grunted as she put the key in the lock.

"You remember him promising, don't you, Mommy?"

Did she remember? Claire gritted her teeth at the pain. The trouble was, she remembered too much. Not only did she remember what had happened, she also remembered things she'd hoped would happen.

She pushed open the door and refixed her grip on the bulging bag. "Molly, we just have to—"

Molly had pushed in first and was now blocking the way. "Molly," Claire said, "don't stop like that. I could trip over you or drop this bag."

The child still didn't move, and suddenly the state of the living room registered on Claire's consciousness. The room was a total, complete disaster. Her mouth moved, but no words came out. Had she mistakenly opened the door to someone else's apartment? Who in the world could be this terrible a housekeeper?

"Somebody made a real mess," Molly said.

No, this was her home. And it wasn't the victim of terrible housekeeping but a ransacking.

"Oh, my God." Claire moved the necessary few steps to get into her kitchen and put the grocery bag on the counter.

Hands shaking, Claire reached out to embrace Molly. She'd been burglarized once before, in that apartment on Logan. She remembered the feeling of violation. They'd only taken a radio and a toaster that time. Drug users, the police had said. They'd sell the items on the street for a few bucks.

This was far worse. She couldn't even see if anything had been stolen. Everything had been turned over and ripped apart. Dishes had been pulled from the cabinets and thrown on the floor. Sofa cushions were lying on the floor, their stuffing hanging out. Someone had done a very thorough job of wrecking their home—of wrecking their lives.

Chapter 7

The elderly couple smiled at Jonathon and held the door open for him. He was tempted to lecture them about letting strangers into the apartment building, but he didn't think they would take it to heart. Besides, right now he was more interested in seeing Claire and apologizing for his anger. He'd been a fool, weaving his dreams of perfection and forgetting that people rarely were flawless. So she'd made some mistakes. Everyone did. If she was as evil as he'd painted her last night, would she have told him about it? No, she cared about him, just as he'd grown to care about her. He'd apologize, he'd take her and the girls out to breakfast, and they'd get this whole mess cleared up.

He took the steps two at a time, rounded the corner in the hallway eagerly, and came to a dead stop. The door to Claire's apartment stood wide open. Was something wrong, or had she just popped out to the laundry room? But even if she expected to be gone only a few minutes, would she leave the apartment door open? He moved forward slowly and cautiously. The scene that greeted his eyes left him speechless with shock and fear.

The apartment looked as if it had been completely destroyed. But the worst of his fears weren't assuaged until his eyes found Claire. His heart started beating again as he watched her moving around in jerky motions, trying to bring some order out of the chaos. Molly was following close behind, a worried look on her face as she tried to pick up the small items that had been dumped on the floor. The poor kid was having a hard time, though. Most of the things were broken, and she didn't seem to know where to put them.

He stepped into the living room. "Claire, what happened?"

She shrieked. Her eyes were wide and filled with fear. Her left hand was balled into a tight fist, and her right clutched at her throat.

"Jonathon," she gasped.

He moved swiftly across the room and crushed her to his chest. "I'm sorry," he said. "It was stupid of me to sneak up on you like that."

"I would have jumped no matter what." Her teeth were chattering.

"I wasn't scared," Molly said, clutching his leg in a steel-clawed grip.

"You weren't?"

"Well, not too much." She hugged him harder.

He picked the little girl up and cradled her with one arm while he hugged Claire tightly with the other.

"Where's Katie?"

"She's at her speech therapy." Claire pushed herself away slightly. "Thank God for that. The poor kid has enough fears. I don't know what this would have done to her."

"Don't sell her short," Jonathon said. "I have a feeling that deep down she's a tough little kid."

"I hope so. What a morning." Claire pushed herself out of his grasp and took Molly by the hand. "We better put the groceries away before the ice cream melts, honey."

"What happened here?" Jonathon asked as he picked his way across the room after them.

Claire shrugged. "I got burglarized."

He stopped and looked around the living room. Drawers

pulled out. Rugs turned over. Seat cushions slashed open. Pictures torn off the walls. This looked nothing like his home the two times he'd been burglarized last year.

He shook his head. "Burglars pop in, snatch a few valuables and split like the wind. They don't take the time to wreck a place, even if you don't have the valuables they expected."

She shrugged again and went into the kitchen. It was no different from the living room. Dishes, food and utensils spilled over the counters and floor. Wanton destruction. Why?

"A mess like this is usually caused either by vandals or by professionals," he said, and watched for her reaction.

"Professionals?" She paused to blink at him.

"Has to be. Vandals are usually a little more personal, a little dirtier, in their destruction. They spray-paint graffiti on the walls, dump garbage, that kind of thing."

"I haven't looked in all the rooms," she said tiredly. "But I don't think anything like that was done."

"Professionals wreck things either as a warning or when they're looking for something specific." He bent down to pick up a cereal box that had been slashed down the front. Its guts were spilling out all over the floor. Sugarcoated chocolate-flavored kids' breakfast food. A shiver went through him. "Something specific and relatively small."

Her eyes seemed somewhat glazed as she stared at the clock on the microwave. "I've got to get this mess cleaned up," she said. "I have to pick Katie up in a half hour."

"Which was it, Claire?" His voice was quiet but firm as he straightened. "A warning or a search?"

Her lower lip trembled slightly. "I don't want Katie to see this mess. She'll get so frightened that she'll never talk again."

He longed to take her in his arms, but he remained where he was. Despite her outward calm, he sensed that she was verging on hysterics. "Claire, I need the truth," he told her. "Everything."

She turned toward him, a frightened look in her eyes. "I wanted to tell you everything last night. But you left."

His heart wanted to break. He was across the kitchen in a

split second, pulling her into his arms. Claire buried her head in his chest and cried softly.

"Mommy?"

"She's fine, Molly," Jonathon said. "Everything's all right now. Why don't you go pack some things? Marilyn wants you guys to stay at her house for a while."

Molly stood there looking puzzled.

Claire lifted her head and sniffed. "That's Paul's mommy, sweetheart."

"Oh." Molly's face lit up in a big smile. "Should I bring my pj's?"

"Everything," Jonathon replied.

"And my teddy?"

"Everything."

"How about my white pussycat?"

"Just pack everything you want, dear," Claire said.

Molly turned to go, then hesitated. "How about Katie's clown?"

"Everything," Jonathon insisted.

"Okay."

After Molly walked off toward the bedrooms, Jonathon could hear Claire chuckling in spite of everything. The sound gave his heart a lift. She'd be all right.

She pulled herself out of his arms and went over to the sink. "Kids can make you forget any problem," she said. "At least for a little while."

He waited as she dabbed some cold water on her eyes. "I was totally stupid last night," he said. "I'll never walk out on you again."

She kept her back to him and wiped her face with a towel.

"I'll be here as long as you need and want me."

She dropped the towel on the counter, but she still didn't turn toward him. His heart sank slightly, but his feet didn't move. He was here to stay, for good or bad. Or was that for better or worse?

He took a deep breath. "Was this job a warning, or were they looking for something? I left my briefcase in your car last night. Could someone just have been after that?"

"Your case is still in the car. I saw it when I put the groceries in this morning," she said. She turned slowly to face him and leaned back against the counter. "As for reasons, I think I've got enemies enough without borrowing yours."

His heart sank, this time with fear for her. He hoped it didn't show on his face. "I'm ready to listen," he said.

She looked at the mess around her, and her shoulders slumped visibly.

"Forget this," Jonathon said. "You and the kids are going to stay at Marilyn's."

Claire took a deep breath and seemed about to speak, but just then Molly walked into the room. "Mommy?" she asked tentatively, with a sideways glance at Jonathon. "Should I pack my swimming suit?"

This wasn't the time or the place for confessions. He pushed himself away from the counter. "Sure, Molly," he said. Then to Claire: "I'll call Marilyn to come pick up Molly and go get Katie. Then you and I can call the police and get this mess taken care of."

She nodded and took Molly's hand. "Come on, honey," she said. "I'll help you."

When they had left, Jonathon dialed his sister's house. "Marilyn," he said, "I need a real special favor. I'd like you to put up Claire and her kids for a while."

"Is something wrong?"

"Yes. I'll explain later, but everything's a real mess right now." The cookie jar lay shattered at his feet, bits of chocolate-chip cookies scattered among the pieces.

"Okay, bring them over anytime. We have the room, and Megan would love to have more people to play with."

He picked up the larger pieces of crockery and tossed them into the sink. What the hell had they been looking for? "There's more," he told Marilyn. "Could you come over and get Molly right now, then pick up Katie at the speech therapist's?"

"Sure."

"One last favor for now. You remember Beth O'Leary? Think you'd have room for her, too?"

"The lady marshal attached to your office? Jonathon, what is going on?"

He closed the cupboards near him. Their gaping emptiness somehow increased his nagging fear. What if Claire and the girls had been here when this had happened? He went back to his conversation. "Do you have room for her?"

There was a long silence. "Sure. I'll send Paul over to your place, and she can have his room."

"I really owe you one," he said.

"Sounds serious," she said.

"Yeah," he replied. "It might be."

He hung up and tried to ignore the destruction around him as he made arrangements with Beth's supervisor to send the woman over to his sister's. After assurances that she would be at Marilyn's within the hour, he finally called the local police.

Marilyn arrived just after he hung up. She stood at the door and looked around the room, whistling softly. "Boy, what a mess! Was it addicts looking for money and jewelry?" she asked.

Jonathon shook his head. "I don't think so. It doesn't look like anything was stolen."

"That's strange."

"Yeah," he agreed.

"Where's Claire?"

"She's in the bedroom," he said, indicating a room with a nod of his head. "Molly was a little scared, and Claire's loading her up on hugs and brave words."

"Poor kid," Marilyn said. "I'd be scared, too, if this happened to my house."

Before Jonathon could reply, Claire walked into the living room with her arm around Molly's shoulder. "I can't tell you how much I appreciate this," she told Marilyn.

"No problem."

"Molly's frightened," Claire said. "I'd hate to think what effect this would have on Katie."

"I'm happy to do it." Then, putting a touch more brusqueness into her voice, Marilyn asked, "Where is Katie's speech therapist located?"

"She—" Claire put her hand to her head. "I can't remember the address. It's in that office park by the tollway."

"You mean the one with those red brick colonial buildings?"

Claire nodded, her hand still at her head. Poor kid, Jonathon thought. She handled the initial shock well, but it was starting to hit her now.

"I still can't remember the address. Her name is Sue Blakely, and she's with the Anchor Medical Group."

"I bet Molly knows where it is," Marilyn said.

The little girl nodded her head solemnly.

"Then let's go." Marilyn held out her hand. "You can show me."

Molly hesitated, looking back at Claire. "Go ahead, honey," Claire said. "I have to wait for the police."

The child still hesitated.

"I'm staying with her," Jonathon assured her.

Molly quickly went to Marilyn's side, and she was clutching her hand as they went out the door.

Jonathon moved forward and put his arm around Claire's shoulder. His heart told him to wrap her in his arms and crush her to his chest, but just as he was about to obey there was a light knock on the door.

"This looks like the place that reported the burglary," the uniformed officer said as he surveyed the chaos around them.

"Yes," Jonathon said, stepping slightly away from Claire. "I placed the call. This is Mrs. Haywood's residence."

The officer nodded and positioned his clipboard in front of himself. "Do you have a list of the valuables that were taken?"

Claire shook her head.

"Can we make one up now?"

"I'm sorry," Claire said. "I'm not communicating very well. What I mean is that nothing's been taken."

"Nothing?" He stared around the room with a perplexed look.

Claire shrugged. "I guess I don't have anything worth taking."

Jonathon's heart ached for Claire, but he also saw the suspicious frown that was building on the police officer's face.

"It's a very strange situation, officer." Jonathon pulled his wallet out and showed his ID. "I'm Jonathon Tyler, with the federal prosecutor's office."

"Oh." The policeman's face softened somewhat, but a trace of suspicion still remained.

"Like I said," Jonathon continued, "this is extremely strange. There's a portable television and a microwave in the kitchen. They're not even unplugged."

The suspicion was now replaced entirely by a perplexed frown. "That sure is weird," the police officer said. "Are they new?"

"I bought them last month," Claire replied.

He shook his head. "Those two items alone would bring forty-fifty bucks on the street. It sure don't look like dopesters."

They silently followed the officer around as he surveyed the damage. "Sure trashed you good," he remarked as he returned to the living room. "And you say nothing of value has been taken? Is that correct, ma'am?"

"As far as we can determine, nothing's been taken," Claire replied.

He shook his head in wonderment and made some notes on his forms. "You got anybody with a serious dislike for you, ma'am?" he asked without looking up from his writing.

Claire looked at Jonathon before she replied in the negative. He saw the fear in her eyes, and heard it echoed in the slight hesitation in her voice. If the police officer noticed, he gave no indication of it as he walked up to examine the door.

"You should lock your door whenever you leave, ma'am," he said as he made further notes.

"I did," Claire said. "I always do."

"Most of us *think* we always do," he said.

"But I did," Claire insisted.

The policeman turned to Jonathon. "There aren't any

scratches around the lock," he said. "Not even the tiniest one. That means the door wasn't locked."

Claire looked as if she were about to cry. Jonathon put his arm around her shoulder. The man could be right, or it could mean that whoever had trashed Claire's apartment had a key. He didn't know which idea would be harder for Claire to handle—that she'd left her door unlocked or that professionals were after her.

"Well, that's it, ma'am." The police officer handed her the clipboard and a pen. "Would you sign here, on the bottom line, please?"

Claire stared at the form.

"Go ahead and sign it," Jonathon said. "It means the officer came by."

She hesitated, holding the pen above the form. "Aren't you going to check for fingerprints?" she asked.

He shook his head. "It's unlikely we'd get a good print, and we really need four fingers for a positive ID. Then we'd have to get a match on them, and I doubt we'd get that."

"Why?" Claire asked.

"This looks like the work of some kids," the policeman replied. "Just bored with the summer."

Claire looked down at the floor, and he turned toward Jonathon.

"If they had any kind of experience, they'd know enough to at least steal the TV and the microwave. Most petty thieves know that small appliances go quick on the street." The officer paused at the door, nodding. "Be sure and lock your door from now on, ma'am."

Claire turned pain-filled eyes toward Jonathon. "I always lock my doors," she whispered.

He went over and took her in his arms.

Claire stared up at him. "Jonathon, I'm scared."

He pulled her close. He was, too, but he didn't tell her that.

"They slashed the girls' mattresses," she said, close to tears again.

They would never get anything covered here. "Let's go out and have a cup of coffee," he said.

"I can't." She shook her head as she looked around the room. "I've got to get this place fixed up."

"No, you don't." He had to fight to keep his voice firm, but he managed. "You and the kids have a place to stay, it looks like Molly took all the stuffed animals and toys the girls own, and you packed their clothes. There's nothing else here you need. We can take care of this later."

She shrugged. "I haven't lived here long, but it felt like home."

"And it will again," he promised as though he'd have more to say about that later. "Come on. We need to talk."

He took her to a little coffee shop on one of the brick-paved alleys that were sprinkled all over the village's downtown area. It was midmorning, and there were few other customers. Even so, they chose a table in the far corner where they would have lots of privacy.

The waitress was busy cleaning the pastry shelves, so he poured a cup of coffee for each of them, then brought over a small pastry tray.

"Cheese, cherry or blueberry?"

"I really can't eat," Claire said.

"That's not an allowable option," he told her.

After making a face, she chose a cheese pastry. He chose a cherry one for himself, then returned the tray. Her appetite had miraculously returned by the time he sat down. He said nothing for a time, allowing her to eat and the horror to dissipate. When he was finished, he wiped off his fingers with a napkin and sat back with his mug of coffee.

"Now," he said. "Let's have the whole story."

Her knuckles whitened slightly as she gripped her mug. "It doesn't make much sense."

"Claire." He leaned forward and took the mug from her hand, clasping both her hands in his. "I'm very sorry about last night. I acted like a fool, thinking only of myself. I want you to tell me everything, and I promise to listen."

She didn't pull away, but she stared out the window for a long time. Jonathon was wondering whether he should prompt her again when she began to speak. "I've covered some of it."

"You mean the money problems," he said. "And the man named Daniels who hired you to keep an eye on me."

She nodded. "The girls and I needed money," she said. "But Brad needed money, too."

A sudden fear clutched at his heart, one that he hadn't even thought of last night. "Aren't you divorced?"

"Oh, yes. I have the papers and the lonely nights to prove it."

He was instantly bathed in relief. "Can't Brad take care of himself?"

She shrugged. "He used to earn a good living, and I suppose he still does." She was silent for a moment. She seemed to be wrestling with private demons. "He also has a number of gambling debts."

"That doesn't have to involve you," he pointed out gently.

Claire's face stiffened, and her voice grew firmer. "That's what I told him. I had problems enough supporting myself and the girls," she said, and took a sip of her coffee.

She was buying time, Jonathon knew. He gave her another moment before pressing her further. "So then what happened?"

"He went to some loan sharks for the money and couldn't pay them back."

"That still isn't your problem." Was she still in love with the louse? He knew that some woman were attracted to the very men who made them unhappy.

"It was made my problem." There was a quiver in her voice, and she began trying with her mug again. "He said that if he didn't come up with the money his creditors were going to hurt the girls."

Anger swept through Jonathon like a brushfire, consuming everything in its path. The slime! How could he endanger his own children like that? No wonder Claire had been driven to desperate measures. She'd been alone, with two little children, and no one to protect them but her. Well, things were different now. She wasn't alone anymore. Trying to harness his anger, Jonathon took her hand again.

"They won't hurt the girls," he promised.

Claire shook her head. "And now Marilyn and her family are involved."

"Claire." He raised his voice slightly to penetrate her fears. "*I'm* involved. And I've been dealing with scum like this all my professional life. Nothing's going to happen to you or the girls."

"They'll find us," she whispered.

"They'll also find a U.S. Marshal who's a top marksperson and has a black belt in karate. The children are well-protected."

Caution still ruled Claire's face, but some of the fear seemed to fade a touch. "A U.S. Marshal?"

"She's an experienced policewoman," Jonathon said as Claire's hand tightened slightly on his. "They'll be fine."

She nodded. The tension in her eyes was almost a memory as hope began to take root there.

"Now let's talk about me," Jonathon said, smiling at her. "In a business way, of course. I want to find out more about this need to report my activities."

"I'm supposed to find a notebook that you have."

He stared at her. "A notebook?"

"A red five-by-seven notebook that was some sort of evidence in a case. Only now it's missing."

"What's in it?"

"Numbers."

"Do I have it?"

"Daniels said you checked it out of the property room and never returned it."

"This is getting a little complex," he said, standing up and stretching. "Let's go downtown and talk this over with my staff."

"Can I call the girls?"

"Sure." He waited while she went into a phone booth. The conversation was short.

"I talked to Paul," she said. "The whole gang of them went to Santa's Village."

"Gang?"

"That's what Paul called them. He said Marilyn, his little sister Megan, Molly, Katie, and someone named Beth."

"Elizabeth O'Leary, the marshal."

Claire stood there, looking helpless. Jonathon went with his emotions and put his arm around her shoulders. "Hey," he said. "They got things to do, and so do we. The sooner we find out what's going on, the sooner it'll all be over."

Claire sat back in the government-issue chair. It was late Wednesday afternoon, the day after the ransacking and the second day she'd spent in Jonathon's office with his staff, trying to make some sense of it all. She was weary to the bone, yet they all seemed no further along in trying to understand the whole mess.

She squinted out the window into the setting sun. It had reached the point where it could shine directly into this conference room high up in the government towers. Jonathon stood to draw the blinds, and she flicked a tiny smile of appreciation in his direction. She wished they were alone.

Without the glare of the sun to claim her attention, Claire let her attention wander around the room. Jonathon and his staff had been at it since yesterday afternoon, and now people were strewn around the conference room in varying states of disarray. All the men had removed their coats, and most also had their ties loosened or completely off. The three women staff members had their shoes off.

"I'm sorry for all this," she blurted out.

Jonathon smiled reassuringly. "It's not your fault."

"I know that," she said. "But it doesn't appear that I'm helping much."

"This isn't a television show," Jonathon said. "We'll probably need more than a couple of hours to resolve the situation."

Her feet suddenly felt constrained in her shoes, and she slipped them half off. Over the last twenty-four hours—minus about eight hours of sleeping time—various members of Jonathon's staff had taken turns talking to her, attempting to glean tiny bits of information that she might have overlooked.

Jonathon stretched his arms high over his head. "Okay," he said, suppressing a yawn. "One more time. Let's see what we have."

"Not much," responded his chief assistant.

"Well, that means we should be out of here soon." Jonathon laughed. "Karen?"

"I spent all morning checking our sources," said a young lawyer with short, curly black hair. "You're not under any kind of investigation."

"Could be superconfidential," Jonathon said.

The woman shook her head. "I checked official and unofficial sources. No way. I called in a lot of markers. If you're under investigation, it's not in this country." She glanced around the room, her eyes half-apologetic. "I even checked out the staff here to see if someone was trying to frame you for something, but I came up negative each time."

Jonathon nodded thoughtfully. Then he rubbed his eyes. Claire longed to reach out and soothe the tension she knew was in his neck and shoulders.

"Walt," Jonathon said through the fingers half covering his face.

"Somebody spent a lot of money on Mrs. Haywood," another young attorney replied, consulting his notes. "And it was all in cash. No way to trace it."

"Any pattern?"

"None. We learned yesterday that an older woman rented the apartment, a young man bought the car, and when I talked to the bank today they didn't know who deposited the money in Mrs. Haywood's account, since it was put into an account she already had."

"Smart," Jonathon said. "That way, no one had to sign anything or show any identification."

"Real smart. He or she made several deposits of two thousand or less. That way, no one was alerted, and nothing had to be reported for oversize cash transactions. And the deposit slips were probably made out by different people, though it could have been one person changing their handwriting.''

Jonathon nodded, then looked at a black man who was sitting in the background. ''Nobody's reporting any missing evidence, not even unofficially.''

''It's a strange one,'' Jonathon said, shaking his head.

''This notebook's got to be worth something,'' the black man said.

''If it really is a notebook they're after,'' Jonathon said. ''It doesn't seem logical. There's no way a piece of evidence could have gotten into my house unless I brought it there, and I haven't. I think they're after something else. They wanted to get Claire into my house for a reason and used the missing notebook as an excuse.''

The man nodded. ''Got to be mob. No one else has the financial resources.''

''Are we discounting any new gangs?'' the curly-headed assistant asked.

The man called Walt spoke up. ''The evidence points to old-line mob.''

Deep frown lines creased Jonathon's face. Claire would have preferred laugh lines, but she was satisfied that these lines came from intensity and not from pain.

''Our biggest mob investigation is that construction kickback scheme on the I-94 repairs.''

Everyone nodded. Claire hoped they would be finished soon. Jonathon kept assuring her that the girls would be fine, and she was sure that the marshal was competent, but she needed to hold the children in her own arms before she could really relax.

''Let's poke at that I-94 case a little bit,'' Jonathon said. ''See what shakes out.''

There was assent, and the aides quickly dispersed, leaving Claire and Jonathon alone. He came over to pull her chair out, and she went into his arms as if she were going home.

''Tired?'' he asked.

''A little.''

"Well, you better not be too tired to eat. Marilyn said the kids are barbecuing dinner for us."

"Hmm," Claire said, closing her eyes and laying her head on his chest. "Dare I hope for a filet, medium rare?"

He grunted in disbelief and held her for a long, sweet moment. "You'd better be prepared for burned burgers and shriveled hot dogs."

She straightened up, refreshed by his closeness and his strength. Now that Jonathon knew about Daniels and the notebook, that horror was over, and maybe Jonathon truly could keep the girls safe. She frowned at her thoughts. Was she being weak in wanting to lean on him, or was she being smart? Her heart said smart, but her mind was still leery. As kind and trustworthy as Jonathon was, she still shouldn't let him become important to her. She'd learned that if you leaned too hard on someone that you'd fall all the harder when he failed you.

Claire hardened her heart. "Any dinner's fine as long as I have my babies with me," she said.

"Does 'your babies' include me?" he asked teasingly as they walked to the door.

"It certainly does not."

"Don't you like me?" he asked.

"You're not a baby."

He stopped her and put his arms around her. "I'm glad you noticed."

For one swift moment, all the shadows disappeared and Claire was caught up in a wave of longing. Jonathon's lips met hers in a blaze of sunlight, and nothing else mattered. Time stood still, fears faded into the twilight, and peace filled her soul. Her scolding, worried mind was silent as his embrace became her shelter, her retreat, her heaven. His mouth spoke to hers of hungers and needs, of lonely nights that would only be distant memories if she but let herself allow it. A flame grew from the smoldering ashes of her past and consumed all memories, leaving nothing in her heart but him.

"Jonathon," she breathed into the stillness when they parted slightly. He was her star in the heavens, her guide across the stormy seas, even if her mind wasn't willing to admit it yet.

"Later," he promised, and let her go. "We've still got a lot to talk about."

He gathered a few papers from his office, and they walked out to the parking lot, their arms linked. Neither of them spoke, but their feelings were still strong and clear. Hearts still called to one another, lips still longed to taste such sweetness again. Now that lies no longer stood in the way, everything could be perfect. They climbed into his car, and he drove out of the lot.

Claire leaned back in her seat and closed her eyes. It would be so good to have someone to lean on, not because she felt weak, but because she felt so much stronger sharing Jonathon's strength. Together they would solve everything.

It was past rush hour when they left Jonathon's office, so they made good time on the expressway. In a few minutes she'd be with the girls, and they all could bask in Jonathon's smile. Little by little, he was chipping away at the wall she'd built around herself, and soon it would be torn down forever. Then she'd be able to love him as she wanted, as he deserved. All she needed was time without worry about keeping the girls safe or guilt at having brought this trouble to Jonathon. The soft music from the radio brought relaxation to her muscles. Thank God, this nightmare was almost over.

"It looks like we have a tail."

"What?" Claire sat bolt upright, trying to focus her eyes on the traffic around her.

"We're being followed," Jonathon said. "I'm sure of it."

Her previous euphoria made a mad dash for oblivion. She'd led Jonathon smack into the middle of danger—her danger.

Chapter 8

Claire spun in her seat to watch the traffic behind them. Suddenly every car seemed to pose a threat, yet none of them looked at all out of the ordinary. Her mouth was dry, and her heart was thudding.

"Which one is it?" she whispered, as if they could be overheard somehow.

"The blue sedan two cars back in the lane to our left." Jonathon's voice was as calm as if he were discussing the weather. His eyes stared straight ahead, and only the tightness of his hands around the steering wheel revealed his tension.

Claire found the car. It looked ordinary, just as the man driving it looked like a businessman driving home after a day's work. But what was his business? She shivered and turned to Jonathon again.

"How can you tell?" she asked.

His glance flicked quickly to the rearview mirror, and he changed lanes. "He's been with us since we left the office."

Claire glanced behind them again. The blue car also changed lanes. "He could work in the same area as you and live out in the western suburbs."

"He could." They were approaching the Harlem Avenue exit, and after a lightning glance to check that the exit lane was clear Jonathon pulled into it.

Claire couldn't help but turn around. The blue car was following them up the ramp. "Oh, Lord," she muttered under her breath.

Jonathon reached over and squeezed her hand. It helped to ease her immediate fears, but not her guilt. "This is all my fault," she said. "It's one of Brad's creditors. I just know it."

"You don't know who it is," he told her. "And I appear to have my own assortment of enemies that have involved you."

They reached the top of the ramp, only to be met by a red light. The other car was right behind them, but Claire refused to turn around. She took a deep breath and tried to relax. "What will they do?" she asked.

The light changed, and Jonathon turned right. She knew without looking that the other car did, too. "I don't imagine they'll do anything," he said. "Since I suspect these are my friends, not yours. No matter what Brad says, his compatriots aren't going to go after you or the girls, because hurting an ex-wife isn't really going to make him pay up. My friends, on the other hand, might be curious as to what you've been doing with me the last few days at my office."

"So they'll just follow us?" she asked.

"As long as they believe you're still helping them that's all they'll do."

But did they still believe that? Jonathon drove in silence for several miles, turning west on Ogden Avenue. Claire's hands stayed clenched tightly in her lap. His arguments made sense, they seemed logical, and they should have eased her fears—except for one thing.

"Daniels knows where you live," she pointed out. "Why would he follow you?"

"He also ought to know how to follow someone without being spotted. There's more than one reason to follow someone. The obvious one is to find out where they're going, but as you said, Daniels, or whatever his name really is, knows where I live. This could be a warning, and in that case, the driver would *want* to be seen."

"A warning? But what—"

"Would he be warning us of?" Jonathon struck the steering wheel with his fist. "Damned if I know. But damned if I know anything about what's going on."

He said this last with a laugh, trying to make light of the whole thing, but Claire had already heard the tension in his voice and seen the worry in his eyes. He wasn't telling her everything. Suddenly it was important that she play a part in this, that she help him in whatever way she could.

"Shouldn't we take his license number?" she asked. "I've got some paper, and—"

"It's 578 DK," he said. "Most likely a rental from O'Hare, where the traffic is so heavy that an agent wouldn't remember an individual customer. I'll have someone check it out to be certain."

"Oh." So much for helping. "Maybe we should stop and call someone. The police, maybe, or your office."

"What could any of them do? He's broken no laws."

"Then are you going to try to lose him?" Her voice was rising, she knew, but she seemed helpless to stop.

"I'm a lawyer, not a stunt driver."

"We can't just drive home and let this guy follow us. We'll lead him right to the girls."

"They aren't interested in the girls, just us."

She tried to accept his words, but gut-wrenching fear kept getting in the way. The girls were everything to her, her whole life. She couldn't just sit here and lead danger straight to their door. Swallowing hard, she allowed herself to glance behind them. The blue car was still there, just as she'd known it would be. She faced forward again, not allowing her eyes to wander any more than her thoughts.

She had to believe Jonathon when he said the girls were safe. After all, who else did she have to lean on? Not Brad, that was for sure. And not Daniels. He had definitely been lying. The "government office" had been empty when Jonathon's staff had gone to check it out. It had never been rented to any government agency. The phone number was an office in the loop, empty except for an answering machine. She only had Jonathon, and no matter what fears her mind conjured up, she trusted him completely.

"Jonathon, I'm afraid," she whispered suddenly. Her words seemed to echo hollowly in the car. The empty, mindless music playing on the radio reminded her of that first visit to Daniels's office. The memory was not reassuring.

Jonathon's hand found hers, though his eyes stayed on the road. "Don't be," he said. "This is all part of the game."

She willed herself to gain strength. Just who was in this game, though, and who was on their side? The car sped on, bringing them closer to the girls.

Claire lost sight of the blue sedan in the rearview mirror once they turned onto York Road, but she wasn't fooled into thinking it was gone. She kept her silence, trying to conquer her doubts and fears, but they reaffirmed themselves when Jonathon pulled into his driveway.

"We'll stay here for a while," he told her, "then cut across the backyards to Marilyn's."

"Fine." It sounded like a good plan, a safe plan, but she was no longer certain of anything. She needed to see the girls, but was afraid of what she might bring in her wake. Gathering up her purse, she let herself out of the car before Jonathon had a chance to come around and open the door for her.

"I'll give Marilyn a call and ask her to hold dinner up a little longer."

They went into the house, and while Jonathon went straight to the phone on the kitchen wall Claire wandered into the dining room. The house was silent and still. It almost seemed to be waiting for something. Even the murmur of Jonathon's voice from the other room couldn't break her lingering uneasiness. This house wasn't a home anymore.

It was strange. She hadn't had that sense the other times she'd been there. It had seemed to be filled with laughter and love just waiting to be claimed. It had seemed such a place of peace and joy that every moment here had seemed special. But coming in with Jonathon today she'd noticed a very different feeling in the air. Something was wrong here. The house held fear now, not love. Could the house be warning her that the girls were in danger? Could Sarah be warning her?

Claire shook off her strange feelings and walked closer to the wide picture window on the other side of the dining room table. The room was in shadow, the drapes partly shut to keep the heat of the daytime sun out, so she had no fear that anyone outside could see her. She looked one way down the street; it was empty. Then down the other way. Far down the block, almost at the corner, sat the blue sedan. It was hard to tell from this distance, but she thought she could see the driver still at the wheel.

"Anything there?" Jonathon's voice broke the stillness.

"The blue car's down near the corner," she said, still staring out the window. "Looks like someone's still in it."

There was a moment of silence behind her. She could feel his frown of tension, even though she couldn't see it. She could sense his hands reaching out to touch her.

"Claire?" he said quietly.

She turned, not certain why, except that his voice held a different note. His eyes were questioning, innocent reminders of her betrayal.

"Did you reach Marilyn?" she asked. "I should have asked to talk to the girls, but..." She couldn't explain that she was afraid that the danger surrounding her might touch them even through a phone call.

A smile touched his lips for a moment. "They were busy making brownies for dessert." Something changed in his eyes. "Marilyn said Katie talked twice again today. Just to Molly, but she talked."

Claire's knees felt wobbly. "Thank God," she murmured, and sank into a chair. "I was so afraid that all this..."

She couldn't finish, but Jonathon understood anyway. He was in front of her, stooped down so that his head was level with hers. His hands took hers in an iron grip that somehow forced her eyes to lock with his.

"It's not going to touch the girls, I promise you," he said. "We're going to keep them safe."

She wanted to believe him. "I don't know how that's possible," she said.

Suddenly she was in his arms, pulled forward so that she was kneeling on the floor in an embrace that promised her heaven. Jonathon's lips found hers and crushed them, and his arms seemed to crush the breath from her body. As she felt her sleeping emotions awaken from his touch, her heart cried out with hope and joy. She wanted so to rest in his arms and know that everything would be all right. Why was she so cautious, so afraid to give her trust, when she knew it was deserved?

For one sweet moment she tasted the promise of love. Jonathon's arms held her, his hands easing the fear and tension from her body as they slid over her back, pulling her ever closer. But even as the fear seeped from her bones a new tension took its place, a sighing, tender tension of awareness, of dreams that interrupted the long nights and awoke the hopes that had lain buried in her soul for so long.

He could make her happy again. He could make her whole. His lips promised a lifetime of wonder, and his hands vowed to heal her wounds. Her heart begged her to believe him, to stop being afraid to take a chance, but there was still a spot deep in her soul that was used to being afraid and wasn't ready to trust anyone—not even Jonathon. She pulled slowly away from him and sat back on her heels.

"I'm afraid," she told him. "Everything's happening so fast, and I don't know who to lean on anymore."

"Lean on me."

Was it that simple? She shook her head. "I've trusted all wrong in the past. First Brad, then this Daniels. I can't afford any more mistakes."

He reached for her hands again, and she let him have them. Her heart was strong now; it could withstand the power of his touch and still stay whole.

"Don't trust anyone, then," he said, his voice so gentle that it wove a spell around her heart. "Take your time to decide who you can trust. Just don't shut me out."

It wasn't what she'd expected him to say, and her heart

wavered indecisively. The hands that held hers were surely ones she could rely on, ones that would keep her and the girls safe. Yet even as the thought crossed her mind she felt as if she were standing on shifting sands that could change at any moment. She got to her feet and went back to the window. The street was empty.

"The car's gone," she said.

Jonathon came up behind her and put his arm around her waist. "We've done what they expected," he said simply. His lips brushed her ear. "You're back here, ready to look for the notebook, so they don't need to watch us anymore."

She sighed and let herself lean back. It was so comfortable to lean against his strength, even if her mind was still watchful and suspicious. "How can you be so sure?"

He turned her around to face him. His eyes had a flame flickering in their depths, a flame that she couldn't totally read but she knew held loneliness. His hands gripped her upper arms tightly. "I'm not in cahoots with them, if that's what you're thinking. I'm just basing my opinions on other cases I've been involved in."

"Oh, Jonathon." She sighed and leaned into him. She couldn't bear that look of lonely isolation. "I never thought you were. I'm just so afraid."

His arms came around her to hold her safe and secure. "I know." She sensed his lips on her hair, feeling the possession of his embrace rather than the pressure of his touch. Peace entered her soul, and she didn't fight to keep it out.

"What do we do now? Go over to Marilyn's?"

"I think we ought to wait a little longer," he said. "Just in case our friend hasn't left."

She nodded. "I suppose we could look for the notebook some more."

He chuckled wryly, the sound rumbling in her ear and tickling. "I suppose that's one thing we could do to kill time, though I have my doubts that it's here. Just where have you looked?"

Her heart fluttered, and a sudden heat claimed her cheeks. She wanted to go back to those other things they could do to kill time, but she knew they couldn't—not now, not yet. There would be time for that later.

"Well, I didn't quite look the 'everywhere' I assured Daniels I had," she admitted. "I didn't feel right about looking in drawers and cabinets."

"Not much of an undercover agent, are you?"

"No, but I warned them."

For a moment, neither of them spoke. They stood, wrapped in each other's arms, safe from the world. This time the silence in the house was peaceful, though. What had changed? Claire wondered.

Just her. Was she being foolish in disregarding her fears for the girls? She closed her eyes to the world and to her thoughts and stayed safe in his arms for a moment longer. The sound of his heartbeat echoed in her ears, and it spelled *forever* to her heart.

Jonathon was relieved to see his assistant Walt's car in Marilyn's driveway when he and Claire arrived. Claire was so anxious to see the girls that it wasn't hard for Jonathon to pull Walt aside for a private talk. The two men went into the breakfast room.

"Anything new?" Jonathon asked.

Walt shook his head. "The I-94 investigation seems clean. No link that we can find to any of this."

"Damn." Jonathon walked to the window, staring out at Claire and the girls, who were on a bench outside. Beth sat off to one side, ever watchful, an ever-present reminder of the danger, even if Claire and the girls seemed not to notice her. Katie rested in Claire's lap, and Molly sat next to them, gesturing wildly, probably about the fun they'd had at the Brookfield Zoo, where Marilyn had taken them today. The love radiating from Claire's face held his gaze. He saw such tenderness there as to make his heart ache.

"What about the car?" he asked. Katie turned to add something to Molly's story, then dissolved into giggles. Claire's hug tightened, and so did his resolve to keep them safe.

"Rental from O'Hare, just like you thought."

"Great. Just great." Jonathon turned away from the window, but the breakfast room offered him little solace, with its brightly colored walls and its bulletin board filled with childish drawings. What kind of people might prey on little children? "What the hell is going on?"

Walt knew an answer wasn't expected, so he turned his attention out the window, toward Claire. "How's she holding up?"

Jonathon shrugged. "All right. She's not sure if she should trust me or not."

Walt looked surprised at that. "You? Boy Scout *extraordinaire*? Hell, I bet you've never even used the library's night return for an overdue book."

Jonathon smiled at that assessment of his personality. "I didn't try to lose the tail."

"The lady was hoping for a hero, eh?"

"And all I could think of was Sarah getting killed by those kids who were driving crazy."

His voice echoed the pain that shot through him as the whole nightmare flashed before him again. The mangled, charred wreck of Sarah's car. The driver of the other vehicle in the hospital emergency room, sobbing that he hadn't meant to hurt anyone. And now, Claire's eyes tinged with fear, begging him to do something while he froze from the fear there would be another accident in which he might lose more than he could bear.

How had Claire come to mean so much to him in barely two weeks? She'd helped to fill the emptiness that Sarah had left behind, but it wasn't only that. Claire wasn't a replacement for Sarah. He treasured her for herself—for the brightness in her smile, for the way she seemed to understand him without words. She made him feel whole and alive. She made him feel enraged that she should be in danger.

Jonathon tried hard to control his anger. "I guess I blew the hero role."

Walt stood up and yawned. "Maybe you'll get another chance at it."

"I'd rather not." He'd have to find some other way to prove to Claire that he cared about her, one that didn't involve putting her in danger.

Chapter 9

In spite of Jonathon's predictions, dinner was wonderful. The burgers weren't burned, and the hot dogs weren't shriveled, only slightly blackened, just the way Claire liked them. The iced tea and potato chips were plentiful, Katie and Molly were at her side, and Jonathon's smile, when he stopped conferring with his assistant and looked her way, made her pulse race. She should have been happy.

But the nagging sense of being watched—and the lingerings of the fear from when they'd been followed—kept her from relaxing. Of course, having a U.S. Marshal on duty at the table didn't help, either.

Claire glanced around Marilyn's backyard in the lengthening shadows of dusk. The six-foot-high stockade fence should have heightened her sense of privacy, but somehow it didn't. It was crazy. Between the fence, the towering oak trees and the thick lilac bushes rimming the yard, no one could see in. She needed to take these moments of peace and security and enjoy them. She needed to see Beth O'Leary as an added protection, not as a reminder of the danger. She had to start believing that nothing could happen to her and the girls here.

"The girls were so good today," Marilyn said, coming to sit next to her. "I know they've been to the zoo before, Molly told me, but they had a ball. Molly loved the dolphin show. She would have stayed there all day if we'd let her. Katie liked feeding the baby goats in the children's zoo best."

"It's kind of you to do all this with them on such short notice."

"It was fun," Marilyn assured her. Then an awkward silence fell over them.

Claire couldn't help but remember the first time she and Marilyn had met. The woman had hardly greeted her with warmth. So why was Marilyn willing to go to such trouble for her now?

"Look, Marilyn," Claire began, then stopped as the woman stared at her. Claire cleared her throat and began again. "I really appreciate all you're doing for us. I know when we first met you weren't too certain of me, and I appreciate it all the more, knowing that."

Marilyn just laughed. "You obviously aren't an older sister, are you?"

Claire shook her head slowly. "No, I was the youngest child. In fact, I was younger than my sister by eleven years, so I was raised more like an only child."

"I thought so," Marilyn said with a laugh. "I was the oldest. Four years older than Jon, and six years older than Mike, our other brother. Being naturally bossy, I became their self-appointed guardian."

"And are still at it," Claire said with a smile. Would Molly always feel the need to watch over Katie? It seemed likely. "Tell me, does Jonathon often need rescuing?"

"Not nearly as often as I'd like," Marilyn said. Her smile stayed in place, but her eyes grew dark. "That's why I was so worried when I first saw you. If he took up with wild women and partied all night long I would have been relieved to see you. But you looked so much like Sarah—" Marilyn frowned suddenly. "Why is it that you don't look so much like her anymore?"

Claire's hand automatically went to her hair. How much had Jonathon told his sister?

"It's your hair," Marilyn said, her frown deepening. "It's different."

"Yes," Claire reluctantly admitted. "I'd curled it before, but it was too much trouble. This is the way I used to wear it."

"It suits you," Marilyn said slowly.

Was Claire imagining things, or did Marilyn's eyes once more narrow with suspicion?

Marilyn turned away just as Jonathon and his assistant got to their feet. She rose, too, and took her daughter by the hand, calling to Molly and Katie, "Hey, kids, want to watch *Sleeping Beauty*?"

"Wow! Sure! Can we, Mom?" Molly asked, not waiting for an answer as she grabbed Katie's hand and led her toward the door. Beth followed unobtrusively.

Marilyn grinned at Claire. "No, the girls don't need your help." Her glance flew next to Jonathon. "And no, Walt does not need you to see him out. The two of you have done enough work at my table."

Although Claire laughed, she felt worry tugging at her soul. How could she let these people be pulled into her trouble? Jonathon had said they were in no danger because of her, but how could he be certain? Maybe the best thing she could do was run. In trying to hold on to Jonathon and the warmth and joy he represented, wasn't she being unfair to everyone?

"We seem to have been left out of all plans," Jonathon said, coming to sit by her side on the bench at the picnic table. Marilyn had taken the girls inside, Walt had left by way of the gate, and Paul and his father had gone in the basement door, talking of eight balls and bumper shots.

Her heart forgot some of its worries as joy flowed through it just in being near his side.

"It seems that way," she said, realizing that they were suddenly alone. Her stomach was jittery, and her mouth was dry. She looked away across the yard, which was rapidly being swallowed up by the night.

"It was awfully good of Marilyn to take us in," she said.

"She likes helping out those in trouble. Marilyn suffers from an exceptionally acute case of big sister syndrome."

"That's not nice," she protested weakly. "I hope she won't get caught up in my problems."

His hand found hers unerringly in the growing darkness. "*Our* problems," he said gently.

Their intertwined hands gave her heart something to focus on. "They were my problems before they were yours."

"Trying to hog them all to yourself?" he asked. "I hadn't realized you were so selfish."

She smiled at his foolishness. The awareness of his strength and the flame of desire flickered in the dark corners of her heart. She *had* to trust him. Their hearts were as intertwined as their hands, as their lives. She had no choice but to share her problems with him.

"Jonathon, what am I supposed to do?" she asked. "How do I get out of the mess I'm in?"

"Refuse to cooperate."

She shook her head, though she knew it was almost too dark for him to see. Splashes of light lay on the patio, light that spilled out from the windows, but none reached them.

"It's not as easy as refusing to cooperate," she said with a sigh. "I've taken Daniels's money. I can't just drop out of sight. That's not going to help you find out who he is and what he wants."

"He's told you what he wants. He said he wants that notebook. I doubt that he's going to tell you much more, but my staff will find out the rest. They're very good at things like this."

His hand slid up her arm. It was a gentle, possessive touch that tried hard to melt the resistance in her soul. She'd like to give in to his logic, to listen only to her heart, which was telling her to take this joy that he was offering and forget the rest. But there was a stubborn streak in her that kept her back straight and her jaw firm. She'd brought this trouble to him. She had to see it through.

"I have an advantage that your staff doesn't have," she

pointed out. "If I just knew what to ask him when he calls next—"

"Drop it, Claire," Jonathon said.

His hand left her arm, and she thought for a moment that he was moving away from her, but she was wrong. He grabbed her upper arms, clutching her tightly in the darkness.

"Stay out of it," he said. His voice was strong and firm. He was obviously accustomed to being obeyed. "There's nothing more you can do. You can look at pictures and see if you can identify him, but no more. You are not to put yourself in further danger."

"I don't like the idea any more than you do," she told him, "but—"

"But nothing. Just stay out of it, Claire. I'm arranging for you and the girls to be taken to a safe house, and you'll stay there until this is all over."

"And when will that be?" she asked. Her heart cried out at the thought of being away from him, even as her mind tried to say it didn't matter. But she didn't like leaving her troubles for someone else to finish. "Are we to put our lives in limbo until you can find the answers to questions I could easily ask him?"

He let go of her. She wanted to touch him, wanted to tell him that she just had to finish what she'd started, but the silence of the night was too deep, too dark, to break.

"I know we've only known each other a short time," he said slowly. His voice was as soft as velvet, but it was strong, too, and it was trembling with barely restrained emotion. "But it feels like forever. It's like we were destined to be together. From that first moment in the park I've felt that we belonged together. I wanted to take you home and never let you out of my sight. You and the girls seemed to already belong to me. I can't bear the thought of losing you."

He grabbed her arm, as if he sensed her fleeting urge to flee and wanted to hold her back.

"I don't know what to say," she said softly, feeling his strength and his concern for her in his touch. "Except that in a way that scares me more than Daniels and all of Brad's bill collectors. I feel something for you, something deep and strong, but I'm not sure I want to look at it too closely or put a name to it.''

"You've been hurt," he said. "You aren't willing to trust yet. I can live with that."

He was so understanding, and she wanted nothing more than to rest in his arms, if only her fears would let her. "It's not that I think you're going to do all that Brad did," she tried to explain. "It's just that he hurt us so badly that it still hurts."

He found her and pulled her into the sweet safety of his embrace. "You need time, that's all. Time to heal. And I'm willing to give it to you. All the time you need. As long as I'm the one there when you're ready."

"I don't know how long it'll take," she warned him, wishing with all her heart that she could just melt into his arms. To lie there, accepting the security, the love, that his embrace promised.

"I'm very patient," he told her.

"Another Boy Scout trait?"

He just laughed. The sound was a quiet rumbling of the chest her head was lying against. Life could be so wonderful, her heart pointed out. It could hold a joy such as she had never known before, if only she was brave enough to put aside her fears.

"Actually," he said, "some people might say it's not patience but stubbornness. While I'm willing to give you time to get used to the idea of my caring about you, I'm not willing to negotiate on the idea of the safe house. It wouldn't be for long, and we can take care of Brad's problems, too."

"Oh, Jonathon," she said with a sigh. "Why couldn't we have met over a head of lettuce in the grocery store?"

His laugh was soft and from the heart, and she didn't have the strength to tell him just yet that she had to stay here with him. She'd send the girls to safety, but she couldn't leave him alone with the troubles she'd started.

Over his shoulder she saw fireflies glittering in the night. Catch a firefly and have good luck, her father had always told her. But she'd always thought that if the glittery little bugs really possessed luck they'd give more to those who refused to catch them than to those who put them in jars. She'd never had the need to put their luck to the test, though. Not until now.

It was just after one o'clock when Claire snuck out of Marilyn's house and hurried through the darkened streets to her apartment. It was just after one o'clock in the morning, and Jonathon trusted that she was in bed.

Claire swallowed hard and unlocked the apartment door. The room was a mess, but it was the same mess as before. She locked the door behind her and crawled over spilled books and torn cushions to the phone. She dialed Daniels's number. Her heart pounded, then the answering machine came on, but she told him to call right away, that she wouldn't be there long. Then there was nothing to do but wait.

She sat down. The living room seemed to stare back at her. The destruction was a violation that still set her knees to trembling. The bedrooms were worse, though, and more than she could face, so she went into the kitchen. They'd have ants if the mess there wasn't cleaned up soon, so she pulled out a garbage bag and began tossing in spilled food and broken bits of crockery.

The unbroken dishes in one pile, the broken into the garbage bag. The unspilled food in one pile, the spilled into the garbage bag. She worked by rote until the worst of the mess was gone. The unbroken, unspilled piles were awfully small, but she refused to think about anything more than the sticky floor that would need mopping. Just think of the things you need to replace, she silently commanded herself.

The phone rang, shrieking in the silence and causing her heart to stop. It seemed a threat in the stillness of the night, but she raced toward it anyway, as if its ringing could be overheard, not in the apartments above or below her, but in a house eight blocks away.

"Hello?" she asked, her breath almost painful.

"Daniels here. I got your call. What's going on?"

His voice had lost its overtones of friendliness. She told

herself his crankiness was because she'd woken him up. That thought stilled the worst of the tremors that shook her.

"I needed to talk to you," she said quickly, trying to remember her prepared speech. "I can't find anything in his house, but I've been to his office. I may get the chance to look there some more, and I thought if I just knew a bit more—"

"We've been over this before," he snapped. "You know what the book looks like."

"Yes, I know that," she said. "But if I knew what kind of case it was missing from, maybe that would help."

"How?"

"Well, I might know better where to look." The apartment suddenly felt still, so threatening. She sank onto the floor so that she at least wouldn't be visible from the windows. "I've been trying so hard to find it and not getting anywhere, I just thought knowing more might help."

"I don't see how," he said. "Either you're working for us or you aren't. Telling you classified information isn't going to win your allegiance back."

"Win my allegiance?" she repeated with a vague laugh. "What are you talking about?"

"You've been spending a great deal of time with him."

"Wasn't that the idea?" The fearful chill in the air came from her heart, not from any door or window—the night air was still warm from the late-June heat.

"The intensity of your search seems to have slackened," he said. "My superiors are concerned that you may be holding out on us."

The demolished kitchen with its small pile of redeemable goods and its stuffed garbage bags full of wreckage mocked her. Was this Daniels's doing? Her heart stood still. Why hadn't she listened to Jonathon?

"How can you suggest that?" she asked, her voice sounding hollow and weak. "Would I have called you if I wasn't still trying to earn that money? I just need some help." She took a deep breath and tried to will courage into her soul. "You throw me into this job with no training and very little information and you expect me to work miracles. The least you can do is tell me why this notebook is so important."

"Because you agreed to find it," he said simply. "And my superiors don't like people to break their promises."

"But I didn't—"

"Perhaps you don't believe that. A demonstration can be arranged."

"No, wait. I—" But the phone line was dead, and Claire was alone in her trashed apartment in the middle of the night.

Her heart in her throat, her breath surely gone forever and her common sense screaming at her for being stupid, Claire grabbed her car keys and raced out the door. It was only once she was back in bed at Marilyn's that she began to breathe again. Trouble was, she was also thinking. What had she done?

She had to tell Jonathon about the call to Daniels, Claire told herself as she showered and dressed the next morning. She hurried the girls through breakfast then waited anxiously at the front door for Jonathon to arrive. Walt came instead.

"Jon wants you to start looking at mug shots today," he said. "But he wants the two of you to ride in separately and see if either of you are followed."

"I see." The logic of the idea didn't make the wait to see Jonathon any easier, and neither did the heavy traffic, which kept them at a crawl.

"It's kind of late for the rush hour, isn't it?" she asked. "I thought the traffic would be lighter by this time." She hoped some conversation would allay the fear she felt.

Walt shrugged. "Not in the summer. People go to the beach, that kind of thing."

Walt didn't appear to care for conversation. She glanced around them and saw the same cars each time. How could you tell if anyone was following?

"Are we being followed?" she asked after a while.

Walt shook his head. "Not that I can tell." The traffic began to open up slightly, and soon his attention was more on changing lanes than on her.

Claire stared at the bread truck in front of them, absently

reading the messages written in the dust and grime on the back door. If they weren't being followed, did that mean Jonathon was? Jonathon had said last night that they were in no danger as long as Daniels believed she was still working for them, but since her phone call she was no longer certain Daniels believed that. Her heart froze with sudden fear. Had her stupidity put Jonathon in danger?

Claire chided herself for being so stubborn for the rest of the ride. Why hadn't she listened to Jonathon when he'd told her to stay out of it?

The ride was endless, parking took forever, and the walk to the federal building seemed to go on for miles. Even the elevators refused to cooperate. The whole bank of express elevators was out of service for cleaning, so they had to take one that stopped at almost every floor.

Jonathon had to be all right. She couldn't bear it if she'd caused him harm. The door to the fourteenth floor finally opened, and there he was, standing at a secretary's desk and talking into a phone. She could almost taste her relief as she sagged against the back wall of the elevator.

"Come on," Walt said, grabbing her arm. "This is our floor."

"Oh, right." She allowed herself to be led over toward Jonathon. Either her knees were decidedly wobbly or the area was suffering an earthquake. She'd known Jonathon had come to mean a lot to her, but she hadn't realized just how much until she'd actually seen him standing there.

All that fluttering her heart had been doing over the past few days was nothing more than that. She cared for him more than she'd known, more than she'd ever felt before. The length of time they'd known each other didn't matter. What did matter was the way they would make the other's life complete. If she could just gather the courage to grasp the brass ring this time around. If she could just stop thinking that the deeper the love was, the deeper the hurt when it came. Pain didn't have to follow love.

Jonathon put down the phone just as she and Walt reached him. "Any problems?" Jonathon asked Walt.

"None that were noticeable."

Jonathon nodded, and his eyes met Claire's briefly. "Everything's set up in the end conference room, if you want to take her down there to get started."

Walt made some reply that Claire barely heard and certainly didn't understand. Her senses were completely concentrated on Jonathon. A cold chill had been in his eyes when he'd looked at her. Was he trying to hold his emotions in check at work? No, he'd been kind and gentle yesterday in front of the others. Had something happened that he didn't want her to know about?

"Down this way, Ms. Haywood," Walt was saying, trying gently to tug her down the hall and away from Jonathon. But she wasn't ready to go.

"Were you followed?" she asked Jonathon.

He'd been reaching for the phone, and he stopped now, his hand in midair. "No, I don't think so."

"I was worried," she admitted. "I thought if they weren't behind us they had to be trailing you."

"Not necessarily."

A heavy, suffocating silence that seemed almost painful settled upon them. She stared at him, afraid to read the look of dismissal in his eyes. Where was the time he'd vowed to give her? Where was the caring he'd said would last forever? Had it already died?

"Ms. Haywood, we really need to get started," Walt said.

But Claire shrugged his arm off. "I need to talk to you, Jonathon."

He frowned, gesturing toward the phone. "I have to—" He sighed. "It'll have to be quick," he said, and led her down the hall to the conference room they'd been in yesterday.

The door had barely closed behind him. "Jonathon what's wrong?" she asked. "Has something happened that I don't know about?"

"What could that be?" he asked. "You know as much about this case as I do. Maybe more," he added.

"Well, since I haven't the faintest idea what's going on, I doubt that." She sank into the nearest chair. The table in the middle of the room was piled high with photographs, video-tapes and albums full of mug shots, just like on television. Would she find Daniels in there?

She turned to Jonathon. "I called Daniels last night," she told him suddenly.

He said nothing, didn't even blink an eye, just kept staring right at her.

"I know it was stupid," she went on, "but I thought I could help."

"And did you?"

She sank back in the chair, her eyes no longer able to meet his. "No. I was terrified. I went back to the apartment and called him. When he finally called back, he was suspicious and unfriendly. He doesn't believe I'm still looking for the notebook. He scared me half to death."

"Too bad you couldn't have gotten that way without sneaking out in the middle of the night."

His voice was different, somehow, and Claire looked up as he eased himself into the chair across from her. The chill about his features was gone, leaving weariness in its place.

"Jonathon?" she whispered.

"We tapped that phone yesterday," he said. "I heard a recording of your conversation the first thing this morning, after a sleepless night because of Beth's report that you'd snuck back to the apartment for an hour. I didn't know what to think," he admitted with a sigh.

"Oh, Jonathon," she said, reaching across the table for his hands. "I'm so sorry. It's just that I've made so many bad mistakes in the past from trusting that others would make things all right. I have to see this thing through."

She tightened her hold on him, as if that could make him understand. "My parents were both older when I was born, and they fussed over me something terrible. Whenever there was the slightest trouble, my father would rush out and take care of it for me. Living with Brad was almost the same, until I found out about his gambling problems, but even then I kept believing him when he promised to fix things. This time I just had to stay and finish things myself."

He shook his head slowly. "This isn't the same as standing up to a grade school bully, you know. You might not be able to finish this."

"I know that now."

He sighed, his shoulders sagged slightly, and he seemed to grow more tired. He reached for the top folder. "We might as well get started trying to find your Mr. Daniels. It could take us all day—if we're lucky."

It wasn't much of a joke, but it was a hint that his sense of humor was still there, buried beneath his worries. She reached for the folder and flipped it open. "I promise I'll stick to my assigned tasks from now on."

"I hope so," he muttered, and got to his feet. "I'll get some coffee."

They went through a lot of coffee and then a tasteless lunch of vending-machine sandwiches and still more coffee before Claire stopped suddenly. She'd just opened a new folder, and there he was, staring up at her. Daniels.

"This is him," she whispered, almost unable to believe that he'd been in the massive pile at all. "This is Daniels."

Jonathon grabbed the photo, and things really began to move. With one quick phone call the room was filled with his assistants, people she hadn't even seen so far that day.

"That's Tinker Denari, alias Fred Cooper, alias Fred Daniels, alias Dan Cooper," Walt said. "He hadn't been heard of for three years. He was supposed to have perished in a fire aboard the yacht *Sea Princess* just off the coast of Florida."

"He's got a record that dates back forty years," the blond woman told them. "Mostly scams and cons. Has more arrests than convictions, though. A *lot* more. He's got a knack for staying very clean. It's hard to prove he's done anything."

"Who's he work for?" Jonathon asked.

"He's a free-lancer," Walt said.

"Mostly," the blonde said. "But he's done some work for Joe Farrell."

Jonathon nodded, and a satisfied smile seemed to envelop him. "Ah, so Mr. Farrell's got his finger in this pie, as well as that I-94 kickback scheme. It figures."

Claire felt lost. Everyone else seemed to find meaning in all that had been said, but she couldn't figure it out. "So he's not a government agent?" she asked.

"Hardly."

"But what's in the notebook, and why does he want it?"

Jonathon laughed. "Hey, we found out who the guy is. Be grateful for small favors. Don't expect miracles."

She began to gather together all the folders she'd paged through. "So what's next?" she asked.

"A decent dinner, and then you and the girls are off to a safe house," Jonathon said.

"Oh, are we?" She'd thought they'd been through all that already, but even as she started to speak she started to stack the albums of mug shots. Some photos slipped sideways out of one, and as Claire grabbed for them one fell to the floor. She bent down to pick it up, and her heart stopped. A deadly chill froze all her emotions—except fear. The photo was of Brad.

Claire told herself she had to be mistaken. The first craving urge of years past was a trick, a product of her weariness. She stared so long that the man's face matter names echoed in her head, but all her brave resolution could not slow the frantic pounding in her heart as she stared at the photo again.

The photo was of several men in suits leaving an office building. The two men in the foreground were clear and in focus, the two following less so, because they were partially blocked by the others. The man she'd thought was Brad was one of the blurry ones. His face was turned slightly away and it was in shadow from off the trees of a doorway. It was possible it could not belong to a stranger, to someone she knew, to a stranger. What she had thought to be a picture of Brad...

"What's wrong?" Jonathon asked.

Claire shook her head, glancing down at the photo again. The same half chill stabbed at her heart. If it was it? If she was mistaken by danger, as it threaded things in on her from every direction. "It's over, Claire," she said. "He said, but she saw his face was still...

Chapter 10

Claire told herself she had to be mistaken. The fear creeping into her heart was just a product of her weariness. She'd been afraid for so long that now she was finding things to terrify her. But all her brave scoldings could not slow the dreadful certainty in her soul as she stared at the photo again.

The picture was of several men in suits leaving an office building. The two men in the foreground were clear and distinct, the two following less so, because they were partially blocked by the others. The man she'd thought was Brad was one in the background. His face was turned slightly away, and it was in shadow. Even as she stared at him, though, at features that individually seemed to belong to a stranger, her sense of familiarity grew stronger. What was Brad doing in a picture of Jonathon's suspects?

"What's wrong?" Jonathon asked.

Claire shook her head, glancing down at the photo again. The same chill clutched at her heart. It was as if she were surrounded by danger, as if it were closing in on her from every direction. "It's crazy, I know," she said, "but this guy here looks like Brad."

She tried to laugh it off, but Jonathon was there, frowning down at the picture. "Which one?" he asked.

Claire pointed to the man. There was something about his stance....

"What case is it from?" Walt asked.

Jonathon flipped the photo over and read him the number, then slipped the photo into a projectorlike machine that sent an enlarged version of the picture onto the far wall. Walt dimmed the lights as he went out. There was no doubt about it. It was Brad. Her stomach twisted into a knot.

"It's him," she said slowly, and took a deep breath. Her soul was still trembling, and her voice echoed it. "What does this mean?"

Jonathon sat down beside her, and his hand found hers. "Maybe nothing." But his voice was hard and distant.

"Or maybe something." She swallowed, fighting back her rising fear. "Don't you think it's an awful coincidence that I just identified Daniels and run across Brad?"

"Sometimes coincidences happen."

His manner was carefully controlled, and Claire couldn't read his thoughts.

"I thought this was all going to be over soon."

"It will be," he promised.

This time there was no misreading the determination in his voice, the strength of his conviction. It didn't matter that it wasn't over yet. She wasn't fighting this alone anymore.

The door opened, and Walt hurried in. "That photo was taken of Michael O'Brien for a tax-evasion case we were preparing. The guy in back is Bradley Bannister, O'Brien's accountant. We did subpoena some files from Bannister's office, but that's his only involvement in the case. Other than getting his picture taken, that is."

"So it really is just a coincidence?" She couldn't quite believe it was that easily explained.

"It looks that way."

"I guess I was foolish to get so worried," she said. A heavy weight slipped off her shoulders with unexpected speed. She felt foolish for having been so afraid, but she felt good anyway. With a smile, she got to her feet.

"You never can tell what's important," Walt said. "Better to be overly observant." He turned off the projector and slipped the photo back in its album.

"What now?" she asked Jonathon.

He had been noticeably silent throughout the exchange with Walt, but she tried to tell herself that it meant nothing, that he had nothing to say because Walt was covering everything. But something told her that she was wrong.

He was still sitting there, staring thoughtfully at the table and sliding a small pad of paper back and forth between his fingers. There was something about the way he was sitting, a tension, not so much in his muscles as in his attitude. The darkness in his eyes held an anger deeper than any she'd ever seen. He was waiting and watching and thinking, and a shiver of awareness ran down her spine. There was more going on than she realized. Whatever Walt said, Jonathon obviously had other ideas about coincidences and their likelihood.

Claire came back toward their table in a secluded corner of a quiet restaurant near Jonathon's office. He watched her as she approached, marveling that such a fragile-looking beauty could bear up so well under the pressures of the past few days. That gentle exterior was built on a framework of steel, but it had been shaken somewhat when she'd found Brad's picture. How had she ever gotten mixed up with such a loser? he wondered.

Claire sat down, and he forced all such thoughts from his mind. She had enough trouble without having the contents of his mind added to her burdens.

"How are the girls?" he asked.

"Okay." She made a slight face. "I guess."

"What do you mean, you guess? Didn't you talk to them?"

"No, I didn't talk to them." She took a sip of her wine, then put the glass down with a sheepish grin. "I asked to talk to them, and Marilyn went outside to tell them it was me on the phone. Apparently they were having a water fight with

Paul and some kids from the neighborhood. They asked if I could call back.''

He laughed and reached over to take her hand. "Here you are, fighting dragons all day to keep them safe, and they're too busy to talk to you."

She shrugged, looking even more embarrassed. "It's not that I don't want them to be happy, but…"

"But you need to hear their voices once in a while to keep going."

She nodded. "I know they're fine, but sometimes I need proof."

His hand on hers tightened. "We'll be home soon, and you'll be able to see that for yourself."

Claire nodded and went back to her dinner. He watched her as he ate his own, waiting for the right moment to say what he had to say. She was so dear to him, and so were the girls. He couldn't leave them in jeopardy, not in any way. She had to understand that.

Once she was done eating, there was no more waiting. "I want to move you and the girls into a safe house," he said.

"We've been through all this," she said, her voice weary.

"This is getting deeper than I'd first thought," he told her. "Every time we turn around, the net closes a little tighter."

"You don't think Brad's involvement in that other case was a coincidence, do you?"

"Let's just say I don't trust coincidences. I'd feel much better if you and the girls were someplace where you'd be protected around the clock and no one could get at you."

"I thought we settled this earlier," she said, shaking her head. Her eyes had been weary a moment before, but now they flared with a deep fire.

"I'm thinking of your safety. We know more now than we knew earlier, and I think it changes things."

Her jaw had a decidedly stubborn set to it. Her aura of fragility had been discarded. Jonathon could see that if he didn't change his tactics his suggestion wouldn't go anywhere except down the tubes. She had to understand his worries.

"I don't want the girls hurt," he said.

Uncertainty brought some of the softness back to her face. "Aren't we safe now? Isn't Beth enough protection?"

"Not really," he replied. He finished the last of his wine and pushed away from the table slightly. "She's only one person, and she has to sleep and eat. She needs help. Plus, it would be safer if the bad guys didn't know where you were."

Claire stared at the tablecloth, playing with one of the ice cubes in her water glass. Uncertainty warred within Jonathon, desire fighting caution. He didn't want to send her away. He wished that all he had to do to keep her safe was to wrap his arms around her, but he'd already learned that that wasn't enough. No single man was enough to protect those he cared about from all harm.

She looked away from him a moment, her eyes wandering over images that only she could see. When her gaze returned, it was harder, more determined.

"I'm your only link," she said.

The words came so softly that he almost didn't hear them. Actually, he wished he hadn't, because they were true. "We'll get a handle on them without you. Don't worry."

"But it will be quicker with me around."

"They're not sure of you anymore," Jonathon pointed out.

"That's right. They're not sure. So they'll keep on working through me. They'll probably be more careful, but I doubt if they'll drop me altogether at this point."

Jonathon clenched his teeth and looked away himself. The images he saw were anything but comforting. The agony of losing one more dear and more precious than life itself. The empty nights when asleep, the miserable thoughts when awake. The knowledge that she was right.

Damn. Not only was she tough, she was smart. What she said was true. Daniels and his pals would still play along and try to use her. They had no other options at this point, but the thought of having her in danger gnawed at him until he could taste the anger and fear.

"Can't someone come in and help Beth keep an eye on the girls?" she asked.

He shook his head. "I don't like the setup, and besides, it puts pressure on Marilyn and her family."

Claire went back to staring at the tablecloth, tracing the damp circle her water glass had left.

This was ridiculous, Jonathon thought. He shouldn't ask. He should just pack them all up and send them to a safe house. What with his staff, the police and the FBI, they'd find Daniels and put him away. If that wasn't enough to catch a few punks, the whole country was in trouble.

"I want the girls out of danger, too," Claire said after a moment. "But I can't let myself leave, and we can't send them to a safe house with someone they hardly know. They've been through too much as it is."

Jonathon nodded his agreement reluctantly.

"Wait a minute." A new light was in her eyes, and the trace of a smile was on her lips. "My parents are elderly, but they'd be happy to have the girls."

His head started shaking of its own volition. What kind of protection would two elderly people be? "Where are your parents located?"

"They live in Fargo."

He could feel the weight slipping off his shoulders. "You mean like in North Dakota?"

"Yes."

"Does Brad know where they live?"

"No." She shook her head. "He never was much into family gatherings, and he only saw them at Christmas and sometimes on the kids' birthdays. There was no reason to tell him when Mom and Dad moved out to Fargo a few months ago to be closer to their relatives."

His mind kicked into high gear. He'd send the kids out under an assumed name, make sure they weren't followed and put Beth on the plane with them for protection.

"Can your parents pick the girls up tonight?"

"Sure." Her eyes started to glow, and a smile came to her lips.

An answering smile spread through his being, but he fought for sternness. "You're only going to get a few days, young lady," he warned her. "If nothing pops in that time, you're off to Fargo."

"Oh, my," she said with a laugh. "Banished to Fargo? For how long?"

How long? How long could he live without her? For seconds, maybe, but that hardly mattered at this point. "For as long as it takes to make sure you're safe," he said.

"That's not very definite."

It was as definite as he was going to get. "Let's go," he said, springing to his feet. "We have a lot of things to put together in a short time."

"How about tickets?"

"You just pack the girls' clothes," he said, pulling her along. "I'll have someone take care of everything else."

Traffic was light, so the ride to Marilyn's was quick, as well as uneventful. Tickets were the least that had to be done. They had to sweep the neighborhood to make sure nobody was watching them. And then they had to get to the airport without anyone following them. They'd be home free once the kids were on the plane. Beth and the kids would use assumed names, so tracing them would be difficult. In fact, he'd send a male marshal along with Beth—put them all under the same name, make them look like a family going on vacation. That would be a good cover.

An hour or so later, Jonathon was at Marilyn's, standing at the bedroom door, leaning against the door frame. Claire had to be under tremendous strain, but she moved quickly and efficiently. The happy let's-go-visit-Grandma-and-Grandpa facade that she had assumed for the girls was still in place. Jonathon could feel the strength radiating from her, and he knew that her happy face would stay in place until Katie and Molly were airborne.

Once the girls were safely on their way, he'd bring her back to his place. A tightness gripped his body. It was for her own protection, he told himself. He certainly couldn't let her go back to her own apartment, and Marilyn's was really no safer. He needed to see her, to talk to her, to touch her to be convinced that she really was safe. His house really would be best.

His house. A thought came to him, a problem that had nagged at him throughout all of this. They'd told Claire to get close to him and look for this notebook. But why? What was the real reason they'd hired her? Why else would they want her in his house?

"Did they ever ask you for anything but the notebook?" he asked.

Claire stopped for a moment. "No. It was always that."

"And they're positive it's somewhere in my house?"

She frowned. "They're positive you have it, and they seemed to think it was at the house, but they never argued when I suggested it might be at your office or even in your car."

Jonathon nodded slowly. It didn't make sense. There was no notebook there, at least none that was like the one Claire described. But if Daniels had another reason for getting Claire close to him, he certainly couldn't think what it was.

"When we get back from the airport," Claire said, "I think we should search the house from top to bottom. We'll find the notebook, and then we'll have all the answers."

It was worth a shot, he supposed. And finding such a notebook did exist certainly would answer a lot of questions.

Claire watched the plane disappear into the darkness, the lights growing smaller and smaller until there was nothing to be seen but the night. Her tears blurred her vision and she tried hard to blink the moisture away before Jonathon noticed. The strength she'd been clinging to was starting to wane. She'd never felt so alone or so worried before. Certainly her parents loved the girls, but could they keep them safe? Even with the federal deputies Jonathon had ordered, would the girls be watched as closely as she would have watched them?

Jonathon squeezed her hand. "They'll be fine," he told her. "Nothing will happen to them."

She nodded. It was easier to pretend to believe it than to start the whole argument over again. She knew she could have gone with the girls. In fact, one part of her heart had insisted she go with them to safety, but another part had refused to leave Jonathon. She had a part to play in this mess, and she was going to play it. She couldn't leave him alone.

Her heart had been tugged first one way, then the other, until it felt ready to break. Now she just felt weary, tired of the whole thing. She wondered if a time would ever come when she'd stop waking up in the night in a cold sweat, re-living the terror of the past days.

"I wish this whole thing was over," she said with a sigh. "I wish I had never gotten involved."

"I don't," Jonathon said. He put his arm around her shoulders and led her away from the wide glass windows that over-looked the runways. "If you hadn't gotten involved, we wouldn't have met, and that would have been a crime."

She smiled at him. His words had taken some of the heaviness from her heart. "It just seems like there should have been an easier way," she said.

They maneuvered around rows of black vinyl chairs. Here and there a newspaper lay discarded, along with paper cups and crumpled cigarette packs. Life had been there and gone. For some reason, that thought made the chill tighten around her heart. The terminal was almost deserted, and she ought to feel safe here. No one could follow them without easily being seen, yet the very emptiness seemed to smell of danger. Maybe she was just too tired to be sensible anymore.

"Why do you think Daniels wants the notebook?" she asked. "Do you think it's something important?"

"If that's really what he wants, it must be important to whoever he's working for. It must have something in it that we don't know the significance of."

Just ahead, passengers were disembarking from another flight, and she pressed even closer to Jonathon. It was crazy. No one coming off a San Francisco flight could pose a threat to her, but her instincts had taught her to fear. His arm tightened around her, and his lips brushed the top of her head. She relaxed slightly.

"It doesn't seem very smart to make such a big deal about

something nobody has noticed yet," she pointed out. "Why don't they just let it go and hope their luck holds?"

Jonathon laughed. It was a deep rumbling sound that spread some of its peace to her. "These guys don't work that way," he told her. "They believe in making their own luck."

"All right, I can buy that, but why are they so sure you have the notebook?"

"That I can't figure out, and that's why I have my doubts that that's what they're really after," he admitted as they walked under the brightly lit Arrival and Departure boards. "I don't keep evidence lying around."

"They said you'd never returned it."

"How can they be so sure?" he muttered. "Have they already got somebody who can check out the evidence room? There are a lot of unanswered questions."

The clerks in the rent-a-car stands watched them idly as they walked by. Her heart skipped a beat when a weary-looking traveler who had been slumped in an uncomfortable chair, apparently trying to sleep, suddenly got up and began to follow them.

"Jonathon," she whispered, for they were heading out to the parking lot. The dark, half-deserted parking lot.

Jonathon slowed down as they passed the last of the rent-a-car booths, stopping to pick up a brochure on the company's latest mileage plan. The man went on past them and into the men's washroom. Claire sagged against Jonathon, feeling absurdly relieved and just plain absurd.

"I guess I'm jumping at shadows."

"No, you're being careful. Nothing wrong with that."

Maybe not, but still she resolved to be stronger. She'd played the part for the girls; she could do it for Jonathon's sake, too. He didn't need to worry that she was going to fall apart on him at any moment.

The parking lot was neither as dark nor as deserted as she had feared. Bright light streamed over the rows of vehicles, and newly arrived travelers were trudging to their cars. There was nothing for her to worry about, she told herself, but still she breathed a sigh of relief when they were inside Jonathon's car.

"So what now?" he asked once they were heading toward the highway.

"I thought we were going to search your place," she said.

He stopped to pay at the parking booth, then headed for the southbound tollway. "We can, but I thought maybe you'd want to do something first. Stop and have some supper or a drink, like regular folks on a regular Saturday night."

Regular people and regular Saturday nights. Would they ever come again?

Stop it, she told herself. She was turning into a wimp. She had a job to do and she would do it, without worrying constantly.

"I think we ought to wait until we're regular people again before we start acting like them," she said. "Besides, I'm anxious to really search your place without jumping at every sound and being afraid you're going to catch me."

He laughed. "Were you really worried? Did I ever come close?"

"Once or twice." She sensed an easing of his tensions as she spoke. How selfish she'd been. Thinking only of her fears and not realizing how worried he was. Just because she refused to think about the future, that didn't mean that his feelings had lessened. Just to show how relaxed she was, she turned on his car radio, hitting the scan button.

"Let's find something that suits our mood," she said.

A country station came on, wailing about cheating lovers looking for stolen moments. "I don't think that's it," Jonathon said with a laugh.

Next came pounding rock with a beat strong enough to wake the dead. "Not too soothing," Claire said, and went on to find a baseball game. "Oops, a little too soothing."

She stopped at a classical station that was playing opera music and sat back. "Now that's just what we need."

"You, an opera fan?" He was clearly surprised.

"Sort of," she said. Leaning back in the seat, she closed her eyes. Cool night air was dancing along her skin, lifting her hair off her neck and bringing the peace that nights had had when she'd been a child. Nights when she'd lain back in her bed and stared out the window at the stars winking high above the lightning bugs. Nights when the wind had rustled the leaves of the crab-apple tree outside her window and old Mr. Romano had played his opera records long into the night.

"I've never seen any operas, and I don't know the stories," she admitted, "but the music reminds me of summer nights as a kid when I'd hear the music from next door."

He shifted so that his arm went around her shoulders. "Well, for that kind of memory I can take opera."

"How kind of you." She laid her head on his shoulder in sweet contentment as the music wove its majestic power over her. Cars whizzed by, their headlights invading the privacy of the car for seconds before going on their way.

The fears that had been gnawing away at her just an hour earlier were relegated to the background. Here, with Jonathon, there was no place for fear, no time for worrying. She felt a delicious warmth creep slowly to every corner of her body, melting the tension and changing her ideas about what was important and what wasn't. The future was still a worry, but she could make time stand still for the moment, could deny that the time would ever come for decisions.

What could she do to stop Brad's loan sharks that she hadn't done? Nothing. What could she do to solve the mystery of Daniels and the notebook? Nothing that she wasn't doing. What could she do about the absolute pleasure of Jonathon's embrace? Enjoy it, her heart whispered. Enjoy it now, before the storm breaks again.

Soon enough they were at Jonathon's house, welcomed by the peace and shelter it offered. They'd left lights burning when they'd left, so the house wasn't dark and sleeping when they went inside. But the welcome Claire felt was more than just lit lamps. It touched her soul, not her eyes. For the moment, they were safe. The trick was to make that safety last forever, and the way to do that was to find the notebook.

"So where do we start?" she asked as she put her purse down on the kitchen table. She sat on the edge of the table

and looked around her. Breakfast dishes still sat in the sink—
a spoon and an empty carton of Häagen-Dazs ice cream. At
least three days' worth of old newspapers sat next to the
toaster, and a long grocery list dangled from the refrigerator
door. This was Jonathon. She cared about him, even loved
him. She wanted to bring a smile to his face and see it in his
eyes, too. In her bravest moments she even wanted to make a
life with him, keeping him from the shadows that wanted to
steal his sunshine. But those moments were just that—moments—and they disappeared quickly when memories of past
hurts came back.

Her glance took in the kitchen cabinets, the cookbook shelf
and the refrigerator. "If you really wanted to hide something
well, it could be anyplace."

"Such as?"

"In the drip pan of the refrigerator."

He knelt on the floor and pulled it out. Nothing but damp
dust. "Where else?"

She frowned. "If it was in the butter compartment, you'd
have noticed. Same thing with the freezer. How about in
among your cookbooks? When was the last time you looked
at them?"

He didn't answer, just pulled out cookbook after cookbook.
French cooking, Italian cooking, dessert books, salad books.
Fish-and-fowl books and low-cal dumpling books, but no
notebooks.

"Well, so much for my ideas." Her enthusiasm had ebbed
a touch, but she refused to notice, for then fear would start to
creep back. She'd start to think that maybe they couldn't win,
and then what chance would she have of growing brave
enough to accept Jonathon's love? "I thought you'd be a great
expert in searching."

"Why? It doesn't come with a law degree." He was sitting
on the floor, cookbooks piled all around him. He leaned back
against the wall. "Let's think logically about all this and assume for the evening that there really is a notebook that Daniels wants. He said I had it. How could he be so sure?"

"He said you checked it out."

"But if I didn't bring it here, who did?"

"Maybe he did. Maybe he's trying to frame you. Have the missing evidence found in your possession."

Jonathon shook his head. "He wouldn't have you involved at all, because your presence could destroy the credibility of his frame. If the notebook was found here I could just say *you* planted it here. Any jury would find that a plausible reason for your presence. No, he wants the notebook for himself, and he doesn't know exactly where it is."

"Maybe one of his men hid it here? But then why wouldn't that man be able to get it back?"

"Maybe he tried to blackmail Daniels and can't anymore. If he'd hidden it well, really well, maybe he figured Daniels would have to meet his demands or never find it himself."

Claire frowned. Her shoulders sagged. "How would we ever find it then? Besides, it doesn't really make sense. Why would one of Daniels's hired hands hide it here? Why not in his own place?"

"Because that's where Daniels would look first."

"It still doesn't make sense. There's a million more reasonable places for a blackmailer to hide evidence than in your house." More than her shoulders was sagging. Her hope was, too. This was an impossible task. None of it made any sense. They'd never find the stupid notebook.

"You need some more optimism," he said, and got to his feet.

"I'd settle for even a slim chance of winning."

He just smiled at her. It was a soft, gentle smile that told her to have faith, that told her that miracles could still happen and that someday she would trust again. A smile that curled her toes inside her shoes and reminded her that notebooks weren't the only things in life. Jonathon went to a cabinet and took out two wineglasses, then took a bottle of wine from another cabinet.

"Want ice? This isn't chilled."

"Ice is fine."

A moment later he was handing her a glass of white wine.

Then he held his own glass out in a toast. "To your search. May it be short, sweet and successful."

"Amen." She sipped at her wine and felt its warmth seep through her. Little by little her tensions unwound. "All right, where do we begin?"

"Why not right here?"

"Why not?" she echoed with a faint smile, putting down her glass.

They set to work with determination, looking everywhere they could possibly think of in the kitchen. The drip pan had already been checked, but they moved the refrigerator out and checked behind it. Nothing but dust. The cabinets held only dishes, the pantry only food, and the space under the dishwasher only two old letters addressed to Occupant that must have fallen off the counter.

"We're not getting very far," she noted.

"We've pretty much eliminated one room."

The dining room was next. All they found was a misplaced spoon that had fallen under the bottom drawer in the china cabinet. Nothing was hidden behind the framed prints on the wall. Nothing was under the Oriental rug except a rug pad. Claire closed the door of the china cabinet and leaned wearily against the wall.

"Didn't you tell me that you had Marilyn redecorate the place? What if the notebook was in something you got rid of?"

He sank down on the floor next to her. "Then we won't find it."

The thought sent a cloud passing over her heart. She couldn't bear living with the uncertainty, with the fear. "Don't say—"

The fear in her heart suddenly seemed to come alive in the ringing of the phone. Her breath caught and her heart stopped as her eyes met Jonathon's. It was almost midnight. Anyone who was calling now had to be bringing bad news.

Jonathon must have read her mind. "Don't jump to conclusions," he said, and got to his feet. "It could be a wrong number."

No, it couldn't. Wrong numbers came when you were in the bathtub. Trouble came late at night.

Jonathon picked up the phone in the middle of the third ring. "Hello?" he said. "Hello?"

He hung up the phone without saying anything else and a new fear stole her heart. They were being watched. It was another warning, just like the ransacking. She got to her feet.

"There was no one there?" she whispered.

"Hey, what did I tell you? A wrong number." He tried to laugh it off, but she shook her head.

"They're watching us. If they know we're here, they may know where the girls are. Something could have happened to them."

He grabbed her by her upper arms as if he could somehow stem the rising panic in her heart. "Nothing has happened to the girls. If anything had, we'd have been called."

"Maybe I should call out there—"

He cut her off. "They can't have even arrived yet. Beth'll get a message to us when they do."

"But—" She cut herself off this time and fell into his arms with a sigh. Just for tonight, she needed his strength, needed his touch to hold her up against the storm. Tomorrow she'd be strong, but tonight it was just too much to battle on her own. His arms closed around her as she buried her face in his chest. The steady rhythm of his heart was reassurance in itself.

"They're going to be fine," he told her, his voice as soft as velvet. "I'm not going to let anything happen to them."

She looked up. It might have been the intensity of his voice that forced her eyes to meet his. His gaze promised her safety and strength if she would just lean a little on him. There was fire in his eyes, too—the flame of desire to meld their lives together and find peace.

"Yes, I know you won't," she said, and her heart believed her words.

His eyes consuming her, his arms holding her in heaven, his lips came down to hers. His touch was gentle, the sweetest thing life had to offer, and she kissed him back. Somehow, in the midst of all the terror and danger, they had found each other, and that was special and right. Her arms closed around him, holding him as fast and tight as he was holding her. Together they could win any battle, conquer any foe.

He held her away from a touch. "What you need is some pampering," he said. "And I know the very thing to make all those worries disappear."

"Oh?" She was willing to try anything. "Hypnosis? Voodoo? Sedatives?"

"A bubble bath."

It was the last thing she'd expected, and her first reaction was to stare. Then a slow smile spread over her lips. "A bubble bath?"

"Guaranteed to relax you," he said. Taking her hand, he led her toward the stairs.

Her common sense made her hold back. "Jonathon, this is crazy. What about searching? We have to find that notebook."

He stopped and looked into her eyes, silently asking questions that never passed his lips. "The notebook's not here," he assured her. "And even if it was, some things are more important than the notebook. You're as tense as an overwound watch."

She smiled wryly. "Now that's poetic."

"The hell with poetry. I'd rather find that damn notebook and know what's going on than have you jumping at the slightest sound." His hand had never left hers, and it slowly drew her forward now. "Claire, I don't know how it happened so fast, or why you touched me like no one has in a long time, but that's the way it is. I care more about you and your well-being than anything else."

"Oh, Jonathon."

It was more of a sigh than actual words. Her heart was speaking, not her mouth, and it was speaking with joy. She went into his arms, not out of fear, not because she needed his strength, but because it was where she belonged. Her heart knew it was all the home she would ever need. Tonight she would be his.

"Does this mean you accept my offer of a bubble bath?" he asked, passion curling through his voice.

"It sounds delightful."

She let him lead her up the stairs, but at the top he slowed. "Now, there are several varieties of bubble bath we offer here at the Hotel Tyler," he said. "There's the basic tub full of suds, clean towels and all the privacy you desire."

"My, what a gentleman you are." In spite of everything, she was starting to feel giddy. "And what are the other kinds?"

"Well, our tourist bath includes the tub, towels and soft music."

She cuddled in his arms. "I usually go deluxe. What would that include?"

He smiled down into her eyes, sending a spark running through her being. "The tub, towels, a glass of wine and a personal back scrubbing."

She smiled back. The spark had become a wild flame, burning and scorching everything in its path. "I'll take deluxe."

"Are you sure, Claire?" he asked. "You're tense and scared. I can hold you if it makes you feel safe. I can hold you all night long. It doesn't have to be anything more than that."

"Jonathon, you are such a dear man," she said simply. She reached up to touch his cheek gently. "I need so badly to be held, to be loved, that I'm not sure I can think straight. But I know that I need you now, like I've never needed anybody else before. Not just to make love to me, but to be there for me."

"I am," he said simply. "You'll find that I do know what's best for you."

He took her into the bedroom and gave her his robe. Navy-blue velour with beige trim, so masculine, so soft. A man can be both, a little voice inside her said.

"Now, you undress and come into the bathroom when you're ready."

Would she ever be ready? she wondered. But her hands obeyed her heart, not her overactive brain, and she slowly took off her blouse, then her skirt. She ought to have been uncomfortable undressing in a strange house, in the bedroom of a man she had only known for two weeks, but she wasn't. The only hesitations in her heart came from a reluctance to admit the eagerness in her soul. The future be damned, she told herself. For once she was going to live for the moment.

When she entered the bathroom, the tub was filled with delightfully rich bubbles. Jonathon waved her toward the tub, laid a thick cream-colored towel over her arm and kissed her neck just below her right ear. A tingle shot through her body, a coursing of desire that shocked her.

"Your tub awaits," he said softly.

He took the back of the robe and gently pulled it from her as she stepped into the tub. She felt her face flush.

"All of a sudden I remembered my stretch marks," she said as the water washed over her, covering her body with wonderful warmth.

"Stretch marks are beautiful," he told her, his eyes confirming his words. He held a rolled-up towel in place for her to lay her head on.

"I'll remember that, too," she promised.

A kiss on the lips was her reward. "Ready for round two?" he asked.

"Sounds like a fight." She wasn't quite at ease yet, though she knew enough to admit that it was her racing heart that was the problem, not Jonathon.

"Or a fabulous meal," he said with a smile, and left the room.

Slow down, Claire silently ordered her heart once she was alone. She lay back a little more in the tub and let the warm, soapy water slosh around her. She closed her eyes, not of her own accord but because she had to. It truly was a relaxing experience. She could feel the tension draining away, making way for more pleasurable sensations.

"We haven't fallen asleep, have we?" Jonathon asked.

Claire opened her eyes to find that he'd returned with a tray holding two glasses of wine and a plate of hors d'oeuvres. A small tape player was tucked under his arm. He put the tray down on top of the hamper, then put the tape player on the floor and flicked a button. Classical music filled the air.

"Not quite opera, but close," he said, handing her a glass of wine. "Is the water warm enough?"

"It's wonderful." The music somehow seemed to be in the water, soothing her with its magic spell, just as the gentle movement of the bubbly water was relaxing her.

"Food for the body, then, to complete the package." He held out the tray, and she took an hors d'oeuvre, a cracker with a strange-looking creamy topping. It tasted cold, rich and delicious.

"It's ice cream on top," she said.

"An early breakfast."

When the ice cream and wine were all gone, he took her glass from her. "Time for the next round," he said.

"More ice cream?"

"A personal back scrubbing," he said.

Her cheeks flushed with sudden heat, but she didn't hesitate. This man was so good for her, so much a part of her life. She couldn't remember ever having been happy when his warmth hadn't been there to bring her sunshine, couldn't imagine how she'd live without it in the future. But no, the past and the future had no place here now.

She leaned forward in the tub. "Scrub away."

At first his hands did just that, scrubbing her back with neat efficiency, but then his hands began to roam slightly, around her sides and up to the edges of her breasts. His touch found new areas that needed caresses, new hungers that needed to be satisfied.

"You certainly run a first-class operation here," she murmured, her skin afire from his touch.

"We try, ma'am. We try." His voice was no longer steady. It trembled with his growing longing.

The flames of desire flared in sudden fury and wanting. Her need to be held and cherished, to belong totally to another, grew into an all-consuming hunger. Jonathon's arms pulled her closer, and eagerly she moved into them, her body pressing into his. Jonathon pulled her deeper into his arms, and she rose onto her knees.

When his lips came to claim hers, she was ready. Dripping

wet, her arms slid around his shoulders, holding him close so that their mouths could cling even more. His tongue was gentle but insistent as it pressed against her lips, demanding admittance. She opened her lips, her heart wanting, needing, to taste of his sweetness and strength.

"I'm dripping wet," she said as his lips moved to taste her shoulders.

"I'll dry," he murmured.

She closed her eyes in perfect happiness as his hands, his lips, slid over her skin. The fire inside her, deep in her heart, grew ever hotter, ever more demanding. His lips came back to hers. She never wanted them to leave. There was a strength in his touch, a power in his nearness, that made her senses explode. This was love. This was the real joining of two souls.

"How much longer are you planning on staying in the tub?" he asked, reaching over for a towel.

Rather than give it to her, he set about drying her dripping body. The towel took over the seduction his hands had begun, roughly but somehow gently skimming over her skin, bringing the fever to an even higher pitch. He dried her breasts, her back and down her leg, and his every touch was slow, exquisite torture. Her arms and then her neck were caressed by the fabric.

"Mmm. Now to test how well I did," he said, and slowly kissed the base of her neck. "Nice." His lips moved down her right side to her breasts. "Very nice," he murmured, and went on with his explorations. Her waist received his approval, and so did her right leg. Then he switched to her left side, his lips moving along her body to send the flames climbing still higher. "Oh, so nice."

All her worries and tensions were far away. This moment became her world. His lips moved to hers again, and the towel fell to the floor. His hands took over where the towel had left off. There was no more time for teasing as real hungers took over.

The night was deep and dark and belonged only to them. Their bodies awakened to each other and spoke in languages without words. Jonathon swept her into his arms and carried her into the bedroom, where they lay together on the bed.

She fumbled slightly with the buttons on his shirt as he rid himself of the rest of his clothes, and then nothing was between them but love. The past, with all its shadows and, the future, with all its worries, both were left behind as Claire and Jonathon soared amid the clouds. The stars seemed to smile and greet them, lighting their way to the heavens.

Touching, tasting, even breathing, became a joy to further their love. There was nothing but them, nothing but the rising splendor of their needs and their embrace. They clung together as sweet ecstasy surrounded and consumed them, and they stayed in each other's arms as they drifted down from passion's heights and found peace in sleep.

Jonathon grabbed the ringing phone and squeezed it tightly as if he were hoping to choke off the sound. "Yes?" he whispered, glancing over his shoulder at Claire. She appeared to be a little restless, but she was still asleep.

"Jonathon? This is Lou. I'm down at the office."

Jonathon peered through the darkness at his clock. "It's two o'clock in the morning. What do you want?"

"You said to call if we found anything, day or night," Lou responded.

"Yeah, so what have you got?"

"We know what the notebook is."

Jonathon waited, then waited some more. "Well, do you want to tell me about it?"

"Yeah." Lou sounded hurt. "I just thought you'd be more excited about it."

"I'm ecstatic."

He hadn't realized how strenuous whispering was. Maybe he should get up and move to another phone, but that might wake—

"Jonathon?"

A gentle touch on his arm told him that he was too late. He turned. Lou was saying something, but all Jonathon knew was Claire, and all he felt was the worry in the air.

"Is it the girls, Jonathon?" she asked, her voice trembling with fear. "Did something happen?"

He shook his head, slipping his hand over the receiver. "No, it's somebody from my office. Nothing for you to worry about."

She lay back, but Jonathon could still feel her tension. She was waiting, listening. He went back to Lou.

"Sorry, Lou, I didn't catch all that. What did you say?"

"Aren't you awake?" Lou asked. "Sounds like your starter needs an overhaul. I said that notebook was in the accountant's files that were subpoenaed for the Michael O'Brien tax-evasion trial about this time last year. Or at least there's a notebook on the property list, but there's no notebook with the actual evidence."

"You're sure?"

"There's been a whole lot of happy campers here, inventorying everything in the property room. We're positive."

"But that case has nothing to do with Joe Farrell." He felt Claire sigh slightly and relax.

"Our reaction exactly," Lou said. "We thought you'd figure out the tie between them, seeing as how you're our head honcho."

"How about if we postpone further miracles until tomorrow?"

"You mean we can actually go home and get some sleep?" Lou asked, punctuating his sentence with a short snort of a laugh.

"Yeah, right. You guys did a good job. You can have a whole hour's sleep, then get back on the case."

"Gee, thanks, chief. You're all heart."

Jonathon hung up the phone on Lou's laughter.

"So things are wrapping up, are they?" Claire asked, a yawn punctuating the end of her question. She was almost asleep again. "Can I really stop worrying?"

"Sure, anytime you like," he said.

But long after Claire's even breathing told him that she was asleep once more, he lay awake. So there really was a notebook after all. Was it in his house, as Daniels apparently believed? And, more importantly, what had Claire's ex-husband been doing with a notebook that a leading mob figure wanted?

Jonathon had told Claire to stop worrying only because he'd decided he'd worry for her. In reality, any way he looked at all this, he saw the walls closing in around her, and he had no idea how to stop them.

Chapter 11

The sunlight streamed through the bedroom windows, sending its blessing down on her. Claire couldn't help think it was a wonderful way to start the day. From down the hall she could hear the sound of Jonathon's shower and his slightly off-key singing. Maybe the past week had been nothing more than a nightmare that she was finally waking up from.

Her body warmed with memories. Well, parts of the last week might have been nightmarish, but other parts certainly hadn't. For instance, last night had been wonderful, better than she'd ever dreamed love could be. But then, it had been a joining not just of their bodies but of their hearts and souls, too.

The girls were safe and happy—she'd been notified this morning that they'd arrived safely—the mess with Daniels would soon be cleared up, and Brad would solve his own problems from now on. She closed her eyes, sliding farther down into the sheets, letting Jonathon's scent surround her. The thought of the future was still a bit scary, but she could put that aside for now and concentrate on her present joy.

"Well, good morning," Jonathon said.

Claire sat up and smiled at him. She hadn't heard him turn off the water, but he couldn't have been out of the shower long. The hair on his chest lay in dark curls against his skin, and drops of water were running down his chest, the broad chest she had lain against in pleasure last night, and into the towel that was wrapped around his waist. Her heart began to race, and her fingers itched to touch him again, to explore anew the depths that were Jonathon Tyler.

"Staying here with you gives new meaning to that phrase," she said with a contented sigh.

He sat on the edge of the bed. Her hand slid over his arm, needing to touch and feel, needing to know that the wonders of the night before hadn't been a dream.

"And to good night," he said, bending down to greet her properly.

His lips said more than words could have. Pressed against hers, they promised a lifetime of good mornings and good nights, of sweet dreams and even sweeter reality. For once the promise didn't leave her skittish, it left her tempted.

"So what's your pleasure for breakfast?" he asked as he stood up. "I'm a whiz at bacon and eggs or omelets."

"What? No ice cream?"

His eyebrows raised in mock horror. "I'm a reformed host, now fully aware of good nutrition," he told her. "Your sweet smile has rid me of my evil ways."

She laughed and reached for the robe he handed her. "Not all of them, I hope."

"Only the ones you're likely to object to." He went over to the dresser and began to get dressed.

She tied the robe's belt around her waist, then rolled the sleeves up slightly so that she didn't look like one of Snow White's dwarfs. Then she sat on the bed and watched him for a little while, feeling a growing sadness that their little interlude was over and the world was claiming them again.

"So what's on the agenda for today?" she asked after a moment. "Any more pictures for me to go through?"

The expression on his face seemed to change. He pulled a dress shirt from a drawer and ripped off the laundry bands.

"No," he said. "It's your day off. You get to stay here, but you can keep looking for that notebook."

"I thought you didn't think there was one."

He shrugged, then looked down at her. His eyes were troubled. "That call I got last night... No, my staff found out that there really is a notebook. It's part of the evidence subpoenaed from Brad's office in that tax-evasion case."

"I don't understand."

"Neither do any of us, at this point, but I think it's time to look a little more closely into Brad's affairs."

Claire frowned. Brad was somehow involved with the notebook? But he was the reason she needed the money. Were his demands for cash just a useful pretense to pressure her into doing a distasteful job? She looked up to find Jonathon buttoning his shirt, and she got to her feet.

"It strikes me as an awful coincidence, the way the same names keep cropping up," she said, shoving her hands into the pockets of the robe.

"Same here."

He went to his closet and pulled out a suit, slipping the pants off the hanger with practiced ease and tossing the jacket on the bed. There was a pleasure in watching the everyday actions, a calming sensation that kept the knot of tension trying to form in her stomach from growing larger. This was the real world, not some wild movie full of gun battles and car chases. Jonathon would take care of everything. And she would find the notebook.

While he finished dressing, she made the bed, pulling the bedspread up and smacking the pillows into shape. "If that notebook's here, I'll find it," she vowed.

"That's the spirit." He picked up his jacket and slung it over his shoulder, leaving his other arm free to go around her. "Now, how about breakfast? You know, double chocolate chip does make a tasty way to start the day."

She laughed, but she wondered as she followed him downstairs how long her courage would last once he was away from her.

"Oh, yeah," he said halfway down the stairs. "They've

fixed it so that your phone at the apartment also rings here in the kitchen. If Daniels should call, play it cool and noncommittal. We don't want you involved anymore, but we don't want him more suspicious than I think he already is. But you don't have to worry, a federal marshal will be watching the house at all times."

Then he handed her a little device that looked like a remote control for a garage door. "We don't want to spook anyone, so we have him sitting in Marilyn's house. If anything bothers you, just press this button and he'll come running."

Claire stared down at the little electronic gizmo, trying to muster some courage. But it had already fled.

Claire felt lonely as soon as Jonathon closed the door. The phone attached to her apartment line sat as a silent but worrisome reminder. She tried to ignore it, reminding herself that the little brown box clipped to her belt would keep her safe. If anything happened all she had to do was press the button and help would come. She told herself she was fine and wandered into the living room. There was no getting away from the storm swirling around them. All that could be done was try to carry on as usual.

She dressed amid all the intimate reminders of Jonathon, remembered to transfer the pager to the pocket of her shorts and came back down to the kitchen, strong enough now to see the phone and not worry. She filled the sink with hot, soapy water and plunged the dishes into it. It was a normal enough action to relax her heart. Marilyn came over just as she was letting the dishwater drain away.

"Jonathon has a dishwasher, you know," she pointed out when Claire started drying the dishes.

"It seems a shame to run it just for a few things," Claire said. "Besides, it gives me something to do."

Marilyn pulled out a chair and sat down. "Didn't you ever hear of leisure time? Loafing around?"

Claire shook her head. "Too much chance to think." She slipped the frying pan into a cabinet, then looked around, giving a last swipe of the towel to some water splashed on the countertop. "I like to stay busy."

Marilyn pretended to shudder. "And when Jonathon asked me to keep you company today I thought I was getting a day off."

Claire laughed. "You can relax. I won't tell."

"No, no. I'll be a good companion. Just tell me we aren't waxing his floors. I hate waxing floors."

"No floors," Claire promised. "We're looking for a notebook that supposedly was hidden here someplace."

"By whom?"

Claire shrugged and hung up the towel. "We don't know. Just that it's some evidence missing from a case and is believed to be here."

"And is that the reason I have two federal agents sitting in my kitchen staring at this house?"

"Partly," Claire admitted, turning away from the sink. "Well, any preference as to where we start? Jonathon and I did the kitchen and dining room last night. I've already gone through his office, the living room and the basement."

Marilyn was on her feet, rubbing her hands together in pretended glee. "Boy, I feel like Nancy Drew, with my very own mystery to solve. Why don't we start at the top and work down?"

"The top? You mean the attic?"

"Sure. It's early in the day, so it'll be cool up there. It's loaded with junk and wasn't touched in the redecorating."

"Sounds fine. Lead on."

The attic was a great place to start, Claire thought as she followed Marilyn upstairs. Not only was it away from that phone that she hoped wouldn't ring, it would also be hidden from the street. Somehow that made her feel more comfortable. Marilyn went into a closet in the back bedroom and pulled a folding set of stairs down from the ceiling.

"Think Nancy Drew started in attics?" Marilyn asked as she climbed the stairs. "Phew! It may be cool outside, but it sure isn't cool up here."

Claire followed her up, climbing onto the wooden platform

next to the stairs. She could just barely stand upright. "It's not that bad," she said. "But it'll only get worse as the day goes on. We might as well get it done now."

"Spoken like a true mother," Marilyn said with a groan. "Let's start over there."

The attic itself was huge, covering the whole second floor of the house, but most of the space was unusable, with no planking over the joists. In the center, around the stairs, flooring had been laid down, and boxes were piled high there. Marilyn took a box from an end pile and plopped it down in the clear space in the middle. Claire pulled the top open.

"Christmas decorations," she said.

"Maybe the notebook was a Christmas present," Marilyn joked as they unpacked everything. "Or a Christmas list."

Christmas lights, ornaments and boxes of silvery tinsel. There was a set of *Sesame Street* ornaments neatly lined up in a box that had to have been Timmy's. Claire touched the little Big Bird gently as a shadow crossed her heart. Molly had a similar set of ornaments, and how she loved them. Timmy must have been just as excited as Molly had when he'd gotten them.

"There's nothing sadder than losing a child, is there?" Marilyn said.

"It must have been devastating for Jonathon to lose his whole family." Claire closed the box and put it with the others, but she knew that the sadness couldn't be put away as easily.

"It was hard the way it happened, too, though I doubt there's an easy way to lose your family," Marilyn said. "Sarah and Timmy had gone up to her parents' cottage in Wisconsin for the weekend, but Jonathon had to work and couldn't get away. They were hit on the way back by some teenagers who were drag racing."

Claire winced. "So on top of the loss he's had to deal with the guilt of not being with them, the question of whether things might have been different if he'd been driving."

"He's getting better, though," Marilyn said. "You've helped him there."

"He's helped me, too." He had, in so many ways. She'd started to trust again, to believe that happiness was possible and that Brad's faults belonged solely to Brad. That they weren't traits shared by all men.

Marilyn put the Christmas decorations aside, and they started on another box. College textbooks. No missing notebook. The next box was filled with yarn and scraps of material.

"Did Sarah sew?" Claire asked. She pictured the woman as the perfect wife and mother—sewing, cooking and knitting to perfection.

"She tried," Marilyn said with a laugh. "Sarah was not particularly domestic. About the only domestic-type skill she had was needlework, and that she perfected when she had layovers as a stewardess."

"She was a stewardess?" Claire asked. "I didn't know that. How glamorous." Somehow her own short career as Brad's secretary before they'd gotten married seemed dull and colorless.

"I guess," Marilyn said vaguely.

The only papers in the box were some knitting instruction books, so they started repacking things.

"The way Sarah used to talk," Marilyn went on after a moment, "it sounded like drudgery, just drudgery forty thousand feet in the air. She did like the traveling, though."

"Did she stop when she was pregnant or when she married Jonathon?" Claire asked as she brought another box over.

"She switched from international flights to domestic when they got married, then quit altogether before Timmy was born," Marilyn said. She opened the new box. It was filled with empty gift boxes, nice, sturdy cartons from the best stores. "Boy, now I know where to come to make my bargain-basement gifts look expensive."

Claire took out the top box. She could tell it was empty just by shaking it. "I used to save gift boxes to carry cupcakes to Molly's preschool in. These are just the right size for two dozen."

Marilyn shook her head as she shook two more boxes.

"Such an honest woman. You put my cheating heart to shame."

Claire laughed and grabbed the next box. Something was in it. Though it seemed too light for the notebook, her heart did a somersault as she fiddled with the cover. But it was just an old greeting card. A wedding card, to be precise.

Claire stared at the card, with its promise of love that lasted forever. Did anything ever happen the way one dreamed? At her own wedding she'd certainly imagined herself living to a ripe old age with Brad at her side. She'd never dreamed that his love of gambling would override his love for her.

Claire looked up. Marilyn had checked all the other gift boxes and was putting them back. "Do you think Jonathon will ever love anyone as much as he loved Sarah?" Claire asked.

Marilyn stopped packing and stared at her. "I should think you could answer that better than me. There is a definite glint in his eye when he watches you."

Claire shook her head. "Oh, I know he cares about me, but I don't know how deeply he cared about Sarah. Was she his once-in-a-lifetime love? It's not that I begrudge her his love.... I just wondered."

"Well, put your mind at rest," Marilyn said, and grabbed up the carton to deposit it with the others. "Theirs was a typical marriage. Love most of the time, but misunderstandings sometimes, too. Neither of them was perfect."

"My ex was a gambler," Claire said suddenly. "I'd say a man who takes care of his family before his bookie comes pretty close to perfect for me."

Marilyn's smile was sympathetic. "I guess real problems make dirty socks under the bed seem rather petty."

"The trick is remembering that when you find another bunch of socks."

Marilyn laughed and went to get another box as Claire stared around the attic. They were about halfway through the boxes, but they hadn't been very successful so far. Was she missing the obvious? Could the notebook be stuck in the space under the planking? Could it be buried in the loose insulation that lay between the joists? Was she making things harder than necessary by looking in obscure places when it might be hidden out in the open?

"What was that?" Marilyn's voice brought Claire back from her thoughts. "Was it the phone?"

"I didn't—" But even as she started speaking she did indeed hear the faint ringing of the phone. The phone from her apartment with its higher pitched sound.

"Oh, Lordy," Claire muttered as she scrambled over the boxes to the stairs.

"Watch your step!" Marilyn called after her. "Whoever it is, they'll call back. It's not worth a broken neck."

But it wasn't falling that Claire was worrying about, it was who was calling and what she would say to them. She almost hoped they'd give up, but the phone was still ringing as she raced down from the second floor and through the dining room to the kitchen. Pausing for a moment to catch her breath, she reached for the phone. She would be in control. One more deep breath, and she picked up the receiver.

"'Bout time you answered," Daniels muttered. "I've been calling so often I almost thought you were avoiding me."

"Nope, I've just been busy." Did they know that she was at Jonathon's and that the phone line had been moved? Just how all-seeing were they?

"Searching for the notebook, I hope." Daniels's voice was low and the words came out slowly and precisely.

She swallowed "I'm doing my best."

"But will that be good enough?"

The air suddenly seemed thick. His words pushed at her with real menace. She took a deep breath, but it didn't help. Her heart was still racing, and her knees were still trembling. Her hands were sticky with sweat, and she wiped them on her shorts. That helped a bit.

"You told me yourself it might not be in his house," she pointed out carefully. "If Tyler took the notebook deliberately, he wouldn't be keeping it around for someone to find. He'd have destroyed it."

"I thought you were so sure of his innocence." Daniels's

voice was low, and he was almost chuckling, though not with humor.

He wasn't a mind reader after all, Claire realized with a start. The knowledge gave her spirits a boost, and her heart slowed its racing a little.

"What did you do?" he asked. "Have a lover's spat?"

"I'm here to do a job, not get involved," she told him.

He did laugh then. It was a cold and deadly sound. "Then get the job done. I'm sure that notebook is there. Find it, or you may find a surprise that isn't to your liking."

So much for her getting the upper hand. She was relegated back to the role of pawn. The line went dead at about the same instant that her knees gave way. She leaned on the kitchen table long enough to pull a chair under her. A surprise that wasn't to her liking? Did he know where the girls were, or was it a threat against her or Jonathon? She hung up the phone slowly, telling herself it was an empty threat. What could he do? He was just trying to pressure her into looking harder, that was all.

Even so, her heart was pounding in her ears, and her mouth was dry. The house seemed so still, so tense. This was what it felt like when you were playing hide-and-seek and you were just about to be found, except that the penalties were steeper in this version.

She had the feeling that she was being watched, that there were eyes everywhere. Shivering, she got to her feet. There were two federal marshals just a few houses away. They would keep a watch over her. She was just being overimaginative.

"Claire?"

With a smothered shriek, Claire jumped up and spun around to find Marilyn standing at the bottom of the stairs. Her hand had flown to her throat. With difficulty, she took a deep breath.

"Claire, are you all right?"

She nodded and sank back onto the chair. "You just startled me, that's all," she said, trying to laugh it off.

"Was it the call?" Marilyn asked. "Is something wrong?"

Claire shook her head, not willing to risk speech for a moment. "No, no. I've just been tense...." She let her words trail off.

Marilyn came into the room with a no-nonsense look on her face. "Why don't I call Jonathon? Obviously, something's wrong. Maybe he can help."

"No," Claire cried, on her feet once more. He was safer where he was. "I'm fine, really." She smiled to prove that her words were true and prayed that the sun streaming in the window would keep Marilyn from looking into her eyes too much. "Let's just keep busy looking for that notebook."

Marilyn left just before lunchtime, when a frantic call about a missing bathing suit sent her home to dry teary eyes. She wanted Claire to come with her, but Claire refused. She didn't need a baby-sitter every minute of the day. She'd gotten over the fear the phone call had brought her, and she was determined to keep looking.

She fixed herself a ham sandwich and a pitcher of iced tea, then settled down with the newspaper. She'd read the first section all the way through when Jonathon strode in.

"Well, hello," she said, putting her sandwich down with a smile. His eyes had no sparkle in them, and fear clutched at her heart, but she pushed it aside. "I didn't expect you back for lunch, or I'd have waited. Want me to fix you something? I make a mean ham on rye."

"I think I'll pass on that for now." He found the pitcher of iced tea in the refrigerator and poured himself a glass. "Where's Marilyn?"

Was that it? "Did she call you?" Claire asked. "I should have known it."

Jonathon had been about to sit down, but he stopped. His frown deepened. "Claire, I already know that Daniels called you. The bug I'd placed on your phone works here, too."

The fear washed over her again, but she had her smile locked in place. "He just wanted a progress report. I couldn't tell if he knew I was here and not back in the apartment."

But Jonathon seemed to wave that aside as unimportant. "But something's obviously scared you."

"His attitude was just a bit much." She put her sandwich down. "You sure I can't get you something? Want to share this sandwich?"

"No, I'm fine." He drank from his glass, then leaned back in his chair.

He looked tired, and her stomach twisted into a knot as she watched him. "Something's wrong, isn't it? Has something happened to the girls?"

"No." He took a deep breath. "They're fine. There's no problem with them."

She leaned forward, her hands tightly clasped on the table before her, like Molly when she was trying to be very, very good. As if that could make a difference.

"All right," Claire said briskly. "The girls are fine. Something's wrong. I can see it in your eyes."

He took a deep breath, then stared down at his glass. Condensation had formed on the sides and was dripping down onto the table. He watched the tiny puddle form for a long, silent moment. Then he looked up, catching her glance with his. Her breathing stopped at the look in his eyes.

"The police found a body over in the northwestern train yard. A white man in his late thirties, murdered sometime last night," he said. "They think it's Brad."

Chapter 12

"**B**rad's dead?" Claire's voice sounded weak and thready even to her, but she seemed to have lost all power to make it stronger. "What happened?"

Jonathon's eyes met hers. She read worry and concern there, but she also saw sympathy. "It was a typical gangland-style slaying," he said. "Small-caliber bullet to the back of the head."

She shook her head, momentarily dumbfounded. This had to be part of the nightmare, this couldn't really be happening. "He was murdered?"

Jonathon just nodded.

Of course it was murder, Claire told herself. Thirty-seven-year-old men didn't die natural deaths out at some railroad yard. It was just that this kind of thing didn't happen to regular people like her. She took a deep breath.

"Do you know why?" she asked.

"We don't even know if it's definitely him," Jonathon said, seriously. "His name was printed on the label in his coat, but that's not enough for a positive ID, and the police can't find any friends to identify the body."

So that was the reason for the extra pain and worry she saw reflected in his gaze. "And you want me to?"

He sat forward then, rage bringing his fist down on the table. "*Want* you to? God, no. I don't want you any more involved in this whole mess than you already are, but it doesn't look like we have any choice in the matter."

She reached across the table, covering his angry fists with her hands, holding them tight until she could feel the storm in him subside a bit. "I don't see how identifying Brad's body is going to make me any more a part of this than I already am," she pointed out.

"I suppose not. It's just that..." His voice seemed to give out on him, and he turned his hands in hers so that he was now the one doing the holding. "It's just that these guys are serious, damn serious, and I'd rather they didn't know you existed."

"I think they know that already." Claire slipped her hands from his and stood up. "I'll get my purse and we can go."

He nodded, and in just a few minutes they were on their way.

Traffic was moderate, mostly cars filled with beach-going families making the midday trek to Lake Michigan. The joy in the cars surrounding her seemed to make Claire's nightmare even more frightening. Outside this car, no one knew of the gnawing pain trying to devour her, of the terrors that kept her awake at night in puny attempts to protect those she loved. She looked away from the other traffic, staring at the factories and warehouses that lined the expressway. The buildings seemed empty and cold even on this sunny Friday in June. Their windows stared vacantly back at her like blinded eyes. Like the eyes of the dead.

Claire swallowed and looked away, taking refuge in staring at the dashboard. Brad was dead. It didn't seem possible. A tiny quiver of pain tried to shake her heart.

She had loved Brad once. He was the father of her children, the first man she had ever really given her heart to. It hadn't been a wise choice, but the wisdom gained from hindsight did nothing to change reality. She didn't love him anymore, his actions had guaranteed that, but she hadn't wanted him dead. She hadn't wanted his actions to catch up with him and get him killed.

"He was killed by his loan sharks, wasn't he?" she asked. "Doesn't that end things with them for me and the girls?"

Jonathon glanced her way, and she got a sudden glimpse of *his* pain. "Loan sharks rarely resort to murder. Sort of cuts down on their chances of being paid," he said. "True, sometimes their methods of serving past-due notices get out of hand and a client dies, but this wasn't like that. It was clean and quick."

She understood that pain now. "Daniels?"

Jonathon shrugged. "Let's just say it's highly doubtful that Brad's demise was due to his debts."

Claire clasped her hands together in her lap, willing all her energy into keeping them still. "All of this is tied in together, isn't it?" she asked. "It wasn't a coincidence that Brad needed money right when Daniels offered me the job, was it?"

"It doesn't seem so, though I doubt he was lying about his debts. Most likely he got the squeeze put on him to cooperate."

"And delivered me and the girls up."

"And then paid the ultimate price."

"I wonder why." Claire closed her eyes, leaning back in her seat and trying to think without fear and the numbness of shock. An unpleasant memory came back to taunt her, and she sat up again.

"Daniels said he was going to provide me with a demonstration of their seriousness. Was this it?" Her stomach churned in protest. "My God, did I cause his death?"

Jonathon's hand found hers. "Don't ever think that. Brad made his own choices. He brought his problems on himself. My guess is that he became expendable and knew too much to keep around."

"But if I hadn't agreed to cooperate…"

"You had no choice, and you know it," Jonathon said.

They were off the expressway now, and he slowed for a stoplight. She glanced behind them and saw the tannish car of the U.S. Marshal. So they had been followed this time, too, but not by the bad guys.

"They found the perfect way to force you to do what they wanted," Jonathon went on.

"I guess." She sagged back in the seat, her spirits sagging along with her body. "And all because I resembled Sarah. What if I hadn't?"

"Then they would have found some other way of getting someone into my house to look for the notebook."

"Why *not* use some other way? They went to an awful lot of trouble with me and still didn't get the notebook. Why not just send in somebody to search your house one day while you're gone?"

"They may have tried that twice, now that I think about it," Jonathon admitted. Claire turned to watch him. "I'd been robbed twice. The first time was just after Sarah died, and it seemed like the final straw, though nothing appeared to have been taken. A month or so later there were a number of burglaries in the neighborhood, my house among them."

"Did you lose anything?"

He shrugged. "Some small stuff—worth a few hundred altogether."

"So maybe that wasn't—"

"No, I'm sure it was them. They could hardly keep breaking into my house and never taking anything. They just didn't find what they wanted and had to try another way."

Claire said nothing for a moment. "It still seems crazy to think I could find it when they couldn't."

"It seems crazy for them to be so certain it's there," he pointed out as he turned into the parking lot at the county medical complex. "But one thing all this says is that whatever's in that notebook must be damned important. A team's going through my house this afternoon to look for it. If it's there, they'll find it. I just can't figure out who Daniels thought had hidden it there."

Whatever was in the notebook was more important than they'd thought. Important enough to kill for. And not just Brad. Claire got out of the car and stared up at the building where the morgue was located. It looked old and tired, its bare windows staring out like empty eyes that couldn't show feeling anymore because they'd seen so much tragedy.

"It's just as depressing inside," Jonathon said.

"Yes," she replied. "I imagine it is."

Jonathon reached across and held her hand before she could open the door. "This could be rough. If you don't want to do it, just say so. They can find somebody else."

"Who?" Claire asked with a shrug. "You said yourself they couldn't find any friends, and that's because Brad had few. His parents are dead, and his only other living relative is a sister somewhere in California."

"They can do it with dental records," he said. "It would take a little while longer to track down his dentist and get the records, but it would keep you out of it."

She shook her head. "I can do it," she said firmly. "I have to. It's the only way to end all this."

"Okay."

He gave her hand a squeeze, and she thanked him with a smile as he led her to a side door in one of the larger buildings. After going downstairs, they made their way down a long hallway that was all brown tile and cinder blocks painted light green. She stared straight ahead, keeping her eyes away from the gurneys covered with green sheets that lined the walls.

A husky man with curly hair and a bushy mustache came toward them. His short-sleeved red knit shirt had a tiny alligator over the pocket, but the animal was lying on his back, its feet straight up in the air. Claire shivered at the macabre humor and was surprised when Jonathon slowed his steps.

"Hello, counselor." The man shook hands with Jonathon. "This the lady?"

"Yes," Jonathon said curtly, his reluctance to have her there obvious. "This is Claire Haywood, the victim's ex-wife." Was he emphasizing the *ex* part? Then he turned to her. "Claire, this is Detective Sergeant Dernoff. He's the investigating officer."

"We appreciate you coming down, ma'am," Dernoff said, reaching out to shake Claire's hand. "We want to get right on this case, so we were glad you were available to make a quick ID."

"No problem," she said, trying to mean it. "I hope that my help will mean a quick arrest."

"We hope so, too."

He waved her down the hall he'd just come from. With each step her heart seemed to slow down. She had to do this, she reminded herself. She'd meant what she'd told Jonathon and Sergeant Dernoff. She wanted to set this investigation in motion so that Brad's killers would be arrested soon. Then maybe she and the girls would be safe. But for all her brave words, her hands were turning to ice and her feet felt leaden. Brad was dead. Murdered. And now she was going to see his body.

"Where was he killed?" Jonathon asked Dernoff.

"Don't know," the other man said. "He was killed someplace else and dumped in the rail yard. A railroad bull found him just after dawn."

The detective stopped at a door, and went through first. Jonathon held it for Claire and then followed. Dernoff flashed his badge at the attendant.

"ID showing for T-47698-89."

The attendant, a tall, muscular black man, barely nodded. He moved slowly along a wall full of stainless-steel drawers, checking the identification numbers on them. The room was very cool, and Claire shivered.

It had been cold the day she and Brad were married, she remembered for some reason. Late August should have been sweltering, but the morning of the wedding a cold front had moved through, and the wedding party, in their chiffons and laces, had all shivered their way through the day. Brad had joked that it was an omen that their life together would be unpredictable. She had laughed with him. That had been one of the happy times. The happy times had come less and less frequently over the years, and finally she and the girls had only been happy when he was gone from their lives.

What a tragedy. It was as if she were here to view the death of her youthful dreams, not Brad. Her heart quivered, and so did her breath. Jonathon was there, taking her hand, knowing her needs.

"You all right?" he asked. "It's not too late to change your mind. It won't be easy. You still may have feelings for him you're not even aware of."

The attendant stopped at a drawer and pulled it out.

Claire shook her head. "No, the only feeling I have toward him is anger. It just seems that so much of his life was a waste. He could have had so much, but he threw it all away." Still, she couldn't make her feet move forward.

"No one is all bad—or all good, for that matter. And no one's life is a total waste," Jonathon said softly. "He gave you the girls and, inadvertently, the strength to go it alone."

She nodded, tears welling up in her eyes. The tears were not for Brad. They were caused by the feelings she had for Jonathon. Even though he didn't want her here, didn't want her mixed up with this murder in any way, even though he had expressed disgust for all Brad had done, Jonathon was willing to give the man back some dignity. Maybe more than Brad had ever deserved. Still, mistakes and all, Brad hadn't deserved to be gunned down.

She walked over to the drawer, and when she stopped in front of it the detective pulled the sheet back. She closed her eyes and took a deep breath.

"Ma'am?" he asked.

Jonathon was at her side, holding her arm and giving her strength. His presence was the only reality she could cling to. She would focus her thoughts on him and let her eyes look at Brad.

"Claire, are you all right?" Jonathon whispered.

She nodded and opened her eyes slowly.

"Take your time, ma'am," the detective said softly.

It was Brad, and yet it wasn't. The vibrancy, the energy that had first attracted her to him, was gone. So was the mocking look that had hurt so often, and the contempt that had been there at the end. But it was the same dark blond hair, the same weak jaw. She took a step backward.

"That's Brad," she said.

"You are identifying the deceased as Mr. Bradley Bannister, formerly your husband?" Dernoff asked, hanging his detective's shield on his voice.

Claire nodded, then realized that wasn't enough. "Yes, I am," she said.

Dernoff waved the attendant over, and Brad was pushed back out of sight. Jonathon put his arm around Claire's shoulder and led her toward the door.

"That it, Dernoff?" he asked, barely giving the man a chance to respond. "We'll be off then."

The detective followed them out into the hall. "You wouldn't know where we could find Mr. Bannister's secretary, ma'am? We have some questions about his office operations. His record keeping seems a bit haphazard in some areas."

Claire stopped and turned to the detective. "I have no idea who he's had working there recently. The woman who replaced me died of cancer about six months ago. I'm afraid I've had little contact with his office since then."

She started to go. Jonathon's touch was urging her away, but the look in Dernoff's face made her pause. "Replaced you?" he repeated. "You worked for Mr. Bannister?"

"Years ago," Claire told him quickly. "That's how I met him. I kept working there until a few months before Molly was born. It's been six years since I did anything there."

"But you could still find things in the files."

"Maybe. It's been a long time."

"Claire, let's go," Jonathon said. "Dernoff, she identified the body for you. Find someone else to question."

The detective ignored him. His eyes were keen and bright, almost hypnotic. "You could identify his handwriting for us, sort out the memos that he wrote from those his secretary did?"

"I suppose." Claire was cautious, though she wasn't certain why. She knew Jonathon wanted her gone, but was there really any harm in helping the police out a little more? What danger was there in that? "You want me to take a look at something else?" she asked.

"If you wouldn't mind."

Jonathon didn't like it, that was obvious. His arm was still around her, as if he were trying to keep Dernoff and all others away, but his voice held a pleading, a warning that it was time to get away.

She looked up at him, telling with her eyes that she wouldn't be free to think of the future as long as the past clung to her skirts. Without Brad's murder solved and the notebook found, what chance did they have?

"Jonathon, I have to do it," she told him.

His mouth slimmed to a tight line, but he said nothing, just led her out to the car.

Jonathon fought back his growing irritation, but it was hard. Dernoff had said he wanted them just to pop in and make a quick ID. Then Jonathon could take Claire and put her on a plane for North Dakota. He would leave her and the girls there, way off the beaten path, until this whole mess was over and done with. They'd be safe there, and he'd be able to breathe. But apparently the Fates hadn't meant for it to work out that way.

"I hadn't realized you'd worked for Brad," Jonathon said as they pulled out of the parking lot.

"That was my first real job," she said. "Actually, my only real job, not counting some waitressing stints over the last few months."

Jonathon nodded, then let the silence ride along with them, using the time for some hard thinking. Since she'd worked for Brad, she could have some sort of useful information. The more information was locked inside her memory, the more valuable she was, to both the police and Daniels. Was it already too late to get her to safety? Did such a thing exist for her?

"Am I coming under the cloud of suspicion, counselor?" she asked, using the title Dernoff had used.

He was startled by her question. "No, of course not."

Her words were tentative, doubtful. "That's good to hear."

"You're not under any kind of suspicion," he repeated.

"It's just that you might know more about Brad's operation than I originally thought."

"I'm not hiding anything."

He stopped, took her hand and looked into her eyes. The woman who had needed his protection was gone, and a strong-willed individual, tired of all the nonsense that had recently come her way, had taken her place.

"I didn't mean that you were," he said. "And I'm sorry if it came out that way. All I was thinking was that you may know more than you realize and that makes you more valuable to all parties involved." He turned at a stoplight and then sighed. "Except to me. You couldn't be any more valuable to me than you already are, and that's what makes me scared for you."

She let her hand touch his. It was a gentle caress that awoke hungers that were anything but gentle. "Life is a risk," she said. "We need to get this all over with so we can breathe easy again. If I can help, then I have to."

He shrugged, his feelings for her fighting with his legal mind. "Maybe you'll remember something when you see Brad's effects, something that will put an end to all this."

She nodded. "Yes, maybe I will."

Jonathon took her hand and kept it as he drove. Driving almost without conscious thought, he began arguing with himself. It was the age-old contest of reason versus emotion. Right now he didn't know which he wanted to win.

When Claire had first dropped into his life, emotion had ruled. Not because of her resemblance to Sarah, but because of the strong, compassionate, understanding woman she was in her own right. Then had come her confession, and reason had taken over; he had become suspicious of her and felt she must be in on the scam. Fortunately, emotion had gained the upper hand, and he had realized Claire was an innocent victim of circumstances. And now? Now reason and emotion stood equal. She could know something that would help them break the case, but at what risk? He didn't want to think anymore.

The silence stayed with them as Jonathon parked and they made their way up to the second floor of an old red brick building that had been a grade school for seventy years before being turned into the Second District detective headquarters. Pointed arches stretched to the sky, and stained-glass windows looked down on government-issue steel desk and cabinets. Scratched tables created central work space, around which detective's desks were grouped. The detectives hollering into phones, and the suspects and victims shouting at each other, made more noise than the building's previous inhabitants could ever have accomplished. Dernoff was already there.

"We got Bannister's stuff in the back interrogation room," he said over his shoulder as he led them into a small room. Besides a square table that was bolted to the floor, the room held four chairs, two rings set into the wall and a mirror. Jonathon glanced at the mirror, which served as a window into the room from the other side.

"Nobody's going to peek at us," Dernoff assured him. "We're not interesting or exciting."

Jonathon was in no mood for precinct-house banter. He turned his attention to the paraphernalia lying on the table. Look through it fast, Claire, he silently prayed. Look at it and find nothing.

"These are the victim's personal effects," Dernoff told her, waving at the table.

Claire picked up a key ring and fingered the keys. "Most of these are for his office files," she said.

"Yeah," the detective said. "We checked them. The others are to his car and apartment. Nothing exciting."

Claire nodded and flipped through his wallet.

"He had two hundred and forty-six dollars in his wallet," Dernoff said.

Claire made a face, and Jonathon knew she was thinking of all the money he owed and the pressure that was put on her and the girls. She pushed aside the comb and handkerchief. Nothing of interest or importance there. Jonathon allowed himself a small sigh of relief. Half done.

"Those the office effects?" Jonathon said, indicating with a nod a calendar, a circular address file and other such items.

"Yeah," Dernoff replied.

Claire picked up a leather folder with a legal-size yellow pad in it and leafed through the handwritten pages as Jonathon watched. What memories did those notes bring to her mind? Would seeing Brad's personal things, notes in his handwriting, break all her defenses down? Brad had been the father of her children. Would Claire break, or was she strong enough?

"At least he was awfully civic-minded," the detective said.

"Brad?" Claire's voice reflected her astonishment. "Why do you say that?"

Dernoff pushed the calendar over to her and flipped to specific days. "Look at this. Here he's attending a fund-raiser— 'Boys Club Luncheon.'"

Jonathon peered over Claire's shoulder at the cryptic message. He hadn't had the impression that Brad had a social conscience.

"And this one is a board meeting for a network of shelters for the homeless," the detective said, pointing to another date. "And here." He pointed to April 16. "'Advertising meeting for Brookfield Zoo animal adoption program.'"

Claire looked away. The room had taken on a strange stillness. Jonathon's lips tightened. Had he misjudged Brad? Had his feelings for Claire made him unwilling to believe that anyone could have been good and right for her but him?

"Brad wasn't the least bit civic-minded, as you put it," Claire said. Her words were harshly said, and her raw anger split the silence. "Brad didn't give a tinker's damn for making this a better world or for solving problems, his own or anyone else's."

Jonathon frowned, watching bitterness spill out instead of tears. Dernoff's look of confusion was comical.

Claire shook her head, looking unutterably weary. Her anger faded visibly. "It's a code," she said. "He used to do that when we were dating and we'd take long lunches together or leave early to go to shows and things."

She looked at them both, then sighed, pushing the calendar away. "You see, he had this thing about being businesslike, so in the office everything was all business. Loving, flirting, had to be done out of the office, during long lunches and

afternoon dates. But rather than leave the office closed up with
no explanation he used to schedule fake appointments, so that
if a client wanted to see him at that time he could point to the
calendar and say he was unavailable. He liked the philanthro-
pist pose. Said it went over big with his clients. I always
thought it was cheating, but I never made much headway in
getting him to actually attend any such events."

"It'd be nice if we could figure out who he was actually
meeting," Dernoff said. "Right, counselor?"

Jonathon did not reply. He tried to ignore the weight of the
detective's words on his conscience. Wasn't that being just
like Brad, though?

"It could just be another girlfriend," Claire said, "but I
never got the impression he was dating anyone else. He
seemed too wrapped up in his business and his debts to have
time for romance."

She took a deep breath and looked at both men. Jonathon
knew what was coming, and he didn't want to hear it. But he
was powerless to keep her from speaking.

"I might be able to put something together by going
through his billing and customer files," Claire said slowly.

Jonathon's heart sank as the detective turned toward him.
Dernoff couldn't hide the gleam in his eye.

"The lady might be able to help us here. I'll get two men
to help carry up the files and sort through them with her. How
about some help from your office? With Ms. Haywood's help,
who knows what we might break open?"

Jonathon looked around. At Dernoff, who was willing to
sacrifice anyone and anything for his ends. At Claire, who was
silently pleading with him to understand.

Chapter 13

Claire watched as the door slammed shut behind Jonathon and felt her heart stop. Had his doubts about her finally overcome everything else? She had felt his anger growing ever since he'd learned that she'd once worked for Brad, but she'd thought he believed in her, thought his feelings for her were enough to wipe out all questions. Was that hoping for too much?

No, it couldn't be. With a quick glance at Dernoff, Claire was out the door. Jonathon wasn't in the hallway, but she found him on the landing in the stairwell, staring down at the former school playground, which was now a parking lot.

"Jonathon?" she said, and came down to a few steps from where he stood. He didn't turn from the window. "Jonathon, I didn't know anything about Brad's deals. Not until the last few days, when you told me he was involved."

He said nothing, didn't even move, so she came down another few steps to the landing. The windows were streaked with dust and grime. Up near the top, a fly buzzed in a futile attempt to escape through the closed window. That was just how she had felt lately.

Reaching out, she touched Jonathon's arm in a silent plea. "Jonathon, please believe me."

He spun around and looked at her as if he hadn't even known she was there, his eyes reflecting his surprise. His arms reached out and pulled her close. "I've never suspected you, Claire. Not even when you told me all about Daniels and his hiring you. I was angry, but I never thought you were a part of it."

His arms tightened around her, and it was heaven resting there in his embrace. She laid her head against his chest, listening to his heartbeat. "I didn't know," she said. "You seemed so angry."

"I am," he admitted. His voice was gravelly, raw with emotion. "But not at you, at the way things have worked out. I just want you to be safe. I was going to ship you to North Dakota tonight so you could be safe with the girls until we caught Brad's killer and put Daniels out of business."

"That was all?" Claire asked, slipping her arms around his waist. "You staged that whole dramatic exit just because you couldn't get rid of me quite as soon as you wanted? And here I thought it was something important."

He didn't join in her laughter. He took her by the upper arms and held her away from him. His eyes glittered with fire. "There is nothing more important than you being safe," he told her.

Love flowed through her, so strong and alive that she trembled under its power. Here was a man she'd give the world to if she could. Failing that, she'd give him all of herself. She wanted to hold him, to love him, to keep the strength in his heart and the trust in his eyes. Life could hold no greater joy than being at his side. In moments like this she was sure of that, her heart and her mind for once in accord. She reached up to touch his cheek, to feel the hunger and strength that lay just beneath the surface.

"I'm very selfish, too, counselor," she told him. "There is no way you're going to lose me."

He caught her hand and brought it to his lips. Then, abandoning that, he crushed her mouth beneath his. There was so much need in his touch, so much wild, barely leashed hunger. Her heart cried out in answer, meeting his passion with her own. Their lips spoke of hope and dreams of tomorrow, their hearts of joys beyond belief. The dangers faded as love's magical powers took over. The storm grew distant and unimportant as sunshine filled their beings.

In the back of her mind Claire heard the noises of the police station. She felt the passing of people on the stairs, but ignored their existence. Reality now was her love for Jonathon. Reality was his lips on hers, his body pressed against hers. Reality was the wonder and peace that was found only in his embrace. But then what was real and vital faded slowly and present problems pushed back in.

Their lips parted, but she remained in his embrace. She couldn't give all of him up at once. She lay against him, treasuring the moment of peace.

"You know, the thing that made me the angriest is that Dernoff is right," Jonathon told her. "He's absolutely right. Brad was obviously some sort of mob accountant, and by deciphering that code we could break any number of cases. Murder, drug deals, extortion. Anything and everything. We'll all be heroes, accomplishing something everybody in law enforcement dreams about. Yet now the chance is right in front of me and I don't want it because it could be endangering you." His voice told her more than his words, for it spoke of warring dreams and ambitions, of different desires that suddenly weren't compatible.

She held him close for what felt like a long time. In actuality, only a few minutes passed, but it felt like a lifetime in terms of the strength and peace she tried to give him. It was time to go back to the battles, but this time they were ready. She tried not to notice the fly still buzzing above her head, trapped and all too likely to remain so.

Jonathon leaned back in his chair, watching as the minute hand inched toward the twelve. Once it got there, they were leaving. He didn't care what Dernoff thought. The man had had Claire's brains to pick for three hours now. That was as much as he was getting at this point, and more than he deserved. If not for Dernoff's probing and pushing, Claire would have been on her way to North Dakota.

Jonathon sighed and put his feet up on the edge of the desk. It wasn't that he minded the prospect of having another night with her, but he did mind the danger she was in as long as she stayed in the area. Besides, his house was being torn apart today by some of his assistants in the so-far-futile search for the notebook. He wasn't looking forward to spending the weekend putting his house back together, but didn't mind doing that and having yet another Friday-evening fish fry with Marilyn's family, as long as he knew Claire was safe.

Another Friday fish fry? Jonathon sat forward with a start, bringing his feet and the front legs of his chair down on the floor with a thud. Lord, this morning he'd told Marilyn he'd be eating with them tonight, certain that Claire would be gone. He guessed he'd better call and cancel.

Marilyn was understanding. "Why don't you both come?"

"I don't know." Jonathon hesitated. "I wish I could just take her out to the Silver Stallion for a thick steak and cherries Jubilee. She really needs to get away and relax." He stared across the room to where Dernoff and two assistants were working with Claire, sorting through a mountain of papers.

"You both do," Marilyn said. "Why don't you go up to the cottage for the night, if you can't get away for the weekend?"

"The cottage? I haven't been there in ages." And he wasn't sure he wanted to go there now.

"You've avoided the place since Sarah died," Marilyn said. "I could understand it before, but not anymore. It seems like the perfect place to get away."

Demons of the past nagged at him. "It's hardly a secure location."

"So have it checked out. They've got police up there in Wisconsin, don't they?"

"It's a two-hour drive, at least. We'd get there way past dinner." As he watched, Claire wearily blew a strand of hair out of her eyes, and his heart shared her exhaustion.

"So eat on the way."

"I don't know, it's—"

"You're making excuses, Jon," Marilyn told him. "You both need a break from the pressure of the past week, and the cottage is perfect. Stop denying it."

Speaking of a break, that minute hand was on the twelve, and it was time they left. He stood up. "I'll give it some thought," he said.

Claire had gotten to her feet, also, and was stretching her arms above her head. Her slender body stirred his in ways that were still surprising. His desire was certainly strong, but his feelings for her went far deeper. He wanted to rush over to her, wanted to take her in his arms and keep her safe. He wanted to make her smile, wanted to hear her laughter, wanted to give her everything in the world she could ever want. Mostly he wanted to share her life, the good times and the bad. He wanted her with him.

With a murmured goodbye to Marilyn, he hung up the phone. Maybe it was time to bury the ghosts of the past once and for all.

Claire awoke feeling stiff and cramped. The steady purr of the car motor had seemed part of her dreams, but now it was part of her waking.

"Feeling better?" Jonathon asked.

"Only my spirit. Everything else seems to have cramped up." She stretched slowly, lazily, like a cat, moving one part of her body at a time. Arms first, out over the dashboard. Then legs outstretched in the small space in front of the front seat. "Any problems while I slept?"

"Only if you consider my left arm getting sunburned a problem." She laughed, and he smiled at her. "I told you not to worry. Between taking the helicopter to Waukegan and renting a car from there we've been impossible to follow. Plus, we've got police behind us, watching the roads after we pass. Nobody can get through."

"I guess feeling safe doesn't quite come naturally anymore.

Or maybe I'm just cranky from the stiff neck that comes with sleeping in the car."

"Well, we're almost there," Jonathon said. "A nice, relaxing dinner by the lake will remove the last of those kinks."

Claire rubbed the back of her neck. "I'm not sure it's possible."

"How about a nice, relaxing, lecherous massage by the lake, then?"

She laid her head on his shoulder with a smile. "Promises, promises."

Around her the Wisconsin countryside sped by, lit by the late-afternoon sun. It was all so peaceful, so restful, so like the picture for a milk ad, that she felt foolish for carrying her worries up here with her. Brad and his violent death could be left behind. That was something she hadn't thought possible a few hours ago.

"Sergeant Dernoff was not particularly pleased when you announced we were leaving," Claire said.

"He didn't really mind," Jonathon assured her. "His grumpiness is all part of the role he plays. He didn't really expect you to stay there all evening."

"Oh, no?"

Jonathon turned off the state highway onto a smaller road. A grazing herd of black-and-white cows ignored their presence. There wasn't another living thing in sight, unless she counted the hawk soaring high above the pasture. Everything was so still, so normal. No wonder she'd fallen asleep soon after they'd left the city traffic.

Part of her still hurt for Brad and all the dreams they'd shared, but her mind was helping to put that behind her. Brad had brought his troubles on himself, and her greater concern was keeping his troubles from touching her and the girls. Here, away from the griminess of the police station, away from the constant threat of Daniels's calls and away from her futile search for the notebook, she was starting to remember that there actually was a world of peace and sunshine to be found.

"Actually, Dernoff got more than he expected from the few hours you were working on Brad's files," Jonathon noted.

"Your suggestion to compare his bank statements with those dates marked on the calendar was a good one."

"He would have thought of it sooner or later."

"So you helped it be sooner."

The cows disappeared from view as they rounded a curve. Even the hawk was swallowed up by the trees, and Claire started to feel unbelievably safe. Danger and violence couldn't live up here in these peaceful surroundings. The good, fresh air and the growing green earth were too pure to permit evil to survive.

"You use the cottage much?" she asked, and caught a glimpse of a lake through the trees. The late-afternoon sun was glittering off the water like a thousand diamonds.

"No, though I can use it any time I want. It actually belongs to Sarah's parents, so she was more in the habit of escaping up here. They live in Hawaii now, so they never use it. I've often wondered why they don't just sell it."

Marilyn's words came back. "Was this where Sarah had gone when she was in the accident?" Claire asked.

"Yes, but I never came here much even before that," he said. "As a rising young attorney with a name to be made I worked long hours and weekends. It didn't leave much time for my family."

His voice was ripe with regret and more than a hint of guilt. It somehow matched the heavy shadows that fell across the road now. The thick pine trees suddenly seemed dark and forbidding, and Claire reached over to squeeze his hand where it lay on the steering wheel.

"You did what you thought best to build for their future," she told him. "There was no way of knowing—"

"That they wouldn't have one?" He sighed and nodded. "You're right. But now that I stand to make giant leaps ahead career-wise I can think of a lot of things I'd rather do with the time."

"Sarah and Timmy came first for you," she told him. "You had a different way of showing it then."

He slowed to make another turn. Though the trees still hung over the road, blocking out the sun, the air seemed lighter and freer. She watched him as the shadows of the trees played over his face, her heart wanting to burst with emotion. At times like this her love was so strong that she was ready to promise him a lifetime and more, but the old panic always came back. It was all just happening so fast.

They turned into a gravel driveway and there was no more time for somber thoughts as they slowed to a stop next to a pale green police car. A uniformed officer got out and walked over to Jonathon's side of the car.

"The cottage is all clear, Mr. Tyler," the man said. "We checked it all out after your call, and there's no sign anyone's been around here for months. Oh, yeah. The checkpoint down the road called in to say no one but local residents have passed since you did. Looks like you're in the clear."

"Thanks." Jonathon waved to the officer as the man went back to his car.

Claire turned to watch the police car until they rounded a curve and lost it in the trees. Then she faced forward again. "Is someone going to keep watching the roads?" A niggling worry had returned to cause a frown between her eyebrows.

"Until we leave."

She took a deep breath and forced the frown away. Jonathon was continuing down the bumpy road, and she looked out the window at the squirrels scampering up tree trunks and the blue jays complaining about the car's invasion. After a few minutes the trees thinned and then ended, making way for a small white cottage and a sparkling lake beyond that. The cool green depths of the water were as life-giving to Claire's soul as water was to the body. Her eyes drank in the beauty and serenity of the scene as Jonathon stopped the car next to the cottage. They stepped out, and she took a deep breath of the damp, pine-scented air. She had never felt so alive, had never expected to feel so vibrant again after the horror of the past few days. The only thing it would take to make the scene was to have the girls here with them.

"It's wonderful, Jonathon."

She turned from the beauty around her to find Jonathon watching her. "So are you," he said softly, his eyes afire.

Suddenly she was in his arms, the tensions of the past day ready to explode. His mouth devoured hers, his tongue insistent against her lips, awakening her need for intimacy and oneness.

There seemed to be no way she could hold him closer, but her arms kept trying. She let her hands roam his back, feeling his muscles through his thin summer shirt and thinking back to last night and ahead to all the pleasures his touch could bring. The fading summer sun held no heat that could compare with the rising hunger in her soul.

She wanted him near her, in her, around her. Even her cautious mind knew that he was her life, her future and her forever. Still, even as she tried to answer the needs crying out in her heart, a nagging doubt in her head stopped her. Finally she and Jonathon pulled apart.

"I think we ought to get settled first," he said, his eyes smoky with desire.

He grabbed the grocery bag full of food from the back seat and came around to lead her down the path toward the lake. The trees that had parted to make room for the house gathered again at the water's edge, making the illusion of seclusion complete. Though Claire could hear the faint sound of laughter and music from along the lake, it seemed that she and Jonathon were the only people on the face of the earth. It was a delicious feeling.

"Well, want to explore the inside or the outside?" Jonathon asked.

"Let's take a peek inside," she said.

But their mood changed from playful to somber when they went inside. The cottage was dark and musty, like someone's old forgotten dreams. The furniture was covered with sheets, the tiled floor felt grimy, and the air itself was stale and tired. A sadness seemed to hang over the place, a weariness of its soul.

Claire pulled back the curtains while Jonathon lifted the shades to solve the darkness problem. Opening the windows would take care of the mustiness, but there was more here that was hurting. The cottage needed to feel life again, to be filled with laughter and love.

"I should have realized it would be filthy after not being used for a year," Jonathon said. He put the grocery bag down on the table in the kitchen area with a frown. "Some getaway."

"Hey, it's only dust. That's easy to take care of." Claire opened a closet near the back door and found an array of mops and pails. "Want to mop or dust?"

"What a choice," he muttered, and took the mop. "You ever a drill sergeant in a former life?"

"I'm a mother in this one."

"That's about the same thing."

"Not quite. I give out kisses for a job well done." She stuck a pail in the sink and turned on the faucet, but nothing came out. "Uh, there is running water up here, isn't there?"

He grinned. "Do I get a kiss if I turn it on?"

"Absolutely."

He disappeared around the back of the cottage and, after a horrendous moment of banging and screeching of metal on metal, rusty brown water gurgled from the pipe. By the time Jonathon got back in the house it was running clear and clean.

"How did I do?" he asked.

"Wonderfully." She leaned over to give him a quick kiss, then poured some soap into the bucket.

"That wasn't the greatest of kisses."

She turned the water off and hauled the pail from the sink. "Up until a moment ago it wasn't the greatest of water." She handed him the bucket and pointed to the living room. "How about if you start in there while I clean up the kitchen enough to handle food?"

"How about if I show you what a real kiss is like?"

He didn't wait for a reply. He swept her into his arms, and his mouth came down on hers like rain on parched earth. His touch brought peace and the promise of life, of days of sunshine and days of hope.

The fires that had burned last night, leaving behind a smoldering memory, ignited once more. The flames leaped at her soul, singeing the shadows that kept her heart from loving. No, loving wasn't the problem, accepting love was. Accepting the burden of responsibility that came with love was. But here and now, in his arms, with his lips crushed into hers, love was all she knew and all she wanted.

"Oh, Jonathon," she said on a breathless sigh a moment later. "How can this be happening so fast?"

"What's fast?" he asked as his hands cupped her face. He rained kisses on her eyes, her nose, her chin, and finally her lips again. "We've known each other forever."

"You're crazy," she whispered—or thought she did—as their mouths met again.

If the last kiss had been spring rain, this one was winter snow, rare and of mystical purity, covering the world until nothing else existed. The sounds out on the lake no longer drifted in through the window. They were silenced by the power of his touch. She shivered as the hunger reached every part of her body.

"Well," he murmured, "what's going to wait? Cleaning or dinner?"

"Why not both?"

Her hands had pulled his shirt from his trousers and were running along the smooth skin of his back. He was a summer night now, heat shimmering along the ground, sleeping and waiting for the coming of the torrid day. His hands felt cool to the touch as they roamed her skin in return, but the trail they left burned. Her body was scorched by his caress, a fire waiting to consume her soul.

She gasped for breath as again and again their lips met. Hungrily they drew strength from the other. Their hands found ways to get beyond the barriers of mere clothes. Her blouse, his shirt. Body to body, soul to soul, they were swept up by the winds of passion, hungering for a bliss that they had but sampled the night before. They had only had a teasing taste of love in the past, and now each new touch promised to outshine the last.

"Oh, Claire," Jonathon said on a moan as he swept her up

in his arms. "Can you feel the earth moving, the thunder in the air?"

All she felt was the wonder of her love for him and the needs of her heart. Was that the earth moving or thunder in the air? It seemed more like standing still or the heavens rising up in celebration, but there was no time to dispute the matter, for he had carried her into the bedroom. Like all the other furniture, the bed was covered with sheets, but they and their dust were easily swept to the floor as love took over.

Hearts, souls, then bodies joined in sweet ecstasy, and the world and all its sorry little woes were left behind for a time. In Jonathon's arms, Claire flew up to the heavens, then slowly fell back to earth like the leaves of autumn, content knowing that spring would come again.

It was dark when Claire awoke. Jonathon's heartbeat at her side was slow and steady, but she knew he was awake.

"How long did I sleep?" she asked.

"Long enough for me to be ravenous."

She felt his body rumble with suppressed laughter, and she sat up. "Come on, it can't be that late."

"It's about ten. Way, way past my dinnertime."

"Poor baby." She leaned over to kiss him. It was a gentle kiss, and it wanted to linger, but she wouldn't let it. Her heart knew what it wanted, but her mind still cried out for caution. Someday they'd both agree. Someday soon, she hoped.

"What do you say we build a fire out by the lake and cook the hot dogs out there?" he suggested.

The bed moved as he got up, and her crazy heart sighed with disappointment. She wanted time, needed time, but she hated it when he gave it to her.

"Sounds much better than tackling that kitchen."

They dressed quickly, and in a few minutes they were sitting out by the lake. The night air was cool, delightfully so, with the smell of water captured by the breeze. With a flashlight they found the ash-littered clearing in the grass by the shore, and Jonathon started a fire. Soon the flames were licking at the air, sending up sparks that went higher and higher.

Claire watched them with a sigh. Had it really only been this afternoon that she'd learned of Brad's death? It seemed to have been in a different time, a different life.

"Looks almost like fireflies," Jonathon said of the sparks as he came to sit on the grass at her side.

He put his arms around her shoulders, and she leaned against him. What was there to be afraid of when he smiled at her that way? Time mattered little when souls intertwined as theirs had. But she remained silent, leaning into him and wishing for a life in which all questions were answered and all decisions were simple.

"My father used to say catching fireflies brought good luck," she said.

"So did you catch many of them?"

She shook her head. "It seemed crazy that they'd give luck to their captors. I always let them go free."

His lips brushed her forehead in the dark. "Maybe that's why you're so lucky."

"Me?" she asked with a laugh. "I have to be about the unluckiest person around."

"Oh, I don't know about that. I know you've had some close calls, but you're safe, and so are the girls."

She nodded. "You believed me when I told you about Daniels and my knowledge of Brad's affairs."

"You were given a job that enabled you to meet me."

"And I'm about to have a delicious dinner that was worth waiting until midnight for."

He laughed and moved slightly away from her, poking at the fire. "It's not almost midnight. Eleven at the latest. And dinner will be delicious, if we can find some long forks to cook the hot dogs on."

"Can't we just use sticks?"

Jonathon got to his feet and pulled her by the hand until she was on her feet, too. "Come on, there's got to be some forks in the kitchen."

Laughing, they raced up to the house and into the lights of the kitchen. The dirt and dust of neglect still remained, but it no longer seemed so oppressive. The house was tired, but somehow it seemed just to be waiting for the courage to love. What a crazy thought, Claire told herself.

"All right, where would they be?" she asked.

"If I knew, would I have dragged you up here to look?"

Jonathon opened a drawer next to the sink. It held corkscrews and can openers and a couple of soup spoons, but no long-handled forks. Claire tried a cabinet. Pots, pans, and a baking dish or two.

"Are you sure we couldn't use sticks?" she asked.

Jonathon didn't bother to answer, just dug through the next drawer. Towels, paper bags and pot holders.

"This is like a scavenger hunt," Claire muttered, opening the cabinet next to the stove. It held a small assortment of canned and dried foods. "They should taste great."

Jonathon peered over her shoulder and pulled out a can of fruit cocktail. "Ah, dessert," he said.

"Right." She spotted a can of coffee in the back and reached for it. "This might be useful now. How long does coffee last?"

"Not as long as that must have been sitting there, I'm sure."

But Claire had already pulled the can down, and through the clear plastic lid she saw something that was definitely uncoffeelike. She pulled the cover off to stare down at a small red notebook.

Chapter 14

Jonathon laughed. "You can't have found the forks in there," he said, turning from the last drawer he'd rifled through. "I can't even believe there's much coffee left."

Claire stared at him for the longest moment, then reached inside and pulled out the notebook.

"Well, I'll be damned," he said after a moment, sounding as if all the air had been knocked from him. "How the hell did it get in there?"

Claire shook her head; he expected no answer to that. "It's got to be the one, don't you think?"

He took it from her and flipped the pages where they both could see. Page after page of numbers in neat vertical columns, with small written notations after some of them.

"It looks like Brad's writing," Claire said.

Jonathon stopped flipping and started to read, turning the pages more slowly. "It's a diary," he said. "It lists times, places and amounts of various transactions."

"Having to do with that tax-evasion case?"

He shook his head. "It doesn't appear so." He turned to

the front of the book again. "It's labeled as if it were, but the inside doesn't match up."

"That sounds like Brad," Claire said. She shoved the coffee can back into the cabinet, the search for the long forks abandoned. "He wrote down everything having to do with money or time. He was almost compulsive about it. He'd either write it in a way no one would understand, like his code, or hide the record some place he figured no one would find."

"Maybe *he* took the forks," Jonathon said with a laugh, leaning against the counter as he continued to leaf through the book. "There is a mint of information in here. I can't believe all he wrote down."

Claire stared at the window seeing not the night beyond or the reflection of them standing in the kitchen but back to the life she used to lead. "Every evening he'd count out his money, including all the loose change he had in his pockets, then list that and every cent he'd spent during the day. If he found a dime on the sidewalk, that got added to the list."

"Different," Jonathon murmured.

She shrugged. "Hey, I was twenty when I met him. Different seemed sort of alluring, not weird. I'd never met anybody like him before. His meticulousness made him seem so in control."

"Well, it's probably what did him in," Jonathon said. "I can't believe that his bosses wanted him to keep these types of records, and when they found out he had he probably became expendable real fast."

He closed the notebook but still held it fast in his hand. His eyes glittered with an intensity that made him seem distant, far away from her.

"Will it help with your cases?" she asked.

He returned to her with a smile. "Help? It'll be the start of a whole mass more of them. This is a windfall," he said, and he swept her up into his arms. The dingy cottage seemed to glitter with excitement. "I can't believe the scum we'll be able to clear off the streets through this. And not just the little guys, either. Some major heads are going to roll."

She was caught up in his happiness, laughing with him and hugging him back, but fingers of worry still poked at her.

"There are things in here that will affect mob figures all over the country," he said. "With some cross-verification of bank accounts and such. And best of all—" he paused to tighten his hold on her "—you and the girls are safe now. There's no way Daniels can get the notebook back through you, so he'll leave you alone."

"That's cause for celebration in itself."

He let go of her, a slight frown creasing his forehead. Some of the darkness of the night seemed to have come inside. "I hate to cut short our getaway, but we really should get this back," he said.

"No problem," she told him, and she meant it. "The sooner it's locked up someplace, the safer I'll feel."

He kissed her again. It was a loving kiss that promised her longer and better getaways in the future if she would just accept them. Her heart responded, and she clung to him just a little. Now that the end of all the danger and worry was actually in sight, she was beginning to think that maybe love could work, maybe it could last.

"Jonathon," she said as he let her go and turned toward the phone. "One thing bothers me. How did the notebook get here?"

He stopped, and his eyes came back to hers. "It had to have been hidden here by somebody."

"But who?" she asked. "It's wonderful that we found it, but finding it here scares me in a way."

His smile wiped away some of her worries, but not all of them. "Hey, relax. Whatever reason somebody had for planting it here, it didn't work. We're home free."

Claire just smiled back at him, pretending her fears had vanished, though they still clung to the walls of her heart. It just didn't make sense. Why would someone plant it here? You planted something in someone's possession so you could catch him with it. If you couldn't turn that something up on demand, then the planting made no sense. If Daniels and his group had hidden it, they would have known where it was.

No, someone else had hidden it, someone Daniels and his group must have known. But then that someone had been unwilling—or unable—to tell Daniels where it was, so Claire had been hired to search.

Claire looked around the cottage. It had no more than a handful of hiding places. More *whys* kept coming. "Why didn't Daniels tell me to search here?" Claire asked.

"He probably didn't know about the place. Like I said, it belongs to Sarah's parents. It's listed on the tax rolls in their name." He picked up the phone. "I'm glad I've always kept the phone here connected. Can you get our things together while I call my office? Then we'll take care of the fire and be on our way."

"Sure," she said, and put the bucket of soapy water up on the counter. Everything was fine. She should stop worrying, relax, and plan what she and the girls were going to do next. But a noise behind her made her turn around before she could spill the water into the sink. Jonathon was flicking the plunger on the phone.

"Jonathon?" The fear raced back to swallow her up.

He turned toward her, his eyes carefully shuttered and devoid of emotion. "The phone's out," he said, then shrugged. "I've kept up the monthly payments, so wires must have been knocked out somewhere."

A prickle of worry crept down her spine, and her breath caught in her throat. "Let's get out of here," she whispered.

He nodded. "We'll send the officer by the road back to put the fire out and lock up."

She grabbed her purse, but even as they turned toward the back door, it opened. Daniels stepped inside. A gun was in his hand.

"I think you have something I want," he said.

Claire took a step backward and came up against Jonathon. Her heart was trembling, but she felt anger radiating from Jonathon, and it steadied her.

"What are you doing here?" Jonathon snapped. Taking hold of Claire's wrist, he pulled her behind him. The position of relative safety made her feel no better.

"Always the gentleman, eh, Tyler?" Daniels said with a sneer. "Or just bringing the notebook closer for me?" He reached out for it.

Jonathon was about to make a protest. Claire could see the muscles on the back of his neck tense, but when Daniels took a step to the side to point the gun at her he gave the notebook up.

"Wise move," the other man said with a laugh. "Not that it'll matter in the long run. Die now, or die in a few minutes."

Claire's stomach clutched in terror. She wasn't ready to die, not now that she'd found so much to live for. But she saw no reaction from Jonathon other than a shake of his head.

"You won't get away with this," he said.

"Who's going to stop me?" Daniels took a step back and flipped through the notebook as if checking to make sure it was what he'd been looking for. "This little baby's going to make me a fortune."

"It's already cost one man his life," Jonathon pointed out.

Daniels just shook his head. "Bannister was a fool. He never should have been writing all this down, and he sure shouldn't have gotten cute and hidden it in another file."

"You mean it got taken by accident?" Claire asked.

"It had nothing to do with Mike O'Brien," Daniels admitted. "But that fool Bannister had it labeled with O'Brien's name. If one of our boys had happened to get suspicious and search the place we would have thought it dealt with O'Brien's account. It was only after O'Brien got caught and those files got confiscated that Bannister confessed. Then he was in real trouble, because certain people were unhappy and wanted it back. Real bad."

"Well, they've got it," Jonathon said. His voice was calm and controlled; no hint of Claire's terror could be heard in it. "What's to be solved by murdering us? Without the book, we've got no proof of anything."

"You're loose ends, and I hate leaving things unfinished."

Jonathon took a step closer to him, a step away from Claire, leaving her feeling abandoned. The open bedroom door beckoned, and she knew what Jonathon was doing, trying to dis-

tract Daniels long enough to give her a chance to escape. Her
terror fled in the face of such courage. She was still afraid,
but she wasn't paralyzed by fear any longer. There had to be
a way for them to escape together.

"Claire's not a loose end," Jonathon argued. "She works
for you."

"I hadn't noticed that lately." Daniels waved the gun at
Jonathon, motioning him back toward the sink. "Let's not try
any cute stuff, or I'll shoot you right here."

Jonathon stepped back, and Claire found his hand, hoping
her squeeze would tell him all the things she hadn't been able
to say. That she loved him, that she was sorry she'd brought
such trouble down on his head. That they were in this together.

"I don't understand any of this," Claire said to Daniels.
Maybe if they could stall long enough, help would come. "I
don't see why you needed me in the first place."

"To do exactly what you did. Find the notebook." Daniels's eyes tested them for a moment, and then his gaze flickered as he slipped the notebook into his pocket. The chance
was gone before they had time to react.

Claire swallowed hard and wiped her free hand on her
shorts. Another chance would come if they could just distract
him.

"You could have found it just as easily if you'd looked,"
Claire said.

"If we'd known about this place, yeah."

Her heart sank. "So we led you up here?" And she'd
thought they were so safe.

"You were a little hard to follow, but not impossible."

But Jonathon's mind was working along other lines. "Wait
a minute," he said. "What made you think I had it? How the
hell did it get here? I sure didn't put it there."

Daniels laughed. It was an unpleasant sound that sent the
fear rocketing through Claire's veins. "You weren't the only
one that came up here."

"I know that," Jonathon snapped. "But why my house? If
you didn't know where the notebook was, why were so sure
it was somewhere in a house of mine?"

Claire saw where they were headed, even if Jonathon didn't. "What difference does any of that make?" she asked, trying to steer them away. "This is all crazy. Why should anyone die over a stupid notebook?"

But Daniels was paying her no mind. "You really don't know, do you?" he asked Jonathon, his voice mocking. "You really haven't figured it out."

"Figured what out?"

Claire could hear the anger building in Jonathon. Both he and Daniels were getting distracted. This should be their chance to get away, but how? She squeezed Jonathon's hand, trying to convey the message to him, trying to remind him to play along and watch for their chance, but she got no reassuring response.

"Figured what out?" Jonathon repeated.

"Figured out who else could have hidden something up here." Daniels's voice was ugly with laughter. "Who else spent as much time in your houses as you? Maybe more. No one else but the devoted little wife."

Jonathon seemed to explode with rage. "That's a filthy lie," he cried, and flew across the room at Daniels.

Claire screamed out her fear for Jonathon, caught unawares by his sudden action. Daniels wasn't, though. He was ready for Jonathon, and he darted back a step and swung out with the gun. He struck Jonathon on the jaw with a solid crack that flung him back against the counter. Claire was at Jonathon's side as he dropped to the floor. His eyes still blazed with anger as he clutched his jaw, but the blinding rage burned out quickly as it had come.

"That's a lie," Jonathon said again. "Sarah wouldn't have done something like that."

Who else could have? Claire wondered, but she said nothing. Anger wasn't going to get them out of here.

"You didn't know the little woman very well," Daniels said mockingly.

His scornful laughter started Jonathon back to his feet, but Claire's pressure on his shoulder brought his gaze to her. Don't let your anger wipe out our chance for escape, she pleaded silently. Don't lose your head fighting the truth. Something in his eyes changed. The fire chilled, and the flames grew low. Jonathon turned back to Daniels.

"Why, then?" he asked. "What hold did you have over her?"

"Who said we needed a hold?" Daniels asked.

Claire felt his rage flare up again briefly, but Jonathon had it under control now. "How long was she helping you?" he asked, his voice raw with pain.

"She started years ago," Daniels said. "She was working for us before she even married you, so we had her longer."

Claire felt Jonathon flinch from the verbal blow, but she could also feel his iron control reassert itself.

"She worked for you while she was a stewardess?" Claire asked.

"Yeah. It was a perfect setup," Daniels said. "Those days the airline crews were never checked very carefully when going through customs. She must've taken millions of dollars through to be laundered for us."

"But why?" Claire asked. "Wasn't it risky?" She could see herself in the same situation, so worried and guilt-stricken that she'd be caught immediately. Could Sarah have been that different from her?

"Why?" Daniels laughed. "Because she was a do-gooder, a soft touch, a pushover."

Jonathon's fists tightened at the mockery in Daniels's voice, but he did nothing, said nothing. Claire kept her hand on his arm.

"She didn't know what she was doing," Claire said. It was a statement, not a question. Her reading of Sarah had been right.

"Not at first, no," Daniels admitted. "She thought she was just taking little presents to a friend's elderly father, and that's all the first few packages were."

"Until she stopped looking," Jonathon said.

Daniels nodded. "She didn't carry stuff for us on every flight, and then not every package was money, but enough were."

"When did she learn what she was doing?" Claire asked.

Daniels frowned. His eyes were evil little slits. "What makes you so sure she did—or that it mattered?"

"She quit the international routes when she found out, didn't she?" Claire said. "She didn't knowingly keep on helping you."

"By that point it hardly mattered," he said, shrugging. "You can't use the same courier for too long, anyway, and she'd just about reached the end of her usefulness. And she didn't know enough to cause us any real trouble."

"That doesn't explain the notebook, though," Jonathon said. "How did she get involved in that?"

"Blackmail?" Claire guessed.

"An even trade," Daniels said with a sneer. "She was quite willing to trade her cooperation for ours. She borrowed the notebook from your office for us, and we agreed not to reveal her former illegal activities."

"Blackmail." Jonathon's voice was flat. Dead. "You're really scum, you know that?"

"Hey, she made her choice," Daniels protested. "She could have refused. No one was stopping her."

"Right."

Jonathon turned his head, staring out at the darkness framed by the back window, coming to terms with his own personal demons. After a moment he came back to Daniels.

"I've got just one question. Did you have anything to do with her death?" he asked.

"Are you kidding?" Daniels asked. "Look at all the trouble it caused us. We'd have to be damn stupid to kill her before we got the notebook. No, we knew she'd gotten the book, she'd told us that much, but there wasn't time for her to hand it over before she died."

Jonathon was lost in his thoughts again, and Claire took his hand. She couldn't tell if he even knew she was there, but that didn't matter. Her love for him kept her close. She turned to glance at Daniels.

"What happened in between?" she asked. "Sarah died

more than a year ago, yet it was only a few weeks ago that you contacted me."

"We tried on our own to find it and came up empty," Daniels said. "It was Bannister, actually, that put us on to you. He'd noticed the resemblance long ago, and he suggested the idea." He shrugged. "Who knows? If it had worked, it might have saved him his skin, but you refused to play ball, so now you get to join him."

The gun suddenly held more menace, his eyes a more deadly intent. Jonathon still seemed lost in the past, and the fear that had stretched Claire's nerves almost to the breaking point doubled. Her mouth went dry as she thought of the girls. At least they were safe, but they'd grow up without her. She wouldn't see them on their first days of school. She wouldn't be there to be their tooth fairy and Santa Claus, to buy green jelly beans for their Easter baskets, to stay up worrying when they went on dates.

No! She wouldn't give up without a fight. She had the girls and she had Jonathon. She had too much to live for to die like a pesky fly. She glanced around wildly, seeking some way to fight back. Jonathon's hand gave hers a sudden squeeze, then let go.

In a split second he turned from her and flung the bucket of soapy water she'd left on the counter at Daniels. The water wasn't hot or plentiful, but the action caught Daniels unawares, and he fell backward against the kitchen table. It was enough. Jonathon grabbed Claire's hand and raced out the door.

The night surrounded them with sudden blackness, and Claire was blind after standing in the lights of the kitchen. She saw their campfire to her left, a flickering glow in the darkness, but Jonathon's hold was pulling her away from its warmth. She stumbled over the stones in the driveway, then felt the softness of grass beneath her feet. The dark shadows of the car was off to their right, but they raced past it.

A shot rang out from behind them. "You can't get away," Daniels called. She heard his feet on the gravel and found speed she hadn't tapped yet.

"Look out," Jonathon muttered under his breath even as they entered the stand of trees.

Branches pulled at her clothes and scratched her face. The scent of pine wafted around them as they raced over the carpet of dried needles, but all Claire smelled was her own fear. She tightened her hold on Jonathon's hand, reaching out with the other one to try to ward off the unseen dangers ahead.

A muttered oath came from behind them, but not far enough behind.

Claire stumbled over a branch. Her ankle twisted, and pain shot up the outside of her leg, but she bit her lip and kept on going. Jonathon's gait changed for a moment. He, too, must have found something in the darkness. It was their enemy now, but it was also their friend. Without the blackness of the night they would be able to see to escape, but Daniels would also be able to see to find them.

"There's a little creek around here someplace," Jonathon told her even as the ground changed abruptly and she slipped to her knees.

Another shot rang out.

Jonathon pulled her back to her feet, but instead of climbing up the other bank of the creek he led her into it. The water was cold, sloshing into her shoes and above her ankles. Its chill had a calming effect. She was still alive, and only a few minutes ago, she'd thought that impossible. Jonathon's hand was holding hers with all the life and love he had in him. Maybe they really could make it.

Stones lined the bottom of the stream, stones that were slippery from the constant wear of the water on them. Claire fought to keep her balance. She wouldn't fall apart again. Wherever Jonathon was leading them, she would be a help, not a hindrance.

There was a splash behind them, then a "Damn." Had Daniels fallen?

Jonathon must have had the same thought, for he suddenly veered from the stream, silently pulling Claire up the bank and into a thicket of bushes. They crouched down, waiting. A branch pressed against her arm, something with tiny feet walked across her cheek, but she didn't need Jonathon's finger across her lips warning her not to move, not to speak. She used the chance to kiss it, and then the noise of Daniels's approach silenced even the beating of her heart.

"Come on, come on," Daniels was muttering as he waded along just a few feet in front of them. "I know you're out here."

Claire's eyes had grown used to the dark, but there wasn't much she could see. Away from the light of the city, the night was very black. The crescent moon threw a faint glow over the land, but what little light it shed was blocked out by the trees. She saw the faint shadow that was Daniels coming closer. He made no effort to be quiet as he splashed through the water, heading past them after what seemed a lifetime.

Even after he had disappeared downstream, neither of them breathed. The night carried sounds all too clearly. But finally Jonathon let out a quiet sigh and sat back on his heels.

"We've got to get to a phone," he whispered.

"Do you think Daniels came alone?"

She felt his shrug. "I doubt it."

He pulled her to her feet and away from the bushes. The branches seemed to crack with the retort of a cannon, announcing their presence. Claire held her breath and followed him as best she could over the rough ground.

The trees were thicker here and the ground was littered with fallen branches and leaves. Every step seemed to shout out their location, and their every breath seemed to echo in the silence around them.

Another shot rang out from their left, and Claire heard the crack when it hit a tree next to her.

"Breathing room," Jonathon said. "That's all we were trying for, and we got it. We've got a good lead."

But would it be good enough? Behind them Daniels seemed to be crashing through the bushes like a herd of elephants. Not as hampered as they were by the need for quiet, he was chasing them with dogged persistence. A faint light coming through the trees brightened with each step as the bushes dwindled to nothing more than grass.

They had run through the trees that separated Sarah's parents' cottage from the next one, and an outside light on the side of the house lit up the clearing. Ahead of them loomed a different type of shadow, a solid darkness that was a building. Her feet hit a smooth pathway with an unexpected suddenness that almost made her fall, but she turned the lost balance into greater speed.

How Jonathon could see in the shadows enough to guide them she had no idea, but somehow he found the door to a shedlike building, and it opened with a loud shriek of its hinges. They rushed inside.

With the light from the yard they could see they were in a boathouse built out over the edge of the lake. The front half of the building had a solid floor. One wall was lined with shelves of tools, while the other had a rowboat leaning against it. The back half of the building, the half over the lake, was floorless, except for the narrow ledge that skirted the walls and surrounded the open space in the middle. Water lapped at the pilings. Across from the door they'd come through, Claire knew, there would be another door, a wide one that could be opened to let the boats in and out. Ropes hung from the ceiling, some over her, some over the water, to hoist the boats in and out of the water. There was no phone, and there was precious little place to hide.

"Over there," Jonathon said, pushing Claire toward a leaning rowboat. Even as he had her crouch next to the boat he grabbed a tool from the floor and hurried to the door.

Jonathon! her heart cried out, but her mouth made no sound. Daniels was almost here. From where she was hiding she could see him approaching by the yard light. He'd been hurrying, but he was slowing down as he came closer and closer to the boathouse. He was at the door, and his gun was clearly visible, pointing ahead of him, at the ready. One step, then another, and he was inside. He turned and then swung the door shut behind him. They were closed in together in the darkness.

Chapter 15

Claire held her breath, feeling as if the slightest sound would be enough to bring the world crashing down around them. She heard footsteps, slow, shuffling movements across the plank floor. It had to be Daniels. Jonathon wouldn't announce his presence that way.

There was a scraping noise, and then the flickering flames of a lighter made a feeble halo around Daniels and reflected with evil intensity off the gun he held. He couldn't see her, and the light he held was far too weak to expose her, yet his eyes seemed fixed on her. He took another step closer, and Claire pulled farther back into the shadows.

A noise came from behind Daniels, and Claire looked out from under the rowboat as he spun around him. A dark shadow that had to be Jonathon was on him, knocking the lighter away and leaving them in darkness once more. A heavy thud told her that the gun had fallen, but the sound of the two men grappling kept her from relaxing.

"Get the gun, Claire," Jonathon called out.

She crawled out from behind the boat. The darkness was complete. She had no idea where the gun could have fallen, except that it had to be near Jonathon and Daniels. There were more sounds of struggle, and then they crashed into a set of shelves. Tools skittered across the metal shelving and fell to the floor. Some sounds were different, duller, and accompanied by grunts of pain. Where was the damn gun?

She crawled across the floor, patting it as she went along as if she were looking for a lost contact lens, but all she felt was dust and dirt and an occasional screw. If only she had some light!

Then, astonishingly, unbelievably, she could see. Not much, just a faint lifting of the blackness. Was it dawn already? The past few hours seemed a lifetime long, but could it really be sunrise? Or had someone opened the doors to the yard? Then, suddenly, it wasn't just a faint glow lighting the boat house, it was full-fledged brightness. She spun toward the source of the light. The wall of the boathouse was in flames! Daniels's lighter must have landed in the rags near the door.

"Jonathon!" Claire cried out, and turned back to the two men.

If they had noticed the fire, they gave no sign as they fought for possession of the large wrench in Daniels's hand. Daniels fought to bring it down on Jonathon, while Jonathon tried hard to pull it loose. A trickle of blood came from Jonathon's forehead, but the look in his eyes was grimly determined.

The gun, Claire thought. She had to find that gun. The fire threw wild shadows everywhere, wild, dancing shadows that mocked her search.

The fire was growing larger, giving off as much heat and smoke as it was light. Its crackling overshadowed the noise of the two men fighting. Claire coughed, gasped for air, and crawled toward another shadow. She sensed a change in the scuffle. Daniels had let go of the wrench, stepped back and hit Jonathon in the stomach. The blow was hard enough to knock the wind from him, hard enough to make Claire wince. Jonathon sank to the floor, and Daniels turned. As he did, Claire saw the gun lying on the floor about halfway between them. But Daniels saw it, too.

They both made it, Claire diving across the floor and Daniels racing toward it. Claire beat him by a split second. Daniels kicked her hand as it closed around the gun. She didn't loosen her hold, even though pain danced across her eyes. She gasped aloud but got her other hand around the gun.

"Give me that, you damn meddler," Daniels snarled, and reached down to try to pull the gun from her hands.

She kicked at him, trying to twist away, but his hands closed around hers, pulling the weapon into a position aiming right at her. She kicked harder, but it seemed to have no effect. Suddenly his hands released their grip and he slumped to the floor next to her. Jonathon stood above her, a grim look on his face and the wrench in his hands.

"You okay?" he asked, sinking to the floor next to her. His face was gray and streaked with dried blood. He crawled over to Daniels's limp body and pulled at his pockets even as sparks rained down on them from the roof.

The air was clearer down on the floor, but the fire's smoke seemed ready to engulf them. Claire looked up. "Jonathon, we've got to get out of here," she said. The door they'd come in was blocked by the fire. That didn't leave many options, but she was too tired to be afraid. Another shower of sparks fell on them, and Jonathon sat back on his heels.

"Damn. It must have fallen out while we were fighting."

"Jonathon." She grabbed him by the shoulders and pulled him around to look at her. "That notebook's not worth dying for. You said that yourself back in the cottage. Let's just get out of here."

She thought for a moment that he was going to argue, but he nodded and grabbed her hand, pulling her over to the edge of the floor.

"Can you swim?" he asked.

"Can I what?" His question made no sense until she looked across the boathouse and saw the other door. All they had to do was swim the twenty feet or so across the water in front of them, then slip under the door, and they'd be safe. Suddenly the air seemed light, and her heart sighed in relief. It truly was almost over. "Yeah, I can swim. Want to see my Girl Scout badge to prove it?"

"Maybe tomorrow," he said, and kissed her quickly on the lips.

The kiss lasted no more than a split second, but that was long enough to tell her about his love and hopes, his dreams and fears, and his plans for their life together. It was also long enough for her to realize she'd be swimming those twenty feet alone.

"Jonathon," she cried out, trying to hold on to him.

Behind him the far wall was totally engulfed by fire, and the flames were spreading up across the ceiling joists. The place would collapse in a matter of minutes. But he wasn't in any mood to listen to her pleas. He pushed her into the water.

The water was cold, a relief after the heat of the air, and she came up sputtering with anger. How dare he decide he would stay and she wouldn't! She'd thought he was above this kind of crazy macho ritual.

"Jonathon, you've got to get out, too," she yelled up to him as she glanced around. The floor was only a few feet above water level, but it was too far for her to reach.

"Get out of here, Claire," he called, partially disappearing from view as he went back to searching through Daniels's pockets.

"Jonathon, this is crazy. What are you trying to prove?" Even as she asked the question, she knew. Sarah. "None of this was Sarah's fault," she called to him. "She wasn't going to give them that notebook. If she was, why would she have hidden it up here? She probably came up to think things over and knew she couldn't do it. Don't throw your life away trying to make up for her mistake."

Flames slithered along a rope suspended from a joist, and a pulley swayed menacingly above her. "Jonathon!" she cried. She couldn't see him anymore.

"Claire, get out!"

She was growing weary from treading water. She knew there was nothing more she could do. If it was folly for him to risk his life for a notebook, it was equal folly for her to risk her life hoping he would come to his senses. Her children needed her.

"I love you, Jonathon Tyler, even if you are a damn stubborn fool," she called out above the roar of the fire. Her momentous announcement received disappointingly little response. A shower of sparks rained down, but she received no answer from Jonathon. Tears streamed down her cheeks. She turned and swam toward the far door.

She got to the door and found it barely skimmed the surface of the water. With a shallow dive, she was under it and free. She swam away from the boathouse, then turned to watch it, treading water in the inky blackness of the night.

It was so silent. She could hear the faint crackling of the fire, but the silence of the night seemed to blank out all other sound. The flames were barely visible. A few were starting to slip through the cracks in the walls and roof, and a golden glow had come over the area. The building would be almost destroyed before anyone would call the fire department.

With a sigh, she swam to shore. She hadn't seen any movement by the light of the fire, and she had to assume that no one had escaped from the boathouse yet. Her feet hit the bottom of the lake, and she pulled herself wearily up onto the sand.

"Jonathon, where are you?" It was her heart speaking, more than her voice, and she knew there would be no answer. All she heard was the faint wail of a siren in the distance. Someone had spotted the fire.

More flames danced across the boathouse roof, and soot rained down on her even where she sat, many yards away. She heard a few cries from across the lake as more people spotted the fire. She could do nothing but sit, watch the water and wait for Jonathon.

How had she managed to find love, a perfect love, then almost lose it like this? Would it have made a difference if she'd told Jonathon of her love earlier? Would he still have been willing to risk all to find that notebook? Somehow she knew it wouldn't have mattered.

A loud cracking noise from the boathouse stopped her breath as some inner timber fell. There was a small explosion, then another, and sparks flew from the roof. Still, the surface of the lake remained calm and even.

"Jonathon!" Claire cried out. "Damn you, Jonathon! Why are you doing this?"

The siren grew louder, and so did the roar of the fire. For a wild, endless moment it flared up toward the heavens, sparks scattered like a million fireflies. Then, with a shudder, the roof slowly caved in, dragging the walls with it.

Claire watched, hopeless tears streaming down her cheeks. It was over, finished. With Brad and Daniels dead, she and the girls were no longer in danger. With Jonathon dead, she no longer had a joy in her life, a hope to cling to. The girls would grow up and away, and all she'd be left with were memories.

She struggled to her feet. The fire trucks would be here soon, and she supposed she should be a visible presence for them to question. They'd have to call Jonathon's office and—

She'd heard a splash out on the water. Her heart was pounding almost too loud to hear, but she strained to listen. Was it only a fish? But no, there it was again, soft and steady. And getting closer.

She knew she ought to hide, to take cover just in case it was Daniels, but her feet refused to move. It had to be him. It had to. She couldn't have come all this way to find love only to lose it in a fire. The approaching swimmer seemed weary, but he moved closer all the while. Her heart in her throat, she watched as the figure struggled into the shallower water. He was dragging something.

"Jonathon?" she cried, though she knew it was him.

She splashed into the water to meet him. He was dragging Daniels's body, and she helped pull it through the last few feet of water.

"Is he alive?" she asked.

"I think so," Jonathon said. "But a timber caught him as I was getting him out, and I didn't stop to check his condition."

They were out of the water now, and they let Daniels go.

He slumped on the sand. Jonathon struggled a few feet beyond him before he collapsed, too. The sirens were close by now.

"Are you all right?" Claire asked, falling to the ground at his side. There was grass here, sparse clumps that were hell to kneel on. She sat down instead.

He nodded. She could see that much in the glow from the fire and the light coming from the side of the house.

He lay on his back, taking in great gulps of air. She brushed the hair away from his forehead. "If anything had happened to you, I think I would have killed you," she told him.

"Vindictive little thing, aren't you?" His voice was weak, but it had a little of the familiar teasing tone. "Lucky for me I got out in time."

"Did you get your precious notebook?"

He patted his pocket. "And it's probably all ruined by the water, too."

The fire trucks pulled into the yard, and they struggled to their feet. Daniels still hadn't moved.

Walt met them in the emergency room of the local hospital and waited while Jonathon got the cut above his eye stitched up and Claire's hand was X-rayed. Claire didn't ask how he'd gotten there so fast. She'd lost all sense of time, and she was hungry for some time alone with Jonathon.

"Daniels didn't pull through," Walt said, as they waited for Claire's X rays to come back. "They think the timber did him in. Saves the taxpayers the cost of convicting him."

Claire found Jonathon's hand. It also kept Sarah's involvement in the case from becoming a matter of public record. Claire was glad. The woman had made mistakes, but she didn't deserve public condemnation.

"What about the notebook?" Jonathon asked.

"Safely in the hands of the head of the police lab. It's being dried out. It looks like most of it will be readable, maybe even all of it. Joe Farrell's being watched to make sure he doesn't skip the country before we get all this sorted out."

Jonathon nodded and sat back in his chair. The lounge was deserted, and through the door they could see an occasional nurse walk by. No one was rushing anywhere. Claire could feel the last of her tension dying away.

Walt got to his feet. "When you're ready you'll be taken to the local airport and flown back to Chicago."

At last Walt left them alone. Jonathon looked up and found Claire's eyes. He smiled.

"Just like the movies, huh?"

"Last time I let you talk me into a quiet weekend at the lake."

His hold on her hand tightened, and his eyes grew warm with love. They both knew that forever lay ahead of them.

Claire frowned for a moment as she thought of how close they'd come to losing their future together. "Why did you risk your life to get the notebook?" she asked. The whole idea was making her angry again.

He didn't answer for a moment. His eyes left hers to stare at their hands where they lay intertwined.

"Why'd you wait around to explain that Sarah might have been going to give it back?" he asked instead.

Claire shrugged, then shivered as a faint siren was heard approaching the hospital. "Because it seemed possible. Because you don't know what really happened." She paused, searching her own mind to find the truth. "Because I didn't want you to hate her. She's still there in the house sometimes, and she wants you to forgive her."

The silence that followed was so still, so deep, that Claire was sorry she'd spoken. He'd think her a fool and have her committed. He leaned forward instead.

"I stayed there to find the notebook for the same reason," he said. "So that she could find peace and we could get on with making our own lives. Over the last year I've thought of selling the house so many times, but something always stopped me. It was Sarah, I think, crazy as that sounds."

"I understand," Claire told him.

"Now the damage is undone. We can get on with the case, and Sarah can rest in peace."

"And the house?" Claire asked.

"I think we can find another one with a swing in the backyard for Molly and lilac bushes for Katie." He paused. "If that's what you want."

"What I want?" she cried, pulling away from him impatiently. "Didn't you hear my great declaration?"

"I certainly did. And I noticed that you didn't give me a chance to tell you how much I love you before you left. I can see what I have to look forward to for the next fifty years. You're always going to want the last word."

He pulled her back down on the seat next to him, and she went quite willingly. Down the hall they heard the doctor's voice and heard a nurse directing him down to the lounge. Their brief interlude was almost over, but there would be time enough in the future.

"Only fifty years?" she asked. "You trying to cut things short?"

He kissed her gently, as if they were both fragile and likely to break under the strain. "Never. I just thought you didn't want to be tied down for a long time, so I was hiding my true intent."

She leaned into him slightly as the doctor came into the lounge. "Well, forever is too short a time for me."

Epilogue

"Higher," Katie screamed. "Higher."

"Are you sure?" Jonathon asked with a laugh. "You trying to fly?"

"Yes."

Molly came over to help Claire set the places for dinner on the picnic table, carefully taking the napkin-wrapped silverware from the picnic basket.

"I like this park," she said.

"Me too." Claire smiled at the simple expanse of green where it had all started almost two months ago.

"You know, I was thinking," Molly said, her little face solemn. "We don't have our old daddy anymore, and Jonathon doesn't have any kids of his very own, so why doesn't he maybe be our daddy?"

"I thought you knew he was going to be," Claire said. "We told you that we're going to get married."

"But that doesn't make him our daddy," Molly told her. "Angie O'Neal's mommy got married again, but Angie kept her old daddy. We don't have an old daddy to keep, so I thought maybe Jonathon could be our real daddy and we could call him Daddy instead of Jonathon.''

"Would you like that?"

Molly nodded, her face lighting up. "He'd make a good daddy." A small cloud passed over her eyes. "You don't think he'd mind if we called him Daddy, do you?"

Mind? Do flowers mind the sun? "No, honey," Claire said with a smile that reflected only a tiny bit of the joy flooding her heart. "I don't think he'd mind. Not one tiny bit."

"Good." Molly ran off to play on the slide and was joined by Katie after a moment or two.

Relieved of his duties, Jonathon came over to Claire's side. "Need some help here?"

She shook her head. "Molly does, though. She's decided she and Katie need a real daddy, and you're to be it, if you don't mind."

He looked puzzled. "But we told them—"

Claire just laughed, feeling as free and happy as the summer sunshine. "Molly is a bit more worldly than we thought. She informed me that just because I'm marrying you doesn't mean you'll be her real daddy. She wants it official so she can call you Daddy."

Jonathon's eyes seemed to mist over. "Sounds good to me," he said simply.

"I thought so, too." Claire took a container of fried chicken out of the cooler. "Especially since it appears you may be getting that title from another someone in about eight months."

"Claire." That one word said it all. Love. Peace. Forever together.

She smiled and went into his arms. "Mind you, I'm not positive, but all signs seem to be affirmative. Hope you're ready for a crowd in your life."

"Ready?" His lips came down on hers to seal the vow of his love. "I've been ready since I brought you home the first day. I knew right from the start you belonged to me."

* * * * * *

SPECIAL EDITION

Stories of love and life, these powerful
novels are tales that you can identify with—
romances with "something special" added in!

Fall in love with the stories of authors such
as **Nora Roberts, Diana Palmer, Ginna Gray**
and many more of your special favorites—as
well as wonderful new voices!

Special Edition brings you
entertainment for the heart!

SSE-GEN

SILHOUETTE®
Desire®

Do you want...

Dangerously handsome heroes

Evocative, everlasting love stories

Sizzling and tantalizing sensuality

Incredibly sexy miniseries like **MAN OF THE MONTH**

Red-hot romance

Enticing entertainment that can't be beat!

You'll find all of this, and much *more* each and
every month in **SILHOUETTE DESIRE**. Don't miss these
unforgettable love stories by some of romance's hottest
authors. Silhouette Desire—where your fantasies will
always come true....

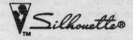

WAYS TO *UNEXPECTEDLY MEET* MR. RIGHT:

♡ *Go out with the sexy-sounding stranger
your daughter secretly set you up with
through a personal ad.*

♡ *RSVP yes to a wedding invitation—soon
it might be your turn to say "I do!"*

♡ *Receive a marriage proposal by mail—
from a man you've never met....*

*These are just a few of the unexpected
ways that written communication
leads to love in Silhouette Yours Truly.*

*Each month, look for two fast-paced, fun and
flirtatious Yours Truly novels
(with entertaining treats and sneak previews
in the back pages) by some of your favorite
authors—and some who are sure to
become favorites.*

YOURS TRULY™:
Love—when you least expect it!

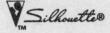

YT-GEN

FIVE UNIQUE SERIES
FOR EVERY WOMAN YOU ARE...

▼ *Silhouette* ROMANCE™

From classic love stories to romantic comedies to emotional heart tuggers, Silhouette Romance is sometimes sweet, sometimes sassy—and always enjoyable! Romance—the way you always knew it could be.

SILHOUETTE® *Desire* ®

Red-hot is what we've got! Sparkling, scintillating, *sensuous* love stories. Once you pick up one you won't be able to put it down...only in Silhouette Desire.

Silhouette ® SPECIAL EDITION ®

Stories of love and life, these powerful novels are tales that you can identify with—romances with "something special" added in! Silhouette Special Edition is entertainment for the heart.

SILHOUETTE·INTIMATE·MOMENTS®

Enter a world where passions run hot and excitement is always high. Dramatic, larger than life and always compelling—Silhouette Intimate Moments provides captivating romance to cherish forever.

▼ SILHOUETTE YOURS TRULY™

A personal ad, a "Dear John" letter, a wedding invitation... Just a few of the ways that written communication unexpectedly leads Miss Unmarried to Mr. "I Do" in Yours Truly novels...in the most fun, fast-paced and flirtatious style!

SGENERIC-R1

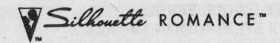

Silhouette ROMANCE™

What's a single dad to do when he needs a wife by next Thursday?

Who's a confirmed bachelor to call when he finds a baby on his doorstep?

How does a plain Jane in love with her gorgeous boss get him to notice her?

From classic love stories to romantic comedies to emotional heart tuggers, **Silhouette Romance** offers six irresistible novels every month by some of your favorite authors! Such as...beloved bestsellers **Diana Palmer, Annette Broadrick, Suzanne Carey, Elizabeth August** and **Marie Ferrarella**, to name just a few—and some sure to become favorites!

Fabulous Fathers...Bundles of Joy...Miniseries... Months of blushing brides and convenient weddings... Holiday celebrations... You'll find all this and much more in **Silhouette Romance**—always emotional, always enjoyable, always about love!

LOOK FOR OUR FOUR FABULOUS MEN!

Each month some of today's bestselling authors bring four new fabulous men to Harlequin American Romance. Whether they're rebel ranchers, millionaire power brokers or sexy single dads, they're all gallant princes—and they're all ready to sweep you into lighthearted fantasies and contemporary fairy tales where anything is possible and where all your dreams come true!

You don't even have to make a wish...Harlequin American Romance will grant your every desire!

Look for Harlequin American Romance wherever Harlequin books are sold!